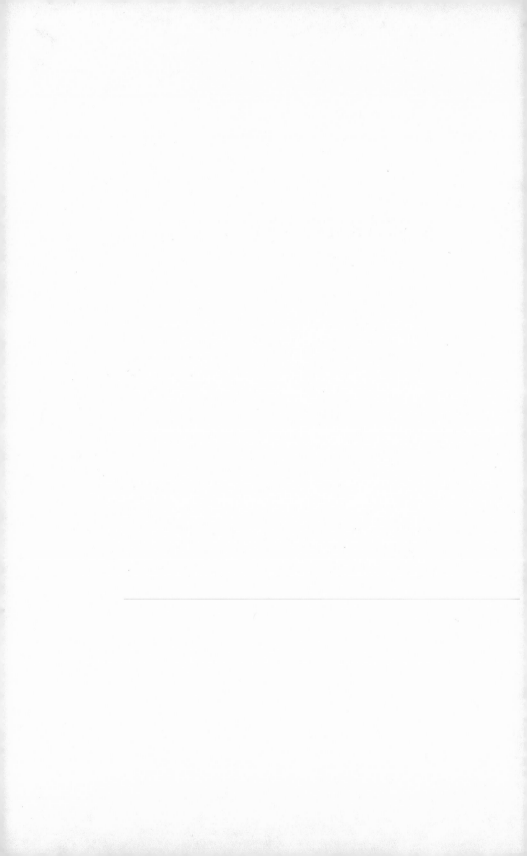

A STAR TO STEER HER BY

A STAR TO STEER HER BY

An Odyssey of Love and Crisis

BASED ON A TRUE STORY

TOMMIE SPEAR

BEVERLY HILLS, CALIFORNIA

A Star to Steer Her By: An Odyssey of Love and Crisis

 Published in the United States by Little Moose Press, a division of Smarketing LLC, California.
269 South Beverly Drive, Suite #1065
Beverly Hills, CA 90212, 866-234-0626
www.littlemoosepress.com

First Edition

Printed and bound in the United States of America on acid-free paper.

Library of Congress Cataloging-In-Publication Data

Spear, Tommie.

    A star to steer her by : an odyssey of love and crisis, based on a true story / Tommie Spear. -- 1st ed.

    p. cm.

    ISBN 0-9786049-4-6 (hardcover with dust jacket : alk. paper)

    1. Voyages around the world--Fiction. I. Title.

PS3619.P4335S73 2006

813'.6--dc22

                      2006018804

Book Designer: Patricia Bacall
Editor: Brookes Nohlgren

DEDICATED TO MIKE FINNELL
WHOSE LOVE AND GENEROSITY MADE MY DREAM
OF THIS BOOK COME TRUE

ACKNOWLEDGEMENTS

I AM DEEPLY GRATEFUL TO my book shepherd and publisher, Ellen Reid of Little Moose Press, for her faith in my book and expertise and patience in leading me through the complexities of the publishing world and to her talented team: my discerning editor, Brookes Nohlgren; my creative cover designer and graphic artist, Patricia Bacall; and my wizard of jacket words, Laren Bright.

I am indebted to my revered writing instructors Jeri Chevalier, Karin Finnel, Susan Gulbransen, Perie Longo, Shelly Lowenkopf, Matthew Pallarmy, Abe Polsky, Laura Taylor, Leonard Tourney, and Duane Unkefer; and to Cork Milner, editor, renowned workshop leader, and friend.

I feel gratitude beyond what I can articulate to my longtime friends and founders of the Santa Barbara Writer's Conference, Mary and Barnaby Conrad. Over the years, Barnaby has critiqued my work, given me ongoing encouragement, and introduced me to my loyal mentors, Christopher Buckley and my much-loved teacher Charles Champlin.

I am grateful for the fine photographic talents of my daughter-in-law, Robin Banks, and the help and encouragement of my two sons, Kendal and William Banks. I acknowledge and honor the skills of my word-processing genius Jo-Anne Wolfe, without whom this book would not have sprung to life.

CHAPTER 1

A man who is not afraid of the sea will soon be drowned...
for he will be going out on a day he shouldn't.

—John Synge

IT WAS THE DAY I decided to jump overboard.

On that late March afternoon, black clouds fat with rain hung over the Santa Barbara Mountains. Small-craft warning was hoisted from the Santa Barbara Harbor Master's flagpole. Its red triangle flag whipped in the wind and whitecaps peaked on the sea outside the breakwater.

I sensed both men's excitement. My husband, Kelly, and Marty, the rigger, were engrossed in studying the new sail. It luffed and filled, the boat heeled over hard. Marty was our best shipwright. Kelly hired him to convert our sloop, *Vagabundita*, to a cutter rig by the addition of a mizzen mast. I knew this sea-trial weighed heavily on them both. This conversion would make or break the *Vagabundita's* performance on our cruise around the world.

I'd warned the men that I'd be throwing myself overboard, but with characteristic lack of caution I didn't say when. I wanted the test of our rescue equipment to have the surprise element of an actual man over-board crisis.

We headed out through the channel into the open sea. The men were occupied up forward so I figured this was as good a time as any. Working my way to the stern, I looked down at the gray, choppy water, momentar-ily regretting my bravado. The westerly should have dropped toward sunset, but it was blowing a good twenty-five knots and there was a big sea running. I took a deep breath, bent my knees, and leapt clear of the propeller. I gasped at the water temperature and inadvertently took a gulp, coming up coughing and choking. My first thought was that I should have worn a wet suit instead of a bikini. Treading water, I yelled at the rapidly disappearing sailboat.

The men were so concentrated on trimming the sails that it took a few moments for them to focus their attention on me. They both froze and didn't immediately spring into action toward the Lifesling as I had expected. I watched in astonishment as they turned back toward the new sail. I felt a brush of fear. Then I realized they had to secure the mizzen sheet.

Both men moved fast now, rushing aft to throw me the orange foam horseshoe. The rope began paying out rapidly. I saw Kelly lunge to grab the end of it, then bend to cleat it down. The lifeline had been attached to nothing. Kelly's figure was growing smaller. I could see him at the wheel, beginning the turn hard alee to come about. For a boat of only thirty-seven feet, it seemed to make a slow, wide arc. Next they dropped sail. The orange horseshoe was barely visible one moment, obscured by a wave the next.

I swam hard toward it, and even without the encumbrance of shoes or heavy clothing (as would be the impediment in an actual man overboard), I made little progress through the heavy chop. Why hadn't I worn my swim fins? I knew that my head, with wet hair the color of seaweed, was almost invisible. I had expected to be in the water for only two or three minutes. How long would it take me to hypothermiate?

Don't be ridiculous, you have hours.

I glanced west to see the red ball of the sun poised just above the horizon.

Unless they lose you.

The irony of being lost at sea before our cruise even began was terrifying. Heavy gray clouds obscured what might have been a brilliant sunset and the darkness fell rapidly.

My peripheral vision caught a movement in the water. Silhouetted against the setting sun I glimpsed the black arc of an evil fin. A sickening rush of adrenaline shot through me. Energized by fear, I flayed my arms and legs harder. The ominous shape half surfaced again. This time my eyes met the curious gaze of a harbor seal, so close I could smell his fishy breath. He must have been intrigued with this pale creature moving so awkwardly through his territory. His usual encounters were no doubt with divers clad in suits as slick and black as his own. "Tomkat, Tomkat, keep going!" Kelly yelled. I heard the anxiety in his voice. In desperation, he threw a white rubber bumper and a flotation cushion overboard.

Trying to swim, I felt immobilized with cold.

It took both men to haul me aboard. I felt like a drowned cat. I had been in the water only fifteen minutes. Kelly hugged my shivering body to him. "Oh Tomkat, I hated to think you were afraid out there. You do know I'd always be able to rescue you no matter what. I was about to dive in when you reached the Lifesling." I smiled, feeling safe in his powerful arms.

We looked at each other for a long moment, certain of our indestructibility. "I thought the Lifesling test was a success though," I said. "At least we know all the difficulties now. I mean if there'd been a bigger sea running, Kel, who knows?"

A week later Kelly and I embarked on our great adventure, sailing romantically for the most remote islands in the world, the Marquesas. After cruising the Southern California coast and Baja, we planned to be five years at sea, circumnavigating the globe. *Five years before the mast*, I called it. At the end of our odyssey, Kelly would be seventy and thought he would be too old for the nomadic sailing life.

For reasons of thrift, he resigned from the California Club and the men's groups and organizations that were his joy during seventeen years as a bachelor before our marriage. He even resigned from his Lost Angels Camp at the Bohemian Grove. I could hardly believe that. Men often waited twenty-five years, until someone died, to be taken in. Kelly's campmates were shocked when they heard, as was I, but I saw the look in his eyes when he told me, "I've done those guy things enough years now, Tomkat. When we get home from the cruise, I only want to be with you."

As Kelly's men friends bewailed his defection from their ranks, my women friends deplored the whole idea of our odyssey. My best friend, Beverlie Latimer, hosted a bon voyage party for me. The women had brought thoughtful gifts I joked about at first.

"This makeup magnifying mirror is perfect! I can use it to reflect the sun and signal passing ships from the life raft!"

"Tommie," one friend, another designer said, "how can you bear to leave your beautiful new house? You and Kelly sweat blood over that—you've decorated it down to the throw pillows."

"Kelly let me have everything I wanted in the house. It'll still be there when we get back."

"How can you go off unprepared with no navigational skills or a radio operational license?" the wife of another sailor asked.

"Only one of us needs to know that stuff." I was beginning to feel ganged-up on.

"How can you leave your only grandchild? Kendal will be almost seven when you get back; you'll have missed her whole young child-hood," the only other grandmother said.

"Yes, I know. That one hurts, but really, you guys, you must know I've thought this through." I parried each concern they raised and thrust back my explanations as if dueling with fencing partners.

Finally, one dared ask, "How can you go off alone, completely out of range of medical help with a sixty-five-year-old man with a heart condi-tion, for God's sake?"

"None of you get it. It's *because* Kelly was diagnosed with a heart con-dition that we decided to go. Dr. De Berry says he'll be fine as long as he takes his heart medication. It's the dream of Kelly's life, don't you see? I'm going to do this with him if it kills me." The women sat there in silence for a moment, absorbing my rationale, then questioned me about what route we'd follow on our circumnavigation.

"You almost have to be looking at a globe to grasp it," I said. "Basically we'll cut our eyeteeth on the Baja Peninsula, sail up into the Sea of Cortez and over to the Mexican mainland for about a year before we make the longest passage, about a month crossing the Pacific from Manzanillo to the Marquesas, cruise French Polynesia and Tahiti, wait out hurricane season in Australia, sail to Indonesia, cross the Bay of Bengal..."

"Okay, okay! We get the picture," they interrupted. Then Beverlie, a surgeon's wife, asked, "What if something happens in mid-ocean?"

That was the question I asked myself daily. That was why I was seeing my therapist weekly about my anxiety attacks. I hadn't even known what an anxiety attack was until I began to experience life-threatening paralysis when driving the freeways. I'd start to sweat, grip the steering wheel, and panic, thinking I'd lose control of the car.

I'd have to pull over and breathe deeply and pray. It seemed more palatable for *me* to die in a car accident than to lose Kelly. The therapist helped me to arrive at that conclusion, and I got some alleviation of my panic attacks in knowing what my unconscious was dishing up.

The therapist recorded relaxation and positive visualization tapes for me to listen to three times a day. They helped a lot and by the time two years passed, as we finished building our new house and refitting the boat, I was over my fear.

It was dark when we finally set sail.

Kelly had been fiddling around in the engine room for a long time during the day. I knew he was checking everything out with his engineer's precision. He had charts of the Southern California coast and Baja spread out all over our multipurpose table, moving the beam of a high-powered flashlight around as he made notations in the log.

I worked in the tiny galley, not more than three feet from him. I had to interrupt his concentration to ask him to clear the table for dinner. It took two hours for the chicken, mushroom, and rice casserole to be ready, what with making the sauce from scratch and pre-cooking all the ingredients on two burners before it went into the oven. A hint of what meal preparation at sea would be, I thought with rueful amusement. Our white-booted gray tabby, Morris, crouched in a corner of the upper book-case watching me intently, knowing he'd get a taste of "people food." We'd hoped he was young enough to adapt to a seagoing life. As a stray kitten he'd come meowing onto our construction site midway through building the house. We fed him daily and when we moved into the completed house, he moved in with us. He'd fallen hard for Kelly and when it came time to depart on the cruise, it seemed cruel to leave him. The fragrance of my hot biscuits began to fill the cabin and Kelly looked up from his charts with a smile. I wanted to serve a hearty dinner to hold us for our first overnight passage, which Kelly said would be "a piece of cake."

During dinner we discussed our plan for standing the night's watch. Kelly suggested three hours on and three hours off as a kinder stint than the traditional four hours, after which we'd relieve each other to go below and hopefully sleep.

By the time he'd reviewed with me our compass course, the Loran and the radar, it was 10 p.m., and I was taking the first watch. I figured he'd relieve me around 1 a.m. and stand his own watch until four. Then we'd be on deck together at dawn to come into San Diego Harbor.

What I had not counted on was that when it was my turn to sleep, I could not begin to relax. I lay in the bunk rigid, agitating into a panic, eyes wide open visualizing Kelly falling overboard into the black water. I threw off the quilt and dropped to my knees on the cabin floor, inclining my face to heaven, hands clasped in prayer. "Please, dear God, please release me from this burden of fear. Keep and protect Kelly. Keep him well and safe. Please, God, I ask only this of you. I've tried to lead a good life, kept your commandments. I promise I will help all who come to me in need, if you will grant my prayer. Please, God, please. I beg of you. I ask only for this. In the name of your son, Jesus Christ, amen."

I felt somewhat calmed but knew there was no way I could sleep. No way I could stay in the warm bunk with Morris.

I took a surreptitious step up toward the cockpit. Kelly was at the wheel on watch, his back to me. We were well out to sea. There was no moon yet. It was much darker than I expected. The only lights winked far away, linking the small coastal towns. I dragged the guilt topside and propped myself in a corner of the cockpit on an urgent watch of my own.

"What's the matter? Can't sleep?" Kelly asked. I mumbled a reply, not admitting to the torturous fear that had brought me to my knees down there, pleading with God.

I finally dozed off and was startled into consciousness out of a half-dream. When I didn't see Kelly at the wheel, I plunged below in a frenzy. He was not in the forepeak, not in the head. Aghast, shouting his name, I rushed up on deck, only to find him calmly refilling the forward lantern. I clutched him to me, my crushing anxiety released in a torrent of tears. Kelly held me until I stopped shaking and my heart no longer pounded, until my breathing quieted.

He rummaged in a locker, turned on the spreader light so he could see, then strung a line all around the deck, securing it to each stanchion as he went, then made lines fitted with snap shackles at both ends for us to wear around our waists and clip on.

"Now we've got a lifeline. Our new rule. I don't want to lose you either, love."

"Oh thank you, Kelly, thank you. I wouldn't ruin the cruise for anything—I hope you know."

The lifeline did alleviate my fear. I went below to write in my log—to write that I'd been given a second chance—but as I did so a dark foreboding closed around my heart, like a shadow lurking just beyond the light.

The need for sleep ceased to be a priority for either of us, drained as we were. It was as if Kelly's lifeline had exorcised a fearful specter—that of his falling overboard—that had possessed me. It would be unthinkable to be apart at that moment. We wanted only to be together and lie close in the cockpit, hand in hand, marveling at the brilliance of the stars, picking out those we knew. The colors of Antares flashed so brightly that at first I thought it was some kind of satellite. I pointed out the North Star, easily located by its proximity to the last star on the Dipper's handle.

"Well, I'm glad you can identify that at least," Kelly joked. "I'm already mistrustful of the Loran, it needs adjustment. But in case our other electronics fail, we can fall back on your celestial navigation."

"And the sextant," I said, proud of my sole navigational skill—of shooting sun sights to determine our position, feeling a kinship with the navigators of yore.

"Look, Orion's rising." Kelly pointed to the north.

"Oh, how funny, lying on his back sleeping. Maybe waking up from a long summer's nap."

I dozed a little then, and this time awoke peacefully. It was still pitch-black, but looking up there was Orion in his familiar upright position striding confidently across the October sky, knife hanging from his three-starred belt. The seas were calm. There was only about a fifteen-knot breeze blowing, just enough to puff the mainsail to steadying function. It was cold in the cockpit and we'd both put on heavy sailing jackets and fleece-lined gloves.

Around 4:30 a.m., Kelly identified the Point Lomas light, clearly sighted and blinking away. Our almost due east course and the huge curving bay of San Diego necessitated heading out to sea to round the Point Lomas peninsula. We lost sight of the glittering golden chain of shore lights. The quarter moon rose late, companionably with Venus, the planet of morning.

Having witnessed few dawns, I hoped for a red-and-gold spectacular. Apparently this one was not going to burst like thunder, but the rising sun lighted the sky so rapidly that the morning star fled, and the moon paled away, disappearing into the blanket of gray cloud cover.

Point Lomas was just off our port bow, and Kelly changed course to begin our entry into the bay. He turned on the engine. The sea was beginning to stir into life, emerging from the camouflage of night. Three harbor seals crowded precariously onto a green bell buoy. It made a droll welcoming committee as serpentinely they moved their heads and barked in tandem with the clang of the bell, a harsh symphony of sound to greet us. Through the binoculars we spotted *Southern Winds*, a ketch of about thirty-six feet, obviously a long-distance cruiser with jerrycans and sailbags lashed on deck. I hugged myself, feeling a thrill of identification with her.

Kelly had made advance arrangements to moor at the San Diego Yacht Club, with which we had reciprocal privileges from our own yacht club in Santa Barbara. He radioed the dock master for our slip location.

"I'm excited about seeing the yacht club, Kel!" I said.

"I know you'll like it," he said. That was the understatement of the day. The magical words *yacht club*, any yacht club, bespoke of hot showers and hot meals in dining rooms festive with burgees from around the world and glass cases displaying silver sailing trophies. I'd always thought them full of the romance of ships and the sea.

After we moored and washed down the *Vagabundita* and ensured that Morris couldn't get out, we donned our Santa Barbara Yacht Club shirts and white pants and made our way up the dock to explore.

"Look at that!" Kelly said.

"What?" I'd been studying the other boats, reading their exotic names and home ports. He pointed, "That sign," *No pets allowed on the docks or aboard*. It was reinforced with a regulation number.

"We're going to have to watch Morris like a hawk. What would they do? Confiscate him?" I felt my chest tightening up.

"Maybe if they saw him walking alone," Kelly said. "I doubt it though. Probably just kick us out. He's got my call sign and 'Vagabundita' on his collar."

"Why are cats so unpopular in marinas these days? I thought there always used to be a ship's cat aboard old sailing vessels."

"True, when rats were feared as a source of the plague. Now cats are thought to wreak havoc in sail lockers. Get in there to bed down and then scratch and pee."

"We've got to be careful. I'd die if we lost Morris," I said. I saw by Kelly's serious face that he couldn't even bear to put words to that possibility.

"It'd be a disaster to get kicked out though. No place to anchor. I've never seen a busier harbor," he said.

As we neared the yacht club we saw that it was decorated in red-white-and-blue bunting with many flags flying. We had unknowingly walked into a reception to view and honor the America's Cup. It was 1990, the year Dennis Conner's racing machine, the *Stars and Stripes*, sailed to victory, reclaiming the Cup for the United States.

Welcomed by the staff, we lunched on the club's deck, sunshine glancing off the sterling silver trophy. Its leather case was lined in blue velvet and fitted to the exact measurements of the elaborate urn. *Louis Vuitton—Made in Paris* was stamped in gold. Handsome young officers, discreetly armed, stood at attention in beribboned dress uniforms. It was an impressive scene. Over lunch, we discussed the profound nature of the America's Cup competition—the commitment of the contenders, the risks and the costs, the broken hearts, the victory of one.

The club's commodore, seeing we were strangers, stopped by our table to introduce himself. Kelly was overcome with our good fortune of stumbling into such an unexpected occasion, the thrill of seeing the ultimate race trophy, and the graciousness of our welcome. As I looked at his happy face, green eyes sparkling, full head of silver hair set off by his deep tan, I'd never thought him more handsome. My heart felt full of our adventure and this auspicious beginning. My spirits rose, flying as high as the white gulls circling above us, as light as the clean sea air, unburdened of the past night's terror.

Knowing this was our last U.S. port, Kelly and I had on our minds a million things to accomplish. Adjustment to the Loran, our all-important positioning device, was paramount, and with that as a goal a trip to West Marine Products headed our list.

Morris wouldn't tolerate being cooped up, and had *nothing* on his mind but escape. We humans with our cluttered agendas have a lot to learn from cats. Not easily distracted like dogs, they have the capability and patience to focus their attention on a single goal, so they usually achieve it. As we two bustled about the boat, poking into storage lockers and under floorboards checking supplies and compiling our busy little lists, Morris sat with half-closed eyes, unobtrusive, awaiting his chance.

We were up on the dock ready to go when Kelly realized he'd forgotten his wallet. When he slid open the cabin hatch, Morris catapulted out onto the dock in a mad dash to freedom with me in hot pursuit. Soon outdistanced, I watched horrified as he jumped aboard a nearby boat, *The Other Woman*. He squeezed his body under its tightly laced canvas cover, the tip of his tail the last part to disappear. With comedic timing a young man dressed in shorts and a baseball cap began to remove the boat covers preparatory to hosing down. Kelly'd joined me by then.

"I don't know whether to tell that guy he's got a cat on board or not," I whispered. "What if he takes the boat out?"

"Maybe we made a mistake with that I.D. collar," Kelly said. I knew he was worried about his reputation with the yacht club—we as reciprocal guests, flaunting our disregard for their pet regulations. "I think it's better not to say anything, wait and take our chances. That fella looks too young to own a yacht like that. He's probably washing down for the owner's day-sail."

"Day-sail? You *hope* day-sail. What if they're going out for the weekend?"

Morris's little caper cost us our afternoon since we didn't dare abandon him to the caprice of the likely wrathful owner when he discovered his feline cargo. Barely breathing, we watched a sailing party approach carrying a cooler and a picnic hamper, then board *The Other Woman*. In full view of everybody, Morris jumped nonchalantly off their bow onto the dock and walked smartly toward his own yacht.

"Do you suppose that was the first of his nine lives?" Kelly said, relief flooding his face.

"How come they *never* have any parts?" I asked. We were waiting at West Marine Products, which felt like our second home.

"Our boat's Eastern manufactured. They can't stock all that inventory." Kelly fumed at the news that it would take at least ten working days to get the Loran repaired.

"Oh well, don't panic, sweetheart. San Diego's fun. We haven't been to Old Town this week. I wouldn't mind seeing the big cats again."

"I've had it with that zoo! We've already taken the bus there three times." Kelly was so seldom cross that I was taken aback, a little frightened. It wasn't his voice.

"You're not wanting to throw in the towel, are you?" I said.

"No, not really. I may sound like it. I'm so fed up right now. God, the hassles! What about you—do you want to call it quits?"

"Who me? Kelly, you must know I've dreamed of this ever since we met."

Kelly sent me off to West Marine Chandlery with a list of items he needed for overhauling the boat's engine. The owner gave me a note that he said had been hand-delivered a few hours before. It was from my first husband, Bill. "I'm spending the morning at the Boat Show. I'd like to stop by and wish you 'Bon Voyage' on my way home." I knew Bill never missed the Boat Show. *Fantasy Yachting*, he called it.

The dock was so hot on my bare feet that I had to dash for patches of shade. As I made my way back to the *Vagabundita*, I wondered if Kelly would resent my first husband coming down to the boat.

"Don't kiss me. I'm all sweaty." Kelly squeezed his body out of the engine room. He smiled in his affable way as I read him Bill's note. "Sure. I'd like to see Bill and show him the boat." Kelly never did put me in the middle on things and frequently joked that he owed a debt of gratitude to Bill for my "sailing training."

"Okay, but you're not going to be able to get your fingernails clean in time," I teased him as I started back to meet Bill.

Knowing Bill would have to walk past the outdoor restaurant Schooner or Later to reach the *Vagabundita's* dock, I waited for him there. I noticed several women's heads turning before he came into my view. He carried himself ramrod-straight and walked with an air of confidence, looking elegantly casual in his moccasin topsiders and ironed white jeans.

He carried a gift-wrapped package and suggested we have a Coke together before going down to the boat. I accepted, knowing Kelly would be grateful for the extra time he needed to finish work in the engine room. "I wanted to give this to you alone," Bill said. "It will bring back memories. Good ones I hope." He sounded wistful.

"How nice," I said as I took the gift. The waitress brought our drinks. "Kelly's dying to show you the boat. He's worked so hard. Passed his ham radio test; took a refresher course in navigation. He ended up tutoring practically the whole class. I'm proud of him."

"You have every reason to be." He paused and swirled his straw around in the glass a few times, then he looked up. "What about *your* skills?" I was distracted and didn't answer. I opened the gift.

"Oh Bill! Our Saint Christopher medal." The talisman, made of brilliant green enamel, was set off with a white rim. As I stared at it, memories of our sailing days floated through my mind. "Bill, this is so special. I forgot we took it off the *Angelita*. Thank you."

"My pleasure. I thought you might need a guardian and I wanted a part of me to go with you on this trip." I stretched out my hand and squeezed his arm. "Tommie, the boys tell me you haven't learned to navigate or even operate the radio. These skills are crucial. What you and Kelly are doing isn't exactly the inland waterway. You're circumnavigating, for God's sake." Bill's parental tone made my hackles rise.

"Yes, I know all that, but it's too late now. Kelly studied navigation for three semesters. He spent hundreds of hours learning Morse code so he could qualify for a ham radio call sign." Bill tapped his gold signet ring against the table rim. "I wish you'd stop that. You're making me nervous," I said.

"I'm making *you* nervous!" He shook his head and made a reproachful sound. "Tommie, I hoped I wouldn't have to bring this up. Kelly has a severe heart condition. What if the worst happened in mid-ocean? What would you do?"

"Not severe."

"What?" Bill stared at me in disbelief.

"I said not severe. It's controlled with medication, and I *do* know how to operate the radio. I'm just not allowed to without a call sign. Of course they'd respond to a Mayday."

"You wouldn't even be able to give your position."

"I would too. Kelly taught me to shoot the sun and stars on the sextant. I'm very good at it." I slid my eyes away. I wasn't about to admit that I usually turned over the next step to Kelly, the computations involved in determining latitude and longitude. Bill looked at me in silence. I took a sip of Coke. The icy soda fizzed in my mouth. I shrugged my shoulders and glanced around the restaurant. "Sure, maybe we're playing the odds a little. We wouldn't be doing this if we weren't fatalists to some extent."

"Like you could be killed tomorrow crossing the street?"

"Yes, but please spare me that old cliché. You know I'm a risk-taker. That's why you brought me this talisman." I saw Bill's lips tighten. "And I thank you again. I'll take all the help I can get. We already have a carving of the Virgin Mary in the master cabin and Saint Anthony prayer cards to wear on watch. Now, thanks to you, we'll have Saint Chris in the main salon. We'll probably pick up some tiki gods in the South Pacific and by the time we hit New Zealand…" I broke off. Bill was making stabbing motions into the ice with his straw. "Bill, I'm not meaning to be cavalier. I made the decision to leave the radio and navigation skills up to Kelly. We've had two horrendous years building the house and refitting the boat. I was working hard on my interior design jobs to help out. We finally ran out of time."

"Well, I can see my suggestions are falling on deaf ears." Bill took off his dark glasses and polished them with a fresh white linen handkerchief.

"Not deaf ears. Technically you're right, but nobody understands what it means to get off on something like this. It's staggering. You're never ready. We weren't. Finally we just had to weigh anchor and sail away."

"So that's your final decision? Just go off unprepared?"

I felt my jaw tighten. My voice went flat. "Kelly let me have every blessed thing I wanted in the new house, even though we went over budget. Now this is what *he* wants, what he's wanted to do all his life, and I'm going to do it with him. That's all there is to it."

Bill's blue eyes challenged my defiant stare. The folly of our undertaking was written all over his face. In one abrupt motion he crumpled his straw and stood up.

"Do me a favor. Have Kelly tape up instructions for Mayday. Promise?"

That evening we put a sign in the rear window of my car, "Tomikat," reading "'82 CAMARO FOR SALE. CLEAN. $1,200." No phone number because we only had a radio telephone aboard the boat and couldn't call in or out without a call sign.

We'd driven less than fifty miles when a potential buyer honked to signal us to pull over. Kelly and the truck driver stood by the side of the road in their shorts and struck a deal. Kelly requested cash; the buyer arranged a time for the next day.

We arrived at Billy and Robin's beach trailer in jubilant spirits. It was fun to all be together for dinner. My eldest son, Billy, was only thirty-three but he'd already made career strides in real estate development. He and his wife, Robin, picked up the trailer for a song. She was a busy professional photographer and since they had no children they used the trailer as a weekend getaway.

Robin set the round glass dinner table with colorful place mats and gaily painted fish napkin rings. She arranged field-picked tomatoes, fresh basil, and mozzarella cheese on cool-looking frosted plates while Billy brushed marinade on the halibut steaks he was grilling. The scent of ginger rose from the barbecue and mingled pleasantly with that of the sea misting in from the breakers crashing on the shore.

After dinner we walked on the Corona del Mar beach. Twenty-two miles off the coast, Catalina Island was etched so clearly that even the deep bay of Avalon and the island's valleys and hillsides stood out. Kelly took my hand and gave me a secret wink. It was the place of our heart, where we'd spent our courtship weekends.

Nobody talked about how long it might be until we four were

together again. The kids walked us out and said goodbye to "Tomikat." and we laughed and hugged. Then Billy looked at me. His tan face made his eyes even bluer. He was a little scruffy with his windblown hair and faded aloha shirt, but it was the same look he gave me at the beginning of an earlier passage through life.

He was seventeen, about to begin the drive up to Berkeley to register for freshman year. He was seated behind the wheel—I don't remember what over-loaded vehicle—and I was standing in the street trying to say goodbye. He looked up at me out of his fine, serious face. Seventeen years of mothering flashed before me like my very life. I loved having sons. They were so appreciative of just being fed. As a little boy Billy never got up from a meal without saying, "Thank you, Mom, for the great breakfast. That was a really good lunch. That was a 'belicious' dinner." He seemed to have been born with manners.

Now he looked at me and our eyes connected. The whole of his child-hood and teenage years were encompassed in that look. "Goodbye, Mother," he said. Before, he'd always called me "Mom."

It was the morning scheduled for the car inspection. Waiting out on a bench by the yacht club's parking lot, I felt a little nervous over what the mechanic might find in his examination of the Camaro's intestines. I watched in anxiety as both men bent over with their heads under the hood, unscrewing things, poking away, and exchanging monosyllables. After a few minutes the mechanic straightened up and clamped down the hood. "Looks okay to me," he announced. The new owner handed over the agreed-upon amount of $1,200. I handed over the Change of Registration form and the pink slip. It was a done deal but somehow I couldn't quite watch "Tomikat" drive away. That nostalgic moment passed, and with great elation I walked the two miles into town to have the money converted into traveler's checks, my "mad money." On an impulse I kept out fifty dollars to surprise Kelly with a restaurant dinner.

I hadn't wanted to waste the dinner money on taxi fare into San Diego. It was kind of a thrill to walk instead of drive to dinner. We went out to the end of the pier to watch the sunset before going to the rather tacky little Polynesian place we liked. Inside the restaurant the décor was vaguely South Seas, with a couple of lighted blowfish and some plastic leis strung from the paddles and surfboards adorning the walls. It was the kind of place that served grated beets on the salad. A cheerful waitress led us to a brown leatherette booth by the window, where we could watch for the "green flash," as she put it.

"Oh no, not that green flash hype again," Kelly said under his breath.

"Don't knock it, Kel. Howard Wright said..."

"Howard Wright said what? I never heard him say anything."

"Well, I did. You must have been off talking to somebody else. He said he and Jane saw the green flash frequently when they were on their year's cruise."

"Frequently? They saw it frequently?"

"Well, several times. Four or five at least. Howard said there's a scientific explanation, something about light refracting from the very last tip of the setting sun through the spectrum. It's too complicated to just reel off, but I wrote it down."

Kelly warmed to the subject. "Well, seeing as how we'll be out there five years, we should have ample opportunity to see it if it exists. How many sunsets would that be?"

The waitress overheard us as she came over with the menus and whipped out her pocket calculator. "That's three hundred and sixty-five sunsets times five equals, let's see, eighteen hundred'n twenty-five. If you haven't seen the green flash by then, you come back here and I'll buy you a drink." We laughed and thanked her and ordered Mai Tais, Kelly's with a Mount Gay Barbados rum float.

"Kelly, let's stop talking about the green flash. We're here to celebrate. Do you realize we're flat out of wheels? That was some kind of peak experience selling my car by the side of the road."

"I felt it too." He looked happily out to sea. The golden light of the sunset lit up his tan face. "Like getting rid of unnecessary baggage. A last link with our old landlubber life."

"Yes," I nodded. "It makes me feel like we're finally off to sea."

Kelly squeezed my hand. "It makes me feel like a kid."

"Throw off the dock lines!" Kelly shouted. There was more exuberance in his voice than I'd heard in three months. Morris sat conspicuously on the forward hatch as if thumbing his nose at the dockmaster and the "No Pets Allowed" regulation of the San Diego Yacht Club. There was a brisk morning breeze and a big sea running. As we headed out under sail into the channel we'd entered at dawn three months earlier, it seemed as if our cruising cat, nose to the wind, shared our excitement of knowing this day finally marked our transition into Mexican waters.

The hug Kelly gave me needed no words. The adventure of our cruise down the Baja Peninsula to Cabo San Lucas, around the tip and up into the Sea of Cortez to La Paz, had begun.

In late October there is a mass exodus of boats from the last U.S. port of San Diego for various locations in Baja or the Gulf of California to the Mexican mainland to loaf away the winter in Puerto Vallarta or Zihuatanejo. The hurricane season officially ends on October twentieth, and usually the skippers wait for this danger to subside. Another popular yardstick is based upon waiting for the water temperature in Baja to reach 72°. Since hurricane Lola was still rampaging off Baja, Kelly and I planned a leisurely perusal of the starkly beautiful 1,200-mile peninsula, stopping to anchor every night wherever we saw fit. Aware of my apprehension, Kelly forewarned me there'd be a couple of all-night passages. I bit my tongue to keep from complaining.

"I'm sorry, sweetheart," he said, "but you'd better get used to them. We'll be close to a month at sea standing night watches on our passage to the Marquesas."

"Don't worry." I shrugged, feigning nonchalance for his sake, swallowing my fear. "By that time I'll have a year of cruising under my belt."

"That's my girl." He bent to kiss me.

CHAPTER 2

Often do the spirits of great events stride on before the events,

And in today already walks tomorrow.

—Samuel Taylor Coleridge

THE FIRST COUPLE of hundred miles were like a gentle dream from which we hoped to never wake. Now we lay at anchor, in an intimate small bay. The morning sun slanted in through the open hatch at an angle, touching curliques on Kelly's chest and transforming the strawberry-blond covering his arms and thighs to a mellow gleam like antique sterling.

"So beautiful," I said. I ran my hands down his length, barely touching. My fingers brushed the twin birthmarks on his inner thighs. We made love with a sweetness born of ten years of trust and deep compatibility.

"I'm glad I married an engineer," I teased him. "You guys know how to make everything work." He beamed me his biggest smile as he swung his tan legs to the cabin floor and wrapped a towel around his hips. Next I heard a giant splash as he dove over the side of the boat. I knew he was backstroking his way through the warm Baja water on what would be a half-mile or more swim. Through the aft porthole of our bed chamber I caught a glimpse of his rhythmically moving arms, then reached for my book.

Long ago I stopped feeling guilty about not accompanying him on his morning regime.

The first year we were married, fall and winter, I donned a cutoff wet suit, thermal cap, and swim fins and bravely waded into the ocean. Kelly was similarly clad and in addition wore earplugs to protect his eardrums, sensitized by years of scuba diving. There was no way he could hear me. Sometimes I called out if the intensity of the rain became daunting, for instance. On one occasion a seal followed me too close for comfort. It didn't matter what the situation was, Kelly never heard me. His uninterrupted stroke put more distance between us by the minute. Since he wasn't worried about his own safety, he wasn't concerned with mine.

I loved ocean swimming in the summer but not when the water temperature hovered in the low fifties and flashes of black sea creatures kept appearing at a disconcerting proximity. *A shark!* I always thought, but it never was, just a curious seal or a troop of playful dolphins.

One gray November morning, after an especially chilling and scary swim, I thought, *Why am I ruining my life doing this? It isn't as though Kelly and I are having a companionable dip together; he's way off about a quarter of a mile away from me. Maybe I'm even cramping his style*, I thought hopefully.

One morning I announced, "Have a nice swim, sweetheart. I'm going to stay in bed and read. Could you please bring me coffee?" Thus began what turned into our new routine. After a cozy awakening together Kelly would be off to the beach while I enjoyed the solitude of the early morning, quietly reading and sipping the coffee he never failed to bring. It was a time of great peace. My alone time. I loved it and consumed about a book a week.

Kelly would come dripping into the kitchen like some big happy Labrador, leaving little puddles of saltwater on the hardwood floor. He'd recite the weather report as he had observed it, sounding like the marine operator. When he emerged from his hot shower, dressed and still chafing his near-frozen hands, I'd laugh at his pleasure in the way he started the day.

This particular morning as I remembered all this, I reluctantly arose from our bunk and stepped up to the cockpit to scan the glassy water of Metention Bay. The sparkling arc of drops from Kelly's powerful backstroke caught my gaze. I went below to brew fresh coffee and serve breakfast. The next order of the day would be Kelly getting on the ham radio. He was part of a network of fellow hams who had a daily communication ranging from world-class sailor Howard Wright in Alamitos Bay near Long Beach, California, to a group of former Southern California sailors who had retired and moved up to the Pacific Northwest. Except for interjections of wit from our odd buddy Howard, who, with his wife, Jane, was only around for brief intervals due to almost constant cruising, the level of the ham radio conversation was, to my ears, embarrassingly trivial.

Kelly was the newest member of the Net. I think they included him because of the exciting nature of our cruise. I was aware that he tried to play down the events of our daily life aboard the *Vagabundita*. He had to be the subject of extreme envy when his contribution would amount to having landed a fifteen-pound tuna while underway from Los Muertos to Las Frailes. They never let him say more than one or two sentences before asking the next man to "Come in, please."

This bright morning Kelly pulled himself up the swimming ladder saying, "Tomkat, hold off serving breakfast, I'd like to take advantage of this early breeze and get underway." I could see the water beginning to ruffle. "We have a long passage to Turtle Bay and I'd like to anchor before dark." I quickly stowed the galley equipment in the two deep stainless steel sinks. The noise of the windlass pulling our anchor up prevented further conversation. A minute later we met in the cockpit, each to our familiar station, Kelly revving up the *Vagabundita's* engine and I on the wheel, in preparation for bringing her up into the wind so he could hoist the mainsail.

The sound of the winch coiling the mainsheet, the flap of the canvas, the feel of the fresh breeze against my sun-warmed shoulders—these were a familiar thrill.

Later, enjoying our simple breakfast in the cockpit and discussing the day's forthcoming passage, we were suddenly amazed at the sight of a gigantic whale, surfacing just off our starboard bow. His Moby Dick eye met mine for a second before he plunged, probably more frightened than we were. I braced for a capsize. We were skimming along at about seven knots and it seemed impossible that the huge creature could clear our draft, but he did. There wasn't even a jolt to the hull, but our coffee mugs slopped over as the boat rolled in the whale's wake.

"My God," Kelly yelled, "I thought we were done for!" He dashed below for the camera and binoculars, but all we saw was a final flip of the whale's tail, a wave goodbye. I smiled a secret smile to think of what my husband would have to say on the next morning's ham radio Net.

Each morning after we got underway we'd set the trolling lines. Kelly had received from a friend a creative bon voyage gift of fishing gear. Packed in its own red zippered waterproof case, the color choice made it readily visible among the morass of gear I was constantly reorganizing and stashing in overcrowded lockers. Each line was individually coiled and fitted with a sinker and a variety of feathered lures in hot pink, silver-and-white, or turquoise, like Las Vegas showgirls in their ostentatious garb and improbable big blue eyes. At first I couldn't believe any self-respecting fish would be attracted by their meritritous glitter, but they were so effective that sometimes we had two simultaneous strikes. Kelly would release the larger of the two fish.

Dorado was our favorite but ran to at least sixteen pounds and made a bloody mess as it thrashed on the cockpit sole. Colored yellow and green like a tropical parrot, it faded to gray as it gasped for water. I always felt a pang for causing its death, but we were dependent on fishing to provide fresh food on our month's passage. I had to rush to throw the canvas pads and cushions below so they wouldn't get splattered with blood, always marveling at how much there was, expecting such a cold-blooded creature to have a pale, watery substance running through its slippery length. I hated the part when Kelly hit the fish in the head with a wrench to end its death throes, but he said it was humane. Appalled by the spectacle, Morris learned early on not to watch, dashing below to hide whenever we hauled a big fish aboard.

With his engineering ability, Kelly rigged a sturdy acrylic board on the stern, positioned so that he could stand upright to clean the fish with a sharp knife and swish the spine and entrails overboard. This procedure always attracted a flock of seagulls appearing out of nowhere, as noisy and effective as garbage trucks on land.

Minutes later Kelly decided how to prepare our catch, sometimes leafing through cookbooks but usually relying on his natural chef's instinct. I was glad he was able to indulge his love of cooking and inventing exotic Don the Beachcomber drinks.

Neither of us ever tired of our fresh fish lunches; there was no finer fare. We often said we dined better at sea than at home. Certainly more time and trouble went into the procurement and preparation when there were no frozen or fast foods available.

One of my birthday presents from Kelly was a sprouts grower, consisting of a cleverly designed three-part clear plastic container with raised mesh bottom and vented top. Water and seeds reliably produced fresh green sprouts in two or three days and they added a satisfying crunch to our sandwiches and tacos.

We wasted a lot of fish. It made us sad to throw it overboard, but without electric refrigeration we knew enough not to keep it overnight even if the temperature dropped. A couple of nights a week the fish ended up as a delicious chowder with the addition of canned clams, celery, onions, and potatoes, or as Mexican-Manhattan with canned chopped tomatoes and salsa cooked down. With this we served my pressure-cooker homemade bread and a good California Chardonnay.

"Tom, when we get home we'll have to invent some stories of roughing it at sea. Nobody'll believe we had it this good."

"Well, we wouldn't if it weren't for your cooking."

"Or your catching."

"Or our fabulous fishing gear," we said in unison, laughing together.

"And just think, I'll be able to write the quintessential book of yacht provisioning and cooking at sea," I said.

I was currently working on a book about life on board, written from Morris's point of view, entitled *All at Sea*. Kelly was a captive audience and laughed and made helpful suggestions as, over cocktails, I read to him what I'd written. Morris stood by uneasily, hearing his name spoken and sensing his dignity was at stake. From 10 a.m. to 12 p.m., when my morning boat chores were done, and again from 2 to 4 p.m., before dinner preparations began, I sat in the cockpit with my pen and yellow legal pad. That was the routine when we were cruising or at anchor. I was surprised at my output and the contentment I felt in my newfound creative direction. Though I didn't realize it then, never again would I be able to spend so much time writing.

"Goddamn cat, Morris!" Kelly's yell startled me awake. He so rarely swore that I was instantly alert. Seldom did anything disturb our night's tranquility as we lay at anchor. The necessary snuggle of our small bunk, senses lulled by lapping water heard through the hull, made for restful sleep. Now I was as disturbed as my husband by the insistent yowl of our ship's cat. If Morris weren't sleeping on our bunk, he always disappeared into his secret hiding places at night.

My fantasy of staying put in our bunk was short-lived. Morris was frantic. With his cat body language on full throttle, he bounded up the companionway into the cockpit, ran to the rail, jumped back down on our bunk, and charged back up. Kelly threw on something and followed him topside. Trying to be loyal, I dragged myself up into the cockpit. The crash of waves on rocks can be a lovely sound, but under midnight conditions it evoked a cold shiver of fear, despite the warmth of the Baja night.

"We're about ten feet away from those rocks of Metention Point." Kelly's voice was hushed. "We've dragged anchor at least a quarter of a mile." His face looked gray and drawn in the moonlight. "If it hadn't been for Morris…" His sentence went unfinished. Moving forward, he quietly ordered, "You start the engine; I'll haul up the anchor. Don't turn on the spreader lights."

That done, he came aft to join me and Morris in the cockpit. We peered intently out over the black water. There were four or five other sailboats rocking peacefully at anchor, identified only by the faint gleam of their forward lanterns. The sound of our diesel engine rudely broke the night's stillness as we powered back to what Kelly deemed a safe anchorage. "Tomkat, do you think any of the other boats *saw* that we dragged anchor?"

I pretended to scrutinize the other boats, hiding my smile. He had so little ego, it surfaced only over his self-perceived lack of anchoring technique. I glanced around at the boats, not a soul stirred aboard any of them, nor did a single beam of light penetrate the blackness. "Don't worry, sweetheart. The only one who knew we dragged anchor was Morris."

That night laid to rest any discussions Kelly and I had about the possibility of adding a third crew member for our long passages. Morris had become that full crew member. He not only stood watch on his own volition, he had proved to be indispensable, possibly saving our lives. Certainly saving that of the *Vagabundita*.

By the time we reached lower Baja we had cruised long enough to have settled into an acceptance of the problems and surprises that occurred almost daily in Mexican waters. The cruising life, by its solitary nature, could be a lonely one, though Kelly and Morris and I created our own jolly company. Often at sea, strangers would reach out to make spontaneous contact unthinkable in our nearly forgotten world ashore.

I had in-depth encounters with other cruising women when we moored in areas urban enough to have a washer and dryer. Clean laundry was a constant challenge at sea. We shared stories as we kicked and cursed the malfunctioning machines that disgorged gray wash at best. In most cases, grumbling, we had to haul the wet laundry back along the docks, to hang from every available boom and line, strung hastily by anxious husbands afraid their wives had "had it" with cruising. We prayed it would dry in the late sun before the evening breeze bore in the salty mist.

I met Barrie Ann at Nuevo Vallarta, the morning of Marina's dockside "garage sale." Excitement ran high as the house flags, hoisted from the spreaders, advertised the many displays in evidence on the dock. Our boat's Mexican name, *Vagabundita*, meaning "little wayward girl," drew smiles and casual introductions from the other cruising boaters.

Every inch of storage space aboard our sailboat counted. After months at sea there was some gear we realized was superfluous and were anxious to dispose of. In my carefully assembled sailing wardrobe—enough to meet any weather contingency first off, then a few girl things for perks— there were some clothes that didn't work, occupying valuable locker space. One was a sleeveless bright-patterned cotton knit T-shirt that looked cheerful when I bought it, but somehow I'd never wanted to put it on. We had a lot of paperback books on display and some items from Kelly's vast stores of parts and repair equipment that even he thought we were long on.

Barrie, a petite blond woman, paused and stretched out a hand when she saw the T-shirt. "This is very pretty, but why is it wet?" she asked.

"Because I dropped it overboard by mistake." I felt chagrined. She laughed uproariously, "Well, join the 'Irretrievable Items Overboard Club,'" she said and we became instant friends.

Barrie was a longtime cruising wife. Her husband, Larry, was a United Airlines captain of such tenure that he could choose his own routes. He moved his wife and yacht around the South Pacific accordingly. Barrie was frequently alone on board for two weeks or more, while Larry was fly- ing. She deserved to have their boat, the *Barrie-Ann*, named after her.

I saw her husband once in the full regalia of his uniform and he was worth waiting for. He considerately enabled his wife to be mobile, by dint of a red jeep they kept in Puerto Vallarta. Barrie was generous in her offers to transport other sailing wives on provisioning trips into the mercado in Puerto Vallarta. That was about as close as I ever got to "lunch with the girls" that year. Once, over a two-hour margarita repast, we explored our favorite topics: "What if?" (worst-case sailing scenarios with our hus- bands) "Why?" (weird that the men love this cruising life so much).

The truth was that marriages of many cruising couples ended in divorce, or with the wife jumping ship to fly home after a year or so. The women who stuck, or even grew to love the life, invariably found ways to define themselves. Barrie had developed a fine artist's hand in watercolor and exhibited at art galleries and local shows in various ports of call. I admired her and was proud to be her friend, even if she was a gorgeous, natural blond with a size-six body.

Kelly and I were delighted to successfully "match up" by radio telephone with Jane and Howard Wright, whom we hoped to meet in La Paz, our mooring location in the Sea of Cortez, but the uncertainty of sailing itineraries, the unpredictability of weather, and the difficulty of communication often thwarted a planned rendezvous.

Happily the Wrights were moored dockside in the marina adjacent to where we were docked at the Marina de La Paz. They were aboard the *Zorba*, a fifty-three-foot wood trawler, painstakingly refitted to Howard's exacting specifications. They left the boat in Baja and flew back and forth to get the most out of the marvelous cruising grounds in the Sea of Cortez.

The old Los Arcos Hotel in La Paz had not changed in the ten years since I had first seen it with Kelly, when we were still courting. We were excited about the Wrights' invitation to join them for a festive luncheon in the charming palmed courtyard of the hotel. I was excited about getting out of my grungy cruising gear and into a long denim skirt and a new top printed with tropical fish. Our conversation revolved around the various anchorages up in the Sea of Cortez where Kelly and I planned to cruise during December and January.

Howard's input was invaluable to us. He took a serious interest in our five-year plan to circumnavigate. I had a sinking feeling that he didn't quite like the *Vagabundita*—maybe didn't quite trust her was more accurate. Our thirty-seven-foot sailboat seemed flimsy compared to the sturdy *Zorba* and their other boat, *The Compadre*, a fifty-five-foot stretch version of a William Lapworth design. She was a full-powered cutter in which Jane and Howard had crossed the Atlantic twice and cruised extensively in the British Isles and the Mediterranean. They'd been cruising Baja since the sixties.

Kelly was grateful for Howard's suggestion to redesign our chain locker to accommodate the 175 feet of anchor chain we carried. It was heavy and awkward but rope lines could not withstand the sharp coral reefs of our destination in the South Pacific. Howard even offered the expertise of his own shipwright, Hymie, who often sailed with them. "So we'll know it's done right," he said.

Both Howard and Kelly knew much of the refitting work on the *Vagabundita* had been done in a slipshod manner while Kelly's back was turned. In his energetic way of shouldering too much at once, Kelly had thought he could divide his time between the boatyard and our new house construction site, as well as simultaneously studying navigation and Morse code at the local city college. Each major project proved to be a yeoman's job and each suffered from lack of his undivided supervision.

I was particularly pleased with the new, more commodious compartment for the chain storage. Though the anchor chain was hauled up by the windlass, an electric winch, I was the one who had to cram my body into the tight forepeak, lie on my stomach and lay the chain out in loose concentric coils to diminish its proclivity to tangle. Sometimes it was covered with a smelly green slime. We hated to stow it aboard in that condition and only did so when it was unavoidable.

I grumbled about my dirty job and complained to Kelly about what it did to my fingernails. Yet, I was secretly thrilled to be the one, by dint of size, to fulfill this important function of stowing the chain. I'd given up on my immaculate French manicures months ago.

I pitied Kelly as he told Howard about our latest equipment failure. It underscored my uneasy feelings about Howard's opinion of our boat. The Global Positioning System (GPS) had gone out. It was a vital electronic navigational device used to determine our position with satellite assistance. Its breakdown clearly emphasized the importance of being skilled in the traditional methods of shooting sun and star sights by sextant. A multiplicity of systems was the safest way to navigate, so we used celestial methods with the sophisticated GPS as a backup.

I remembered well Kelly's excitement when he explained the GPS, or "Magellan," as he called it. He had a true engineer's love of electronic gadgets and I knew that each addition of the latest in technology was a big part of his enjoyment of readying the boat for her finest hour. Not so me. I've always been intimidated by electronics and machines in general, and had been rightfully accused by Kelly of barely being able to operate my own vacuum cleaner. The sextant was another matter. We had been given a fine old one as a bon voyage gift by another sailing friend. I loved taking it out of its beautiful fitted wooden box and navigating in the same way as the ancient explorers. I grew expert at bringing the wobbly little green sun-image down to kiss the horizon and yelling "Mark!" while Kelly reconciled the time on his chronometer with Greenwich Mean Time. He patiently taught me how to work out the computations. Always slow at math, it took a week for me to trust my accuracy, but I finally mastered it.

It was going to be a real pain to ship the GPS back to the U.S. for repair. Horror stories were told regarding packages coming and going that never made it through Mexican customs. Our savvy U.S. postal department refused to insure to Mexico. We could just imagine our $2,000 GPS sent under these conditions. Jane Wright offered to take it back on the plane with her to Los Angeles to facilitate its reaching the appropriate repair service. Kelly could have cried, he was so grateful. We stood at the end of the marina's dock waving the Wrights off on their cruise to a favorite Sea of Cortez island, Isla Espiritu Santo.

The wind made whitecaps on the water and luffed the Wrights' canvas for a moment before it caught and filled the ample sails. The *Zorba* moved like a stout matron on her course. I linked my arm through Kelly's. At this moment I could read his mind. I thought hard about picking the right words to alleviate his concern. "Kell, isn't it wonderful we love our sailboat so much? I don't envy the Wrights that big motor sailer and I don't envy Howard's shipwright, but I sure envy Jane's spice locker!" It was always with a tug at the heart that we watched friends sail away, to meet perhaps again on some far-flung shore.

After much discussion of our finances, Kelly and I decided to invite all five of our collective children, three with spouses, to meet us for Christmas in La Paz. The airfare was reasonable. We could accommodate two couples on board and put the overflow up at one of the small, tile-roofed courtyard hotels near the marina. We wouldn't need any rental cars and our gifts to each other would be our company.

Christmas fell midweek that year and sadly the kids were all too busy working to get away. It was a disappointment. Kelly especially wanted them to see firsthand what this cruising life of ours was all about. Characteristically, my youngest son, Kenny, was the only one who came.

Storms raged off Baja that late December. We wondered where the locals got the ski parkas they donned for the unaccustomed cold. We tried to laugh a little about day after day of unrelenting rain that overflowed the sidewalks and dumped mud into the anchorage, dirtying our white hull and turning the sea to an ugly brown.

Kelly occupied himself writing our newsletter, to be mailed to a long list of friends at New Year's. I experimented with Mexican recipes, sometimes scalding our tongues with an unfamiliar red or green pepper. I was proud to perfect Chile Rellenos. Fish tacos became our luncheon specialty once I'd learned to make them well. Rosa, the Mexican woman who ran the fish taco stand outside the marina, invited me home to her dark little kitchen one afternoon and took the gringo yacht lady in hand and taught me to make tortillas from scratch. She shook her head sadly as she told me the present generation of young girls wouldn't make them anymore, preferring to buy them ready-made. I could tell my new friend was ashamed of her pupil when I failed to produce her perfect circles, rolling the little golf balls of dough out on her floured marble slab with an old Tequila bottle. I did my best, but mine turned out oblong or pear-shaped instead of round. Too polite to comment, Rosa just turned away. Nevertheless, I was thrilled to acquire the skill, and proud to promise Kelly fish tacos in mid-passage on our forthcoming monthlong Pacific crossing.

We decorated the boat with homemade ornaments and even bought an artificial tree at the mercado, since there was not a fresh fir or spruce to be found. Almost every night one string of lights went out, so we spent hours testing each tiny bulb. We shopped for fixings for Christmas dinner. Over our years of spending most Thanksgivings anchored somewhere off Santa Cruz Island, we'd polished our technique of turning out a turkey dinner with all the trimmings. Stuffing, giblet gravy, creamed onions, mashed potatoes, and yams with pineapple, even homemade pumpkin pie, were produced from one oven and two burners, no microwave.

Christmas Eve.

The downpour was so intense, the visibility zero, that our taxi driver was afraid to negotiate the roads and made so many wrong turns we were afraid we'd be late for Kenny's Air Mexicana flight from L.A. The modest airport was crowded with people waiting to meet the Christmas Eve plane. It looked like a funeral crowd, there were so many old ladies dressed in black. Not a single red scarf enlivened the somber crowd.

"Kelly, do you think they're all widows?"

"Sure. They're here to meet their grandkids who've made good in California." The intensity with which the women worked their rosaries made me think they knew something I didn't. Beads slipped through gnarled fingers, their murmuring Hail Marys nearly drowned out by the loudspeaker announcing further delays in the arrival of Kenny's flight. The plane was already forty-five minutes late.

Suddenly the lights in the airport went out. We rushed to the windows. Nothing but darkness and deluge. The landing strip was entirely blacked out. I gripped Kelly's arm, praying hard, wishing I too had a rosary to occupy my trembling hands. The loudspeaker announced that they were out of radio contact with Flight 874. *Why did they have to tell us that?* My temples throbbed and I pulled my sailing jacket with the broken zipper closer. Cold from the concrete floor crept up my legs through the sodden soles of my espadrilles.

"Kelly, maybe the weather report was so bad the plane didn't leave L.A. Maybe Kenny's not on it. They have such terrible radio transmission," I finished angrily.

"That would be expected in this storm." Kelly was interrupted as the exterior doors pushed open. Passengers looking like refugees, drenched from the short walk from the plane, crowded into the dim waiting room. Kenny's height and his bright ski parka distinguished him from the morass of dark figures. I rushed forward, almost choked by relief, not forgetting to thank God for answered prayers.

The violence of the storm spent itself overnight and Christmas dawned with a tender stillness and an innocent blue sky.

We'd planned to cast off about midmorning and head up into the Sea of Cortez to our favorite anchorage off Isla Espiritu Santo. "Let's not disturb Kenny," I said. "He's exhausted from the trip. When we get there he'll wake up in paradise."

Kenny did wake up about halfway through our two-hour sail. He greeted us, but he didn't join us in the cockpit. I was surprised when he went up forward, wearing a headset, Dos Equis in hand. He lay flat on the sun-warmed deck looking like he needed to absorb the heat into a hurting body.

"Kelly," I said, "Kenny's in a lot of pain. I'm glad he came but I have this feeling like, I don't know, maybe I can't help him with it. Do you see what I'm talking about?"

"Sort of. When he went up forward and downed a beer and just lay there by himself, I thought something must be wrong, but I don't feel it like you must as a mother."

"I bet it's him and Mindy. They're splitting up for good. It's killing him."

"Are you sure?" Kelly looked incredulous.

"Of course I'm sure. Why do you think he came by himself?"

Kelly passed his hand over his brow and sighed, "Will you ever forget how much in love they were?"

"I know. Only four years ago."

Kenny, then twenty-seven, worked for Hobie Sports in Laguna Beach. One day he called in a fever and said, "Please try and come down, Mom. I really want you and Kelly to meet Mindy. Oh, and she's got a little girl." A few days later, we met at a restaurant in Laguna for breakfast. Mindy hardly said anything at first, just laughed a lot. I wasn't able to get much of a read on her. Judging from the age of her daughter, I guessed Mindy was a couple of years younger than Kenny. She was dressed in khakis and a white shirt, becoming against her tan face and shoulder-length dark hair. I noticed her beautiful long-fingered hands and sandaled feet when she got up to take her pretty six-year-old daughter, Jennifer, to the ladies' room. Mindy seemed to regard me with a certain wariness, understandable, as she was meeting her boyfriend's mother for the first time. There was an odd, partially concealed assurance about her, like she knew a secret she wasn't telling—and much more that I sensed but couldn't put a finger on.

Holding hands under the table, Kenny and Mindy looked at each other as if they were all alone in the café. Their ardor enveloped us like the fragrance of hot bread and coffee wafting in from the kitchen. Loath to intrude, I was finally overcome by curiosity and asked, "So how did you two meet?"

"I came into Hobie Sports one day and there he was," Mindy said. "I took one look and said 'That man is the one for me.'" I was taken aback by her candor and glanced at Kelly. "You wouldn't believe how much I spent on sports clothes in there trying to get his attention. He was always in the back selling a surfboard or something."

"Come on. I noticed you," Kenny put in.

"Not until I asked you to stop by after work." She turned a beaming face to us. "He moved in the next day."

"It wasn't *that* fast," Kenny said, trying to save face.

"By the weekend anyway."

"And that was how long ago?" Kelly asked.

"A *month*," they said in unison. They looked into each other's faces, eyes alight; laughter they could not contain spilled out of their mouths. No wonder my son hadn't called me in the last four weeks. They'd been busy.

Jennifer curtsied as she thanked us for breakfast and said it was nice meeting us. Kenny and Mindy hugged us and went outside as we stopped at the cashier.

They stood on the curb waiting for the walk signal. Kenny's arm was around Mindy's waist. He pulled her to him and kissed her on the mouth. Their bodies clasped together even as the light changed, lovers oblivious to the summer tourists laden with beach chairs and boogie boards who surged across the street, brushing by them. Jennifer hopped up and down on one foot, pulling on Kenny's shirt until he broke out of the embrace and turned around. "What, Pest?" he said, ruffling her hair.

"Take us to the beach," she begged.

"Where else? It's Sunday, isn't it?" Kenny took their hands to safely cross the street. As they approached the parking lot, he slung Jennifer onto his shoulders and jogged her along piggyback. Riding jockey style she shrieked in mock terror. Kelly and I glimpsed the exuberant face she turned to her mother. They piled into their Jeep, Jennifer yelling, "The beach, the beach!"

Kelly took my hand as we watched from the corner. In mute accord we didn't move to catch up with them. No one looked back to wave.

I'd been struck by Mindy's allure and tried to analyze it. A uniqueness, something that went far beyond her youth and beauty. She was truly one in a million of the pretty girls who flocked Laguna's streets.

As Kelly and I got to know her better we learned a little of her past. She'd seen to her daughter's welfare since she'd given birth at eighteen, getting little help from the ex-husband of the brief marriage.

A successful IBM computer broker, she was well-known in her field. Firms from coast to coast competed to hire her. So much for her assurance, well-earned by hard work and self-sufficiency, but floating just beneath the surface was a contradictory vulnerability that, coupled with her physical fragility, endowed her with powerful magnetism. Right away I'd fallen for her. Kelly felt the pull too. It made us want to help her, give her things, turn ourselves inside out for her.

Kenny brought Mindy up to Santa Barbara the next weekend after our Laguna Beach breakfast to show her the lay of the land. Kelly and I took them to lunch at the yacht club and conversation turned to our long-range cruising and house-building plans. After lunch we walked down the marina dock to show Mindy the boat and then drove over to our lot on Ortega Ridge, where the excavation looked like a great bite was taken out of the steep slope that ran from the street down to meet the Valley Club Golf Course.

They were engaged a few weeks after that—in love and impetuously married three months later.

Kenny and I stayed up in the cockpit a while after Kelly went to bed. I lay on my back, watching the incredible stars of Baja pop out one by one. Kenny was below, pouring us each a small snifter of brandy. Sometimes Kenny could be closemouthed about his personal life. I hoped we could talk. "What's going on, sweetheart?" I said. "I know things aren't good."

"I don't want to go all into it, Mom. Mindy and I've been haranguing for months. Basically she's this high-powered IBM computer broker with a six-figure salary. She's got to be in New York."

"I know all that but she always said she didn't care how much money you made, that she loved you, loved having your precious Kendal."

"Mom, I'm a surfboard salesman and a part-time ski instructor. What can I possibly do in New York?" That silenced me as I cast about in my mind, feeling like I should intervene, but it was their decision. I couldn't think of anything to say. I leaned over and hugged Kenny. "I feel so bad for you, Kenny. I think I know how much you love Mindy, Jennifer, and Kendal."

These thoughts plagued me as the *Vagabundita* creaked and swayed, sound and motion that usually put me to sleep, but I couldn't get the breakup out of my mind and whispered to Kelly about it that night as we snuggled in our bunk. "Oh Kelly, I had such high hopes for that marriage, so thrilled with our first granddaughter after all our boys. Remember when Mindy left Kendal with us?"

"She could barely walk. She went up and down our stairs on her hands and knees."

"You carried her in a backpack when we walked on the beach," I said.

"Remember when she saw the divers?"

"It was good you had to leave for Houston before Mindy picked her up. You fell in love with Kendal that week."

The next morning I raised a cup of the special coffee Kenny'd brought, saying, "Here's to Christmas at sea."

"Too bad the rest of the kids couldn't make it, but we're glad you're here, Kenny."

"This is pretty amazing," Kenny looked out over the sparkling water, his cheerful spirits resumed. "I can hardly believe I flew into La Paz last night. We're so remote here—not another boat in sight."

"That's because of Christmas," Kelly said. "Usually there's a couple of fishing boats at least. The fishermen are probably whooping it up in La Paz. I hope so anyway. They're hardworking. They deserve a holiday."

"That rocky area looks like it'd be good diving," Kenny indicated the rock-lined points extending out from both sides of the beach running along the deep cove Kelly'd anchored in.

"Let's go for it," I said, anticipating sharing a much-loved activity with my son. "The water's perfect. You won't even need a wet suit."

"You two go along," Kelly said, "I want to finish our Christmas letter." I knew he was giving me the opportunity to experience rare time alone with my son. We hoped to find lobster, so plentiful along the Baja Peninsula, but agreed it would be wrong to dislodge abalone. Once known as "the world's greatest fish trap," we were sensitive to the changing environment in the Sea of Cortez, its dwindling fish stocks and fragile ecosystem.

We surfaced at intervals to discuss various forms of marine life we spotted, intrigued with the rough-surfaced, blackish-gray, shell-like formations clinging to the rocks. I watched through my mask as Kenny gently probed one with his ab-iron. It had the suction-like apparatus of an abalone but was much smaller and camouflaged, just enough to make spotting them a challenge. Eventually we got cold and swam back to the boat, exhilarated from the saltwater.

Kelly applauded our empty booty bags. He was putting the finishing touch of grated cheese on the Coquille Saint Jacques he'd whipped up for our Christmas Eve dinner.

"Wow, Kelly," Kenny said, always impressed with his stepfather's culinary skills and no doubt starved after two hours of diving. "What's that gourmet-looking thing?"

"Scallops in cream sauce, fresh from the La Paz fish market."

"Scallops—of course! I used to dive for them and pick them off the rocks. Mom, that's what those weird-looking shell things we saw were."

"You're right, and we were so tempted to take them."

Most of the lights on the plastic tree were working now and I had a few simple gifts wrapped, things like fishing lures and squeeze flashlights. Kenny'd brought us carefully selected paperbacks, tapes of our kind of music, and decorative packages of fancy coffees.

The cabin had a festive air and we sipped champagne watching the early sunset, the spectrum of pale pink to orange dramatic against a frieze of black clouds heralding an approaching storm. The peace of the evening was short-lived. When the storm hit, accompanied by the inevitable roll, we were just sitting down to our turkey dinner. At first it was exciting to listen to the sounds of the storm, but soon felt claustrophobic to be stuck below with everything battened down instead of up on deck enjoying the fresh air and breeze that sailing is all about. We went to bed at an embarrassingly early hour.

The next morning, as the threatening sky scowled down, we weighed anchor and powered back to La Paz. Rain or no rain at least we could show Kenny the town in his remaining two days.

I took Kenny on a tour of the mercado with its grisly meat market displaying the severed heads of farm animals and its plethora of fresh, though un-iced, fish. We picked up fruit and vegetables that I'd learned to wash in chlorox-treated water from a bucket on the dock. Poor Kenny was experiencing ominous rumblings of the possible onset of tourista, the same symptoms that had laid Kelly and me low over Thanksgiving in Cabo.

"You're going to think this is nuts," I said, "but you're also going to love it. I've got a cure. A doctor in Turtle Bay who gave Kelly a tetanus shot told us about it—margaritas. He said there's something about the tequila and the lime juice that kills the amoeba."

"That's the craziest thing I've ever heard," Kenny said, looking skeptical.

"Well, if you feel up to it let's give it a try." Kelly'd been on a quest to find someplace that could fax our Christmas letter and a silly picture of Morris leaning against a "Bon Voyage" pillow with a book entitled *How to Shop Mexico* propped in front of him. Our secretary, Marie Koutoulas, was ready with addressed envelopes to mail it out for New Year's to our friends.

Kelly and I'd discussed meeting somewhere in town in the early evening to watch the sunset. I knew it would be spectacular, alighting the storm clouds hanging out at sea. "N6YNL, N6YNL, come in please. This is Foxtrot." I tried Kelly's radio call sign repeatedly on my shortwave walkie-talkie, as I called it, to no avail. I turned a disappointed face to Kenny. "He's not reading me. We carry these things for fun but they don't have much range."

"Don't worry, Mom, we'll go back to the boat soon. Let's try your remedy now." He'd spotted an attractive café overlooking the balustraded walk that ran along the beachside promenade. The whole front of the restaurant was open.

It was fun to sit and look out at the rain that had started again as our birdbath margaritas were served. I punched in Kelly's call sign again, hating to think of him left out of our fun, but there was no answer.

"It's okay, Mom. Stop trying to get Kelly. I need this time alone with you." I heard a serious note in his voice and he looked away from me a moment, fiddling with the salt on the rim of his glass.

I jumped in with, "Is it something else about you and Mindy?" The bomb he'd already dropped about their decision to divorce was bad enough, along with the pain I'd detected when he talked about his daughter, Kendal.

"No, Mom. It's about you and Kelly. He doesn't look well to me. He isn't himself."

"What! Doesn't look well? He's *never* been more tan and fit," I said defensively. "He swims over a mile a day; we walk everywhere."

Kenny interrupted. "Stop, Mother. You see him every day so you don't notice. It's like a pallor under his tan. He doesn't seem to be all there sometimes, like he doesn't hear me. He seems kind of vague."

"He has this new little hearing aid, maybe he didn't have it on. I don't know what you're talking about, Kenny. Right before we left Santa Barbara, Dr. De Berry gave him a thorough physical, even an EKG. I carry the chart with me."

"Why?" Kenny asked.

"In case there's a problem, they can compare the new EKG to the normal one."

"Normal! There's no normal here. He already *has* a heart condition."

"No, just an uneven heartbeat. Fibrillation. It's completely regulated by medication. I have a three-month supply. Twice as much as we need to get us to Papeete. I don't know why we have to dredge all this up again." I glanced away in irritation.

"Because I'm concerned. Really worried about *you*, Mother." He reached out and took my hand. "You and Kelly are headed for this crazy month's crossing of the Pacific Ocean to the most remote islands in the world. He's sixty-five and he's got a heart condition, whether you're willing to admit it or not. I want you to hire a hand, or better yet, a professional skipper to go with you for the crossing."

"No way. It's *our* adventure. We've been cruising for almost a year now. I've got the feel of it. A third person would be a third wheel; it'd wreck the romance."

"The *romance*!" Kenny shook his head, pulled his hand away, and signaled the waitress for another round.

"We need something in our stomachs," I said. "Order some quesadillas or salsa and chips, guacamole."

"Wait. Listen, Mom, you and Kelly love Mexico. I can see that, all your funny stories. You're having the time of your lives."

"Yes, that's the point," I interjected.

"Well then, here's a simple solution. Winter in Zuitaneo, then come

back here and cruise the Sea of Cortez. It's what most of these other cruising people seem to be doing." He gestured around the restaurant at the
gray-haired couples dressed in waterproof jackets and boat shoes.

"No, Kenny. I wouldn't even suggest that to Kelly. It would seem like
I was chickening out on the Pacific passage. It would break his heart if I
backed out now. Not fair."

"I'm only saying to *postpone* the Marquesas. Finish out your first year
in Mexico. It's enough of an adventure. At least you're not entirely out of
range of help."

"We can't just change the whole plan now. We're going around the
world!"

"You've allocated *five years*. What's a six-month delay? I have a bad
feeling about it, Mother. Really bad."

"What, are you psychic now or something?" He fell silent despite my
sarcasm.

"No, but *you* are. You can't tell me you haven't had any premoni-
tions." I knew he saw my eyes drop.

"Not anything you could really put your finger on." He just stared at
me as my voice trailed off. We both knew I was lying.

"Listen, Kenny. I want to tell you something to make you feel better
about all this. You know the mail packet Marie sends when we make each
major port?"

"Mother." I heard his exasperated exhalation. He slumped his body
back into his chair like an old man, "You're changing the subject."

"No, I'm not. Just hear me out, Kenny, please." I stretched out a hand
to touch his arm but he pulled away, folding his arms across his chest, his
body language speaking more eloquently than the angry tone of his
voice. "I was starting to say about the mail packet. It's scary what happens
to people with no warning. In just the last three months, with our
friends...two couples our age lost adult children. One of Kelly's best male
friends just died way too young. They'd been in each other's weddings.
Kids your age with babies getting divorced..."

"Okay, Mother, *okay!*"

"No, I didn't mean you and Mindy. Really, I'm getting to the point."

I held up a hand as if to ward off the interruption I knew was coming. "There was a letter from Barry McNulty—you remember my college boyfriend, you met him in Laguna years ago."

"Of course, Mom."

Back to "Mom" at least. "He had that incredible tragedy. His son and granddaughter going down in that plane together..."

"Yes," Kenny said, propping his chin in his hand, pain in his eyes. "Yes, I even remember her name, Annabel Lee, because she'd be Kendal's age. Good God, how do people get over a thing like that?" Kenny didn't sound angry anymore. I had his attention.

"They don't. They couldn't; only some grow so bitter they turn it all inside and others reach out—that's what Barry's trying to do. He wrote to me, 'No matter where you are in the world, no matter what happens, if you need me I will come. I will know if you need me.' Kenny, it's been over thirty years. He's a port in a storm for me; he'd be there, no matter what."

"But, Mom," my son reached out for me now, his young face naked, his voice low and grave, "Don't you know I'd come for you too?"

CHAPTER 3

There is, one knows not what sweet mystery about this sea.

—Herman Melville

I T HAD BEEN WONDERFUL to see Kenny but Kelly and I were glad to be off to a new anchorage. Las Hadas considered itself a very exclusive resort, barely tolerating the sailboat "Yachties," as we were called. Huge powerboats paid substantial sums for dockside slips. Their skippers ran gigantic generators to power what we sailors considered an ostentatious array of freezers, appliances, and overkill lighting. Our sleep was disturbed nightly by the noise. We developed warm friendships with the other sailors anchored for free out in the ample bay.

Amused to be under constant scrutiny by the white-uniformed hotel attendants hired to keep the riffraff out of the pool area and off the beach, our goal was to gain credibility by sporting a monogrammed Las Hadas towel, if we could snitch one. I tried to dress as a guest of the hotel: white shorts, glitzy sandals instead of worn topsiders, and designer sunglasses, a great status symbol in Mexico. Kelly usually blew our image in his grungy old shorts and T-shirts.

One afternoon I spiffed Kelly up in his one unfaded bathing suit and an awful gold braid-trimmed captain's cap he'd received as a joke farewell gift. The outfit was convincing and he spent an entire afternoon luxuriating by the pool. I sent him over a fancy rum drink from "a secret admirer." He almost fell off the chaise when the white-coated waiter appeared with the pineapple-and-umbrella-festooned concoction. I signaled him from across the pool with a seductive glance from over lowered sunglasses.

One hot afternoon Kelly went into Manzanillo by taxi with Jim Gustin, one of the yachtsmen we'd met. The men were in search of the most reliable and cheapest source for diesel fuel, needed to top off our tanks before our Pacific passages. Even though we intended to be under sail for the entire voyage, we would need some fuel to run our generators and charge batteries. We were warned the next chance to obtain diesel would be questionable in the remote Isles de Marquesas.

I'd spent the morning cleaning the boat and was enjoying a rare afternoon of reading in the cockpit, half dozing, dropping my book at intervals when a heavy jolt to the hull set the boat rocking wildly. I jumped fully awake and dashed forward, fearing a collision. Two of the largest dolphins I had ever seen were scratching their backs on our anchor chain. I smiled at their playful antics. Standing on the bowsprit, I could have reached down and touched them. We were in such close proximity that our eyes met in what seemed like recognition. I felt that we shared an ancient bond, as if they were nebulous ghosts from a much-loved former life. Once, in Hawaii, I swam with the dolphins, holding to their dorsal fins as they took turns carefully carrying me around the circular tank. They dove only to the depth of my limited lungs. I marveled at the gentle way they brushed against my body, intuiting that I was in an alien element.

Kelly returned to the boat just in time to see them. By now they had been playing about our bow for some two hours. People on the neighboring boats had gathered to watch. Some called over, asking enviously, "What is it about the *Vagabundita* that attracts them?" The sleek dolphins answered in high-pitched squeaks, as if trying to tell us something.

Kelly called his Santa Barbara ham radio contact, Dr. George Austin, at their appointed time that evening. George said my son Billy and his wife, Robin, had called with wonderful news. We would have a grandchild in seven months. I told Kelly I believed the dolphins were trying to communicate this to us.

In celebration, we decided to disregard our budget and splurge on dinner. I got all dressed up in my long blue-and-white skirt, sarong-tied over a sleeveless white top. Dangling shell earrings and a pink hibiscus in my hair completed the outfit. "You look like a South Sea island girl already," Kelly said, buttoning his peach-and-blue aloha shirt over white pants— those white pants I had "a thing" about, hand-washing and bleaching them in the sun on laundry days. He took my hand as we walked over the rope bridge spanning the vast island-studded pool to the hotel. Ascending three floors, we were seated at a romantic, pink-clothed table set with amber-rimmed, handblown Mexican glass. Candlelight illuminated the cascading bougainvillea on the balustrades as we listened to enchanting Latin melodies played by mariachis on classical violin and guitar.

"Sweetheart, let's toast the baby," Kelly said. His eyes locked on mine as we clinked glasses. In his gaze was the pain of his lost grandchild and the thrill of the impending birth of mine.

"It will be your grandbaby too, Kelly. Any little child would love you for a grandfather; you're such a big teddy bear of a guy." He smiled back at me, joy written on his face. As the wine dwindled, Kelly reached across the table for my hand.

"I know what a big thing this grandchild is to you, Tomkat. I've been thinking. We'll be sitting out hurricane season in Australia when the baby is due in mid-November. We could fly home for the birth and stay in California for Christmas." Candlelight coming from the ornate wrought-iron hurricane lanterns adorning our balcony table illuminated Kelly's face. Not the slightest flicker in his expression betrayed the caring in his words. Tears filled my eyes. I knew we couldn't afford two round-trip airfares from Australia, a cat sitter for Morris, and slip fees for the boat.

"Kelly, you make me happy saying that, but you don't get it." I covered his hand with mine and leaned close. "I love this crazy, seagoing, nomadic life. I want us to go on doing this together, maybe forever. Think now. We have five grown children—two married and one already getting divorced—plus your mother to look after. In the next five years a lot of unforeseen things will happen in their lives. I don't want to diminish what we're doing out here by running home every time there's a crisis, good or bad."

His face lit up. We looked out over the dark, palm-lined beach, across the lighted water, and picked out the *Vagabundita* from among the other anchored sailboats, her forward lantern gently swaying, beckoning us back aboard.

The next afternoon at the same hour as before, the two oversized dolphins returned to our sailboat. Laughing, I called to them, "It's okay, you guys, we know about the baby!" Obviously confident in knowing their message was received, they squeaked a farewell, dove under the hull, and surfaced in gleaming arcs on the other side. Mission accomplished, they leapt joyfully out to sea.

We could talk of nothing but the grandchild. When George radioed in that evening, Kelly could hardly wait to tell him about the dolphins bringing us the news. "Oh come on, Kelly, you don't really believe all that nonsense, do you?"

"Uh-oh. Tommie overheard that. I'm afraid you're in for it now, old boy. She's about to quote you chapter and verse." I'd already taken a book down and was leafing through it. Kelly held the phone for me.

"Listen, George, *nobody* puts down my dolphins. I've got Jacques Cousteau's book here and I'm going to read you something that will change your tune. Okay, ready? 'There have been several dolphins who have acquired more or less permanent fame by associating with humans. One of the most celebrated of them was Pelorus Jack, who became known in 1888. Pelorus Jack lived in Cook Strait, which separates the two principal islands of New Zealand, between French Pass and Pelorus Sound. He was fascinated by ships and there was hardly a vessel which entered Cook

Strait that Jack did not accompany. The *Penguin*, a steamer which frequently passed through the Strait, on one occasion inadvertently rammed
Pelorus Jack and the dolphin was rather seriously injured. From then on,
whenever the *Penguin* entered the Strait, Jack was careful to keep his distance from that particular vessel.'"

"Interesting story," George said, "but it's only one isolated case."

"Listen. Cousteau was a serious scientist. This book *Dolphins* deals
with his studies and even *he* intimates that anthropomorphic connec-
tions exist between humans and dolphins, especially in the area of
communication, so there!"

Kelly took the phone. "I think she's implying that you brain surgeons
think you know everything, old boy!"

Anchored out in the bay at Las Hadas for a week, we were enjoying
one of the best aspects of the cruising life—reunions with cruising couples
we'd met along the way. Our socializing took place after dark, since there
were barely enough hours in the day to conduct our endless chores of
maintenance and provisioning.

A typical workday for me meant starting my bread dough's first rise,
rowing the dirty laundry ashore, and, using hose and bucket, doing a gar-
gantuan wash, including my hair and the cat. I feared a flea infestation
almost as much as one of cockroaches. Horror stories abounded, reinforced by the sight of the multitudes of the loathsome insects that'd
scurried underfoot in La Paz, around the beer cooler where scraps of food
were dropped. Infested boats would have to be stripped, hauled, and
tented like in house exterminations. We'd been warned the inch-long
insects could come aboard hiding in cartons from the mercado, so we
unloaded everything on the dock, carefully wiped the jars, and varnished
the cans to prevent rust. Morris always sat and monitored the procedure
to make sure we'd bought his favorite brand of cat food. I hadn't been
able to get it since San Diego, necessitating an elaborate deception.
Kelly'd sneak off to another dock with the new kibble and Morris's

original plastic Purina Deli-Cat container. After refilling it and throwing away the evidence of the substitute bag, he'd come on board shaking the jug. Hearing his familiar dinner-bell signal, Morris would leap to meet him. One time he was so eager he didn't realize the steps leading down to the main salon were removed and he went flying through the air like a bat.

Kelly was so eternally busy he might as well have been a professional shipwright. Now he was getting out the teak rungs he'd had custom-made at Abrole's Yard in La Paz. He stained them, then strung them with rope lines ascending to the spreaders, port, and starboard. He'd been badly disappointed when Gabrielle, his runner, came back with Manila line. "The cheapest, Señor," he'd said, meaning well.

"It's murder on the hands, Kel," I said. I thought of how I used to chafe my hands on the *Angelita's* hemp lines, back in the early days when nylon line was considered unsalty. The fibers from the Manila would work into your skin like splinters, causing painful minor infections.

I pitied Kelly working aloft to secure the new ratlines. The sight of him up there with his legs dangling caused a scary flashback of the one time I'd been hoisted up in a boson's chair to change a spreader light. Even tied up at dock, the boat's motion was multiplied by ten from that height and the deck appeared minute, the potential fall lethal.

"Don't look down," the two men yelled, feet securely planted on the dock. No, I'd been there. "Sorry, Kel. I can't do it. Hire one of the local boys."

"No, we'd just be shouting back and forth in my pidgin Spanish. He wouldn't know what to do." Kelly hoisted his own weight, hand over hand, by means of a pulley. I was even afraid to tail the line for fear I'd drop him. It took all morning to secure and make taut the rope ladders.

I felt guilty and offered to try them once they were up. "They're great! We're looking more like a South Seas cruising boat every day," I yelled from my terrifying vantage point. I knew he struggled to make the lines tight but when I climbed up, the narrow rungs killed my bare feet and were so wobbly I knew I'd fall if I missed a step or a handhold. The Manila line felt like coarse sandpaper in my hands. "They're not too bad," I called down, "but I hope you won't have to send me up in a mid-ocean storm."

I tried to joke, knowing I wouldn't have the strength to hang on, to hold my own weight against a gale.

We had a full day ashore planned with Jim and Janice Gustin. Word travels fast through the network of cruisers and it turned out that they were headed to the Marquesas on an itinerary identical to ours, so we teamed up for our last day of official business and provisioning.

The first order of the day was the elaborate procedure of checking out of Mexican waters through the office of the Port Captain. Knowing the officials loathed hippies and primed with the drug-bust stories of the seventies, when people simply disappeared into Mexican jails, Janice and I were demurely attired in longish skirts, modest blouses, and straw hats. The men (both growing rather suspect beards) wore long pants and searsucker jackets. Our copious documentation was sorted and ready. Office after office stamped us through. The lengthy procedure went off without a hitch. That done, we walked into the main part of Manzanillo to check out provisioning sources.

The Gustins had discovered a bar, The Capitol, which served a veritable free lunch for the price of four margaritas, a powerful incentive for our shoestring budgets. Over the repast we discovered we were bound for the same bay, Taiohae, on the same island of Nuku Hiva. We clinked glasses as we agreed to make the Pacific passage to the Marquesas in tandem. I made a silent prayer of thanks to my guardian angel.

The Gustins' list of items for *Loki Lani* was as long as ours for *Vagabundita*, so we decided to convene in a day or two, hopefully before the crush of the upcoming Easter weekend, to decide what day to leave. "But definitely not on a Friday," Kelly said, voicing the sailor's superstition that if one did, you'd never return to that place again.

Janice and I joked over our produce purchases, wiping out the entire stock of first one little stand and then the next, as if provisioning for a hotel rather than a Pacific passage of a month's duration.

We each bought and packed into canvas carry-on bags:

60 potatoes

40 onions

50 green tomatoes   }   To be stored, foil

12 unripe avocados   }   wrapped, said to

                             }   last two weeks.

4 heads cabbage   }   Iffy cabin life in

2 heads celery   }   the heat. Neither

2 heads lettuce   }   of us would have

                             }   ice beyond 4 or 5

                             }   days

2 melons

12 each grapefruit, lemons, oranges

Plenty of limes – to season fish

4 dozen eggs – to coat in Vaseline and rotate every other day
to keep yolks from settling

At one of the last stalls we lucked out, finding the very thing we
needed to stow the produce in—seven-foot-long blue mesh hammocks.
We each bought one, chattering excitedly as we lugged everything back.
"Wow, sixty potatoes!" Kelly said. "Are we having them every night?"

"Not necessarily, Kelly, but there's baked, mashed, fried, and diced for
clam chowder…"

"Don't forget Vichyssoise," Janice put it.

"Oh yeah, sure, with fresh cream and minced chives. Done in the
blender," I said.

"You girls are going to have fruit flies in three days," Jim said.

"Come off it, Jim, you guys'll eat like kings."

Excitement ran high. For us women, the ever present laundry that
grew like mushrooms overnight and the three square meals a day were the
big challenge, nor did we then know what an important role good food
would play in keeping our men's spirits up. For them the challenge was
the responsibility of having spare parts and know-how to repair any of the
hundreds of things that might break, plus the maintenance of the water,
fuel, electrical, and electronic systems, not to mention the crucial sails.

When we got back to the boat, Kelly radioed our soon-to-be-departing buddies: "Bon voyage cocktail party aboard yacht *Vagabundita*. This evening at eighteen hundred hours. Bring ice if you can spare it." A cocktail party at sea carried none of the fuss of a shore-bash. Just cold cerveza, vodka and tonic (if near a mercado), tequila and rum (if cruising). Nobody served scotch or gin (too expensive in Mexico). Nobody could store enough white wine to serve at a party either. Wine was reserved for celebratory dinners, champagne for crossing the equator and making landfall.

Kelly and I laughed and agreed we hoped never again to serve or be served the kind of hors d'oeuvres all we sailors brought out for our boat parties. Little canned sausages dipped in Kelly's "21 Club" sauce, a mixture of ketchup and mustard with a thimble of brandy. Anchovies pinwheeled around capers, which nobody ever took. Ghastly little smoked oysters. Limp crackers hastily heated and accidentally burned in the oven. Planters peanuts going slightly rancid. The occasional can of macadamia nuts from the Hawaii cruisers *was* a treat. Here in Mexico, the ever prevalent fresh salsa, guacamole, and chips saved the day.

Aloha shirts and shorts for the men, a pareau tied on over a sleeveless T-shirt for the girls was our attire, except for Janice and her pearls. We hoisted the cocktail flag, and mariachi music pulsed from the tape deck.

Morris was not in a party mood. He was wearing his grumpy face, stretched out full length in the cockpit, taking up room we needed for seating people. A half-circle of inflatable dinghies bobbed around our stern as our friends came aboard. Morris, the only cruising pet in the fleet, was warmly greeted by all but, for some terrible reason of his own, bit anyone who tried to pet him. He didn't quite break the skin but it was unpleasantly startling and guests would jerk their hands back in alarm. It was embarrassing, like trying to show off a sulking grandchild. He hadn't budged from his spot and rumbled low in his throat and fixed Kelly with an insolent stare when he tried to nudge him down. To get even, I got out Morris's cat life preserver and made him model it. When everybody laughed, Morris slunk below.

"He's mad we left him all day. He didn't approve of the new hammock, and now he's jealous of our friends." Kelly's pronouncement was correct. We knew Morris's moods changed like the tides.

Chatter and laughter escalated on round two of the drinks as Janice regaled the women with our provisioning tips and the men made little deals to swap parts.

"...Calling N6YNL, come in please," the radio crackled.

"Please, shush a second everybody—it's Dr. Austin, Kelly's Santa Barbara radio contact." We'd missed George's calls the last two evenings, fouled up by the daylight savings time change. Kelly repeated his call sign, identifying us as the yacht *Vagabundita*, and we heard George's voice clearly.

"Sorry, old man—I've got bad news. Your mother died last night, pretty much in her sleep. There was no crisis anyway, no pain. We'd brought her home from the hospital, Sherry and me—well, you knew that. At least she had her granddaughter with her. I'm sorry, so sorry, old man. Let me know what I can do." They signed off. Kelly went white and quiet, not in shock exactly. We already knew his mother, Pinky, had had a minor stroke. We'd even talked to her, calling through the hotel operator, agonizing over whether to fly home when we heard her weak voice, or wait a few days and see. Well, Kelly'd be flying home now.

I held Kelly in my arms, knowing my love was all I could give him. Of course it was awkward for our guests. Everyone murmured condolences and made offers to help any way they could. I assured them it was okay to leave, that we had so much to discuss now, that we'd radio them tomorrow when we'd worked out our plans with the 360° directional change. *God, we've already checked out of Mexico.* It was the only thought I addressed amid the multitude that jostled in my brain.

"Sweetheart, of course we have to talk and work everything out, but you need a while to just absorb this. We've had a couple of drinks. I'm taking you ashore to the Italian place. You're going to need your strength."

The cheer of the red-and-white checkered tablecloths and the hanging lanterns, the soft Latin melodies playing in the little bistro created an ambiance preferable to that of our dark cabin, made gloomy by bad news, where George's words still hung in the air, *"Your mother died last night."*

Kelly did eat some salad and spaghetti, obedient as a child, absentmindedly raising forkfuls to his mouth and chewing. Mainly he talked and talked about Pinky—her youth, her marriages, her happiness—like he was trying to figure out what her life had meant. Finally, when he'd seemed to reach the end of his reminiscence, he dropped his head into his hands. His shoulders began to shake. It was the only time I'd ever seen him cry.

Kelly finally went into a fitful sleep, tossing and mumbling, thrashing around in the sheets. I knew the radical change in our plans was eating at him. He was on the radio telephone to George at first light. I was impressed with the concise instructions Kelly read off, knowing his buddy was honored to be of help. "Contact Gethen Hughes at All Saints by the Sea to make the funeral arrangements. Put everything else in our secretary, Marie's, hands, she can delegate what's paramount to Sherry and Pinky's friends. I'll fly home today as soon as I can get a flight. Good God, it's almost Easter weekend. We've already provisioned and checked out of Mexican waters. Mucho regulations. Tommie will have to stay with Morris and the boat. I'm calling the Las Hadas Port Captain next to move them off our mooring into a dockside slip." Though he'd thought of everything, it seemed overwhelming, conducting two separate agendas. I heard the words of my son. My scalp prickled.

"Put the passage off, Mom. Stay in Mexico. What's six months?"

"Goddamn cat, Morris," I said under my breath. I loved him so much I didn't quite feel like shouting it out as loudly as my frustration warranted. I suspected he'd jumped ship again. I had awakened in some anxiety because he was not sleeping beside me in the aft-cabin bunk, his usual nocturnal habitation. Sleepily trying to reconstruct the events prior to his disappearance, I tried to remember the last time I'd seen him. But who can keep tabs on a cat? He slunk about the boat—a shadow. We always made a thorough search before casting off, fearing that Morris, lured by the warmth of the engine room, would be fatally caught in its machinery. Frequently it was only the glimpse of a white paw sticking out that revealed our illusive cat's hiding place.

Now I felt guilty, having locked him in the forward cabin so he couldn't run around and leave little cat footprints in my fresh varnish. I still had a big job ahead of me, sanding and adding two more coats to all the teak trim prior to its exposure to the equatorial sun. I couldn't risk any foul-ups at this late date. Morris gave me a dirty look, as only a cat can do, grumpily settling himself on a pile of faded blue canvas cockpit covers. I made sure the forward porthole was open for ventilation. Morris was accustomed to coming and going through it. I heard a little warning bell ringing faintly in my brain, but I brushed the intrusion aside.

Kelly was worried about leaving me anchored alone out in the bay, so he made arrangements to rent a slip while he was gone. Since moving to the dock, we were now Med-tied—bow out to sea, stern to the dock. Morris was used to the reverse tie-up procedure, enabling him to jump through the forward porthole and land safely on the dock. To attempt this now would cast him into the murky channel waters.

For a while I searched for him through the tightly packed forward cabin. I knew it was futile. The porthole gaped at me like an open mouth, screaming its accusation of my carelessness. I thought of Morris struggling in the black water, desperate to gain a claw-hold against our slick fiber-glass hull. His only chance would be to make it to the dock, probably too high above his reach during the night's low tide. I clung to this hope, though, knowing there was little I could do except put food out and get word to the neighboring boats.

It was a still, sunny morning, perfect for varnishing. My first stop was at the Tahls' big powerboat. Connie and John were recent arrivals who had been especially friendly, knowing I was alone in my husband's absence, manning the sailboat and caring for our ship's cat. I'd told them the stress-ful arrangements of Kelly's spur-of-the-moment trip home to Santa Barbara for his mother's funeral, and now about Morris's disappearance.

Connie poured me fresh-brewed coffee as she listened in concern to my story. She was a devout Catholic and offered to pray to Saint Anthony for the safe recovery of my truant cat.

"Connie, you've just said the magic words. I've had miraculous recovery of cats and dogs, even lost jewelry, thanks to Saint Anthony. He doesn't seem to care that I'm not Catholic. I've got the Saint Anthony prayer card on board and another one that protects against a whole lot of things including death by drowning. Kelly humors me by wearing it around his neck on night watches." I tried to play down this admission with a smile and a rueful little shrug. I could tell by the way she looked at me that she understood. Connie frequently cruised down the Baja Peninsula from Newport Beach and crossed to the Mexican mainland alone with her sixty-something husband. We cruising wives shared a deep bond. It was a bond of fear, hinted at but left unspoken. In her efforts to help me, she suggested I make some "lost cat" posters offering a reward and enlisting the help of the Las Hadas dock boys and even the Port Captain.

"Really? Do you think the Port Captain would take notice?"

"Well, you sure can try."

I rushed back to the boat in a fever to begin. I rummaged around and came up with enough bits and pieces of old Christmas stuff to manage a couple of acceptable posters. I had to sacrifice two treasured photograph album pages to do it and, after much cutting and pasting, was somewhat satisfied with the results.

I spruced up as best I could for this unscheduled meeting with the Port Captain of Las Hadas, but after cruising for almost a year my best white shorts were distinctly dingy. I hoped to trade heavily on the mileage of my blue eyes and sun-bleached blond hair. Being a huera held some clout in Mexico. Even though I was a woman "of a certain age," Kelly never ceased to be amused at the smoldering stares bestowed on me by young men the ages of our grown sons. I prayed that the Latin males' eternal fascination with blondes would serve me now.

Señor Ernesto simply gleamed. I stared openmouthed. He was every inch the Port Captain. I had never seen a more handsome Latin man clad in a more immaculate uniform. The gold buttons on his starched jacket winked in the morning sun and the fringed epaulets on his shoulders flashed as he moved. As I said, he was every inch the Port Captain.

"Señor Ernesto, I have a big favor to ask," I implored. "You see, our cruising cat, Morris, disappeared. Kelly had to fly to California to conduct his mother's funeral." I tried to control my voice. "I'm alone on the sailboat and desperate."

"Señora," Ernesto's dusky eyes turned liquid and filled with sorrow. He flung up his hands in a helpless gesture. "I am devastated to give you so little hope of the recovery of Morris. You see, this is our time of passion for the cats." He shook his head in despair at being unable to help me.

Cat mating season—that was all I needed.

Ernesto went on, his concern genuine. "There are at least three hundred cats hanging around the kitchens of Las Hadas right now." As he spoke he reached over to his desk and produced a framed picture, showing three cats. I suppressed a smile. This dignified man was a cat fancier, probably a little crazy, like the rest of us. "My own cat, Jose, has been gone over a week." He pointed with a meticulously manicured finger. "See, he's the one in the middle. He is, as you say, a Tom." There was a flash of white teeth and he thrust out his chest in macho identification with the tomcat. I averted my eyes discreetly and took a deep breath.

"Señor Ernesto, I am hoping for a miracle. I have been praying to Saint Anthony, but just in case he is not listening, would you be willing to display this in your office window?" He was so elegant that I had scant hope he would agree to my request. I pulled one of my amateurish posters from behind my back. It displayed a flashy gold star offering a substantial reward for the recovery of Morris. The photograph was the best part. He looked no less than an impressive African cat, stalking along in his stripes and white boots. I watched Señor Ernesto's face intently as he weighed my request.

"Of course, Señora, I will be happy to display this. We will add my Port Captain's telephone number to your poster, and I will be personally in touch with you on your sailboat by radio." I almost hugged him but extended my hand instead, thanking him profusely. "Lady, I wish you luck and the help of our dear Santo Antonio." Ernesto had a beautiful spirit to match his looks. I also knew that beneath his white captain's jacket beat a marshmallow heart.

Kelly and I talked daily on the phone, but even when we had pre-arranged the time, it was a difficult procedure. We were both in stressful situations. In the elegant whitewashed lobby of the hotel, there was always a line waiting to use the one telephone. The operators never spoke a word of English. I had been waiting some forty-five minutes for my call to go through. I glanced around at the palms and watched the beautifully turned-out Señoras vacationing for Easter weekend with their husbands and children. Eventually there was a click and I heard Kelly's voice. "Finally! Hi Tomkat."

"Hi, sweetheart. Listen, Kel, if you think for one minute I'm lounging around the pool, soaking up the sun, and relaxing..." I broke off, wondering how I could say the words I knew would break his heart.

I had never known of such a love affair between a man and his cat. Morris would sit in rapt admiration on Kelly's bathroom counter, watching his master shave, rotating his head in rhythm with the strokes of the razor. He also sat hundreds of hours on the desk while Kelly, perfecting his technique to qualify for his ham radio license, tapped out the Morse code.

When I told him Morris was missing, there was such a long silence I thought we'd been disconnected. Finally, I heard his voice. "Tom, please try very hard to find him."

"Kelly, I already have the word out. Posters displayed, rewards offered, everything I can think of. Pray to Saint Anthony, please, sweetheart. It works. Don't try to call me tomorrow night; I'll be out beating the bushes for Morris."

First thing Saturday morning I upped the reward on the posters to 100,000 pesos. Unbeknownst to the management, every guard in Las Hadas was now focused on finding our cat. I was also involved in the second go-round of sanding and varnishing, so my cat search was highly inconvenient.

Morris had been gone for two nights now. I was loath to leave the boat for even a minute in case I got a call from Ernesto or anyone else who might have spotted him. I took comfort in the fact that two or three people an hour stopped by the boat to ask about Morris, so the word was definitely out.

Kelly's voice shook on the line when he asked if there was any news. I so wanted to reassure him. I prayed that I wouldn't have to tell him that Morris had been found, washed up on the black sand beach, identified by the tag he wore on his collar. I had walked the surf line, terrified I might find him lying there. "I have high hopes, Kel. I've upped the reward to a hundred thousand pesos."

"A hundred thousand pesos! Ye Gods! How much is that?" Kelly shouted.

"Relax. It's only about thirty dollars, but still that's a lot of money for just returning a cat. He's got that tag with *Vagabundita* and your radio call sign on it, so he'd be easy to identify."

"I think he'd run away if anybody tried to catch him," Kelly said. His voice sounded so tired.

"How are things going at your mother's?" I asked.

"Alex and Chan got here all right, but otherwise I'm pretty much overwhelmed."

"I'm going to make…" I was going to say, "one last try," but changed it to, "another good effort this afternoon. I'm going around to all the guards with Morris's picture. We're quite the buddies now over all this." I hoped my laughter didn't sound forced. "I love you."

"I love you too, sweetheart."

My last undertaking was a discouraging proposition. No one had any news. When I got back to the boat, I looked reproachfully at the radio telephone. There was no blinking red light indicating a call. Well, at least I've finished the varnishing, I thought. Kelly will be pleased over that. I made a generous gin and tonic and headed for the cockpit, relieved to put my feet up. Barely settled, I heard someone calling my name and looked up to see Connie running toward me along the dock. "Tommie! We just heard a cat meowing over near those rocks!"

"What? Oh no, it's just that Mexican bird that sounds like a cat. I know what you mean though. I thought it was Morris too at first." I wasn't going to let myself be lured by a false hope. Their boat was only two slips down from the *Vagabundita*, and I hadn't heard a thing.

"It really *is* a cat. We're sure of it. Come on down to our boat and listen." It was growing dark as we hurried down the dock, gin and tonic in hand. I chewed on my thumbnail, thinking about another night without Morris. I felt as if I'd been dragging the bay for him during the last forty-eight hours.

"There it is! Hear that?"

Suddenly my eyes and ears were on the alert. I heard a faint meow. "Oh Morris, Morris, is that you?" I hardly dared allow the hope. As I called his name the meows grew louder and louder, reaching a crescendo, and then I saw a face and two white paws emerge from the rocks. Connie and I hugged each other and I cried. I could see that Morris would have to swim to reach the dock and I knew he wasn't about to do that.

"Wait, Morris! I'm coming to the rescue. Connie, stay here and talk to him." I thrust my glass into her hand. "I'm going for the dinghy." Thank God it was tied up alongside. I didn't even consider the outboard. It would have been quick, but much too heavy for me to lift down from the aft stanchion.

The sun had set. Moving fast I stumbled in the gathering darkness, terrified that Morris would split again before I could reach him. I had to row all the way out through the channel and down along the sea side of the breakwater.

Morris was pitifully glad to see me but so scared that he wouldn't come out. I had to climb up over the precipitous rocks and carry him back to the dinghy, rowing as best I could while holding his trembling body. I would never know the story of his adventure, or ordeal, whatever it was. The minute we were back on board, Morris rushed to use the cat box. *Wow*, I thought, *that must have been the worst of it.*

Easter morning! Morris was restored to me. The Resurrection held new significance. I excused myself to God and Saint Anthony for my sacrilegious association and crossed myself just in case. Then I set to work giving credit. I stuck a piece of lime-green masking tape across my original posters of Morris. GATO PERDIDO was now half obscured with ENCANTRADO! Ernesto gave me this word and it loosely meant "Jubilantly Found." The bottom of the poster acknowledged the role of our dear Saint Anthony. Black magic marker on lime-green tape proclaimed, "Gracias, Santo Antonio."

I was glad I'd awakened early and dressed. I was already up in the cockpit with my coffee when it began. Nothing could have prepared me for the parade of families coming to see the celebrity cat. Morris held court regally as hordes of dressed-up little children reached out to pet him. He was like a rock star accepting accolades. He would have signed autographs if he could. I held my breath in fear that he'd start biting people when he'd had enough of fame. I watched, charmed to see two- and three-year-olds crossing themselves with chubby fingers and lisping, "Gracias, Santo Antonio." Fortunately they were all on their way to Easter services so we had about a two-hour respite before it began again. Morris seemed dimly aware of his responsibility to his fans. He sat stoically on a canvas cushion, unperturbed by all the little hands that reached out to touch him. I counted up on my fingers—he'd already gone through three of his nine lives by now.

Since Kelly's return from his mother's funeral in California, we expected each day of provisioning to be the last before our Pacific crossing. But daily some unforeseen emergency arose. We lingered another week.

I was disappointed that our plans to make the Pacific passage in tandem with Jim and Janice fell through. They had long ago arranged for her sister to join them in the South Pacific for cruising in the Tuamotus and the time lost when Kelly flew home put us out of sync. They went on to the Marquesas ahead of us, with a promise to keep in radio contact. I felt a twinge of chagrin and uncertainty in discovering that Janice had a radio license, while I possessed only the skills of the sextant.

Arrangements for Pinky's house and property had to be made, involving detailed instructions for our secretary, Marie, regarding the settlement of the estate. These concerns took the edge off the excitement of our preparations, and I felt bad for Kelly that he couldn't direct his attention solely to last-minute plans. I wanted these final days to be fun for him. Things seemed somehow to be falling apart in every direction and I couldn't help but recall my son Kenny's concerns. Not wanting to squelch Kelly's big moment, I kept my thoughts to myself.

Still, it was a heady time anticipating the adventure of our great crossing. Exhausted each night we fell into our bunk, sharing the excitement of the events of that particular day, alternately bemoaning and laughing over the glitches and delays of Mexico. Holding each other through the night in our little-bit-too-small bunk made everything seem all right. Every morning we stumbled along, still groggy with sleep, as Morris led the way up into the cockpit and down to the galley, meowing for breakfast. Minutes later our hands gripped hot mugs of coffee. As the sun warmed the morning, our spirits brimmed with the anticipation of what the day's events would bring.

CHAPTER 4

Never trust her at any time,

when the calm sea shows her false, alluring smile.

—Titus Lucretius

FINALLY OUR DAY OF "JUMPING OFF," as the yachtsman called it, arrived. We were ready to sail. I could have been the ballast in the hull, so weighed down was I with a leaden feeling. The morning had not dawned sunny. I looked up at the white stucco walls, and impossible fairytale turrets of Las Hadas eerily glimpsed through the morning mist. I didn't say anything, but I felt like the life had drained out of me. I knew with certainty that we were gazing on this scene for the last time.

With the engine warming up, Kelly directed me to take the wheel while he cast off the dock lines. "Put her in forward gear," he ordered. We had a tight turn to make getting clear of the packed slips of huge sport fishers, their massive bowsprits protruding far into the narrow channel. I anticipated a familiar lurch as Kelly jumped aboard, but glancing back to my horror I saw him still on the dock, struggling to free up a last mooring line.

"I don't like this, Kelly," I yelled. I was already midway into the narrow channel.

"Quick, throw her into reverse," he shouted. Unaccustomed to backing procedure, I felt the sweat break out on my body in ugly prickles. *Oh God, I'm going to crash the boat before we've even left.* We carried no insurance on *Vagabundita*. This thought induced a sickening rush of adrenaline. I drew a ragged breath. I had to perform right.

The *Vagabundita* had a quick response fore-and-aft-gear mechanism and Kelly leapt aboard just short of my ramming the dock. Relieved, I was also angry with him for putting me through this. "For a minute there it felt like I was starting on the passage by myself, Kelly." I saw him bite his lip above the beard he was growing.

Now we were around the end of the rock breakwater and even the cheerful Las Hadas sign "Vaya con Dios" struck an inappropriate note, like wedding bells at a funeral. I looked ahead out to sea. No horizon was visible through the gray mist. I thought of the month's passage ahead.

It was a wretched start. We'd worked so hard to have everything ready and ship-shape, but the boat was filthy with the grime of Manzanillo. I sloshed buckets of saltwater over the decks. It only smeared the dirt and trickled it down our once immaculate topsides. I had to scrub with brush and bucket on hands and knees.

The light morning breeze averaged four and a half knots as Kelly put up the main and jib. It increased to ten and Kelly yelled at me to clip on. At twenty knots he put me at the helm, directing me to luff the main so he could put in a reef. *Christ! We're in the thick of it already.* I hated to see Kelly precariously balanced, hands engaged in tying reef points, forgetting his lifeline. In steering back on course, I overcompensated and gybed, causing the boom to slam violently, nearly knocking Kelly overboard. My hazardous mistake drained the last of my confidence. To gybe was an amateurish embarrassment at sea.

Kelly saw my quick tears. Every small error carried the germ of terminal disaster. Always kind and calm, he soothed my anxiety by labeling it "First-day-out jitters," claiming to share the malady. "Well, if it *had* been my first day out it would have been my *last*, that's for sure," I said.

"This is an unpleasant start," Kelly admitted, "but at least you never get seasick. Think of it that way." My warning stare stopped him. A black depression fell over me as I looked at the ugly, scary sea surrounding us. "I promise I'll stop trying to cheer you up," Kelly said. He couldn't help the bright flash of his dimples. "But honest, sweetheart, you'll love sailing again once we hit the trades."

A nice relaxing drink and a good dinner eased the tension, cheering us both. I got through my 10 a.m. to 1:30 p.m. watch with Jane Eyre on tape and Morris on my lap. The seas were down, wind steady at six knots. I'd seen a lighted cruise ship—a fairy galleon made of spun glass—maybe it wasn't going to be so bad...

I startled awake to my own scream. The drenching impact of water engulfed our warm, sleeping bodies and soaked the sheets and foam mattress of our bunk. A good four inches sloshed over the cabin sole. "For God's sake, Kelly, what happened?" I shouted. "We've had those aft ports open every night for almost a year." I was nearly hysterical from the shock and outrage of our awakening.

"Rogue wave," he announced calmly. "Dumped in about thirty gallons." Water sloshed back and forth with the boat's roll. I saw it surge to the level of the locker where our clothes hung.

I yelled at Kelly as if the crisis was his fault. "For God's sake, turn on the bilge pumps!" All this water had to drain somewhere and I knew it had already seeped into the aft lazarette, where we stored our paper goods and auxiliary provisions. I hoped the plastic baggies held.

Giving in to my displeasure, I bitched at each new disastrous revelation. At the sight of our bunk sagging under the weight of its soaked bedding, my patience snapped and I flung my hand toward the mess. "Now we've got a wet bed to sleep in—one of our few comforts."

Kelly's big happy-face further irritated me, with his ever-present smile, dimples flashing. "Tomkat, in this tropical heat our mattress will be dry in no time." I watched with annoyance as he dragged the heavy, sodden foam topside. He seemed thrilled to have experienced the rogue wave phenomenon and began to regale me with frightening, often fatal accounts of how rogue waves would appear from nowhere and sweep unsuspecting sailors, drowsing on their night watches, right out of the cockpit to a watery grave. I continued venting my frustration over our sheets. "Kelly, these itchy salt-encrusted sheets are going to drive us crazy.

Can't we spare a little freshwater to launder them?"

"I'm sorry, Tomkat. We'll have to wait for another squall. We need all our freshwater to drink." Sighing deeply, I resigned myself to the discomfort of the unwashed sheets, forced to abandon thoughts of using my makeshift washing machine.

A friend and Santa Barbara restaurant owner, Kathy Becker, had given me the huge plastic pickle container as a bon voyage gift. It doubled as a washing machine and as a receptacle for non-biodegradable wrappings we did not want to throw overboard. The roll of the sailboat provided the remarkably efficient agitating action. Still, I was always limited to a paltry amount of freshwater for laundry. It was a rare treat to have fresh sheets on our bunk.

Daily I decanted five quarts from our main tank into a storage container to keep careful track of our allocation—two quarts each to drink and one for dishwashing. The day after our rogue wave immersion, my first attempt yielded a squirt, the next a dribble. Pumping madly, I yelled in a panic, "Kelly—we're all out of water!"

"What? That's impossible." He was already at my side, trying the pump himself. We spent a discouraging two days tracing the water lines in search of possible leaks. This involved emptying all the under-bunk storage compartments of their hundreds of canned foods and sock-wrapped bottles, which then rolled precariously around on the cabin sole and dangerously impeded our progress through the main salon. Morris expressed his distaste for the mess we had made by sitting on the bunk, regarding our human desperation with contempt.

With his left-brained engineer's mind, Kelly had thought of everything and had a fail-safe remedy for what was a sailor's worst fear—no freshwater. We had a pump that miraculously converted saltwater into palatable freshwater, but it had to work very hard all day to yield two gallons. I didn't dare ask Kelly what we would do if it broke down. I quietly inventoried our cans of juice and bottles of beer, wine, rum, even including the juice from canned fruit. I figured we could just make it on these liquids if necessary for the projected three weeks we still had to go. We probably wouldn't quite die of thirst, but we'd sure be drunk.

Kelly never found a leak or came up with a valid explanation for the loss of our precious freshwater supply. Finally he deduced an air bubble block must have occurred when I filled the tanks at Las Hadas. I did not recall ever being warned of the air block hazard and Kelly never blamed or scolded me, still it was another sobering reminder of our vulnerability. Our cautionary joke, "There are no plumbers at sea," referring to the care needed in operating the head's pump mechanism now became, "There is no Sparkletts man at sea."

"Kelly, I'm going to have to put these soiled, salty sheets back on and it makes me sick. Where are all these squalls we're supposed to run into?"

"Don't worry, sweetheart. They're out there. I'm afraid you'll be singing a different song when they hit." That evening at cocktail hour, I asked Kelly to explain the rogue wave phenomenon. Though this one had only caused inconvenience, it was frightening to think a person could actually be swept overboard. It made me rethink our clip-on precautions. Kelly and I had a firm rule to stay clipped on to our lifeline at all times during night watches, but in daylight we made our way about the boat untethered and often perched in precarious places to try to catch a breeze or to tan the light underside of an arm or leg. We even kept Morris attached to a long rope at night. He had his own cat-sized orange foam life preserver too. The same one everyone'd laughed at in Las Hadas, but it was for real, designed to keep a small creature's head above water in an overboard accident or an abandon-ship crisis. Another rule, which soon became second nature, was to keep each other in sight at all times and announce when we were going forward or aft of the cockpit, and below.

Morris never ventured along the slippery decks. He was always either asleep below or sitting with us in the cockpit like an old salt, face to weather, ears laid back. His presence was real company on the night watches.

The GPS had gone out again. "I think that damn thing is a lemon, Kel. Doesn't it have some kind of guarantee?"

"Yeah, sure. But in the meantime here we are…we'll have to start getting star sights with your sextant."

"I notice you say *my* sextant," I said, thrilled at the prospect of working with the star finder. In addition to the failure of the GPS, we could hardly ever get an evening sun-sight because the horizon was usually ringed 360o with huge, puffy, white clouds, beautiful to look at but impossible for purposes of navigation. I'd trained Kelly to watch for images in the cloud formations. We played "cloud shapes" every evening at cocktail hour. It made me happy when he'd suddenly yell, "Look, quick! There's two people kissing"—"There's a whole theatre audience watching a play!"

But, oh, those night skies in the low latitudes! On my solitary watches, star finder chart in hand, lying propped against the cockpit cushions, I never tired of looking at the heavens. The descent of a meteor, dropping soundlessly down through the night sky, dazzled my gaze. Did it then splash into some distant sea? I'd ask Kelly if that was what caused rogue waves. *Seems plausible*, I thought sleepily.

The last thing I'd do on my watch was put on the tea kettle. When it whistled, I went to wake Kelly. I knew the stories of his Trans-Pac Honolulu race passages and how his shipmates would roll him out of his hammock yelling, "Your watch." I woke him with a gentle stroke of my hand and a soft murmur. "Coffee, tea, or hot chocolate?"

"You sound for all the world like a flight attendant in first class," Kelly said.

"How would you know?" I challenged. "We always fly steerage, just like we sail." Giggling, I dodged his swat. "Kelly, if you want to listen to *Wuthering Heights*, it's really good. Just rewind it." We had a whole collection of books on tape—some classics, some mysteries, and some recent bestsellers—they were our salvation on watches. I couldn't read with a flashlight. We needed sharp eyesight to make frequent visual sweeps of the horizon to spot other vessels. The possibility of being run down by a freighter was a constant concern, even though we were not in the major shipping lanes.

"This is our worst roll so far," observed Kelly. He kissed me as he surfaced into the cockpit at dawn to relieve my watch. "I doubt you'll be able to get much sleep. Try bracing your feet against the bulkhead." He was right. There was too much motion to relax.

I opted instead to prepare an energizing meal. My husband's powerful torso had grown lean over our months of cruising, and I was always pleased to surprise him with something special to eat. Today, however, I cast a lingering glance after the half-rotted oranges and grapefruits I tossed overboard. "Say goodbye to the last of the citrus, darling. I can just squeak out a small fruit cup. Lots of limes left though."

"We seem to be running short of all our perks at once," he observed ruefully. "I really don't mind except for the water." The forty gallons we had inexplicably lost meant not only a careful rationing but a heartbreaking sacrifice of our precious freshwater solar showers, enjoyed by a spare rinse from a water bag fitted with a sprayer and hung aloft from the spreader. Deprived of that refreshment, we suffered constantly in the 90° equatorial heat. Our salt-encrusted skin itched unmercifully. "Hard to believe how we used to take showers for granted," he beamed with his unfailing good humor.

"And worse, how I used to bitch about no hot water in Mexico." I laughed.

"A hand for yourself and one for the ship" was indeed accurate sailor's lore. Preparing even a simple breakfast below while holding on with one hand was a difficult process. Just as I was in the midst of it, I was interrupted by Kelly's jubilant announcement of an approaching squall, coming in fast off our port bow. It moved toward us through the leaden clouds with astonishing speed, barely preceded by a few huge drops. We each raced to our preparations.

Impeded by heavy roll and gusting wind, Kelly rushed forward to take down the spinnaker pole. I was prevented from my usual exclamations of anxiety over his hazardous task by my own need to scramble aft to close the portholes and get the cockpit cushions stowed before the rain hit. Hoping it would be more than a momentary drenching, I tore off our bunk sheets and grabbed an armful of salty towels. Done altering sail, Kelly was tying buckets to the liferails. We were both shrieking with elation at this answer to our prayers.

"It seems so crazy to be this thrilled by yet more water," he effused as we stripped naked.

"Everything is going to be clean, including my hair!" I shouted. "How about a shampoo?" Morris watched from below, appalled as the two silly humans cavorted and exalted in the deluge. An hour later rain still descended in unbelievable quantities. All the available containers were full and the solar-shower bag bulged to capacity. Kelly made a batch of margaritas out of the obliging limes, and giggling we took naughty nude photographs of each other, just modest enough for our future slide show, we hoped. In unspoken celebration we came together and made love in the warm downpour, almost drowning in our kisses.

By day four the wind dropped considerably. The seas turned a deep marine blue with no trace of green. We'd only made a disappointing fifty miles, down from our first three days of 140, 145, then an astounding record of 165.

Awakening day five to heat and stillness, steering a course of 220° through glassy seas—we'd hit the dreaded doldrums, zone of boredom, with variable or nearly zero winds and squalls likely, caused by the meeting of the northeast and southeast trades. We were just below latitude 10° North, 113° West when George, our Santa Barbara ham radio buddy, radioed in. He said the Miami Hurricane Center suggested a heading of 200° to get through the high-pressure ridge.

Visually it was a stunning change, with clouds reflected in water like a still lake, sky indistinguishable from sea. Suspended in a vast blue void, our sails lay slack without a breath of air. "This is going to be our shortest run so far," Kelly predicted. He was right. With sails sheeted down, all day we slatted along, both sound and motion a harsh irritation to the senses. Whenever the breeze freshened, even a little, the genoa had to be raised again to catch the zephyr, our spirits rising in tandem, but always a short-lived hope as the wind died again. "This may be our worst day," Kelly said. "A sailboat with no wind is a useless thing."

"Come on, Kel. Cheer up. At least we're not in any danger. All you care about is speed. The doldrums are more annoying than anything."

Kelly's "worst day" prediction was borne out as it stretched tediously on. It was also the day our produce heaved a last sigh and died from lack of refrigeration. Sautéing every salvageable scrap with soups and stews in the menu of my mind, I wore only an apron to protect my bare skin from the pain of hot olive oil. Kelly made suggestive remarks about my bare, tan bum. I was too hot to flirt.

"Kelly, will you look at that!" Stringy residue of celery, rotted cabbage leaves, and snippets of red and green peppers drifted past, gained our bow and floated on out of sight. "That stuff you threw overboard is making more way than the boat," Kelly said. It was my turn to laugh. Our garbage seemed to mock us.

By afternoon we were totally becalmed. I couldn't concentrate to write. It was too hot to make love. "The torpor of the tropics" Kelly called it. Sizzling in our own sweat we dove over the side for long, listless swims. Boat dead in the water, we hardly needed to be tethered but were so for safety.

Barnacles had grown overnight in the warm, still sea, lying thick along our waterline and around the propeller. They had strange, protruding gooseneck-like tubes. For once, it was an easy job to scrape them off, but Kelly worried about them covering the zinc plates that protected our hull from electrolysis.

"Come on, Kel, stop complaining. It's not like you. I'm going to make us a nice cup of tea and then we're going to talk about something *fun*."

"Tea?! In this heat?"

"Why not? The Brits were always talking about a nice restorative cup of tea, and it had to be this hot in India and Africa." I came back on deck with the tea and slices of my homemade bread with butter and marmalade. *Kelly had heard me.*

"I'd really like to be in Papeete for your birthday, Tom—staying over Bastille Day mid-July. I want to show you all the places I saw when I was there on the Trans-Pac race in the fifties."

"Yes, but that was before the jets—it'll be all changed now..."

"Sure, Quinn's Bar's gone, but we'll go to Bali Hai. The guys know me." Kelly was talking about the resort made famous by the four Southern California men who in the mid fifties abandoned their predictable lives to "go native," as it was called then. They took Tahitian wives, set to work, and Bali Hai was born. It had been considered a shocking scandal then. I was full of questions and Kelly told me all he knew, then veered off on another subject. "I've been thinking. We'll have to be in Australia by the end of September at the latest to wait out hurricane season. I'm considering looking for another boat there—a little bigger."

"What?!" I was incredulous. "After all that re-fitting on the *Vagabundita*?"

"I know, but she was never designed to be a long-distance cruising boat—taking the kind of beating she's been taking—but I didn't feel we could afford to replace her. Now, with what mother left me, we could." He looked ashamed.

"Kelly, stop. Pinky would be thrilled to finance a safer, more comfortable cruise. Think of it." He looked grateful for my words. "But we're not going to give up our day-sail picnics, are we?"

"Of course not. Those come first anyway."

For fun and to augment our income, we'd planned to run day-sail picnics on the *Vagabundita* out of the South Pacific beach resorts. We'd worked out the menus and written to the hotels about our idea. I could see Kelly, in his element, ruggedly at the helm, spinning romantic yarns of our cruising adventures to the enthralled passengers.

"Getting the new boat will take some time. We *will* go back for your grandchild's birth—and drop off Morris at the kids'." We both looked to where he lay stretched out below, sides heaving. "To get back to the itinerary," Kelly said, "we'll have half of July and all of August cruising the Tuamotus." His face glowed at the prospect. "While we're waiting out hurricane season, we can rent a car and tour Australia—New Zealand too."

"Exciting!" I said.

"We'll have short hops from then on. We're sure cutting our eyeteeth on this one!" I went below to boil rice for an exotic curry dinner inspired by our romantic plans. Kelly joined me in the galley and got out a bottle of champagne and the crystal schooner glasses. "What are we celebrating?" I asked.

"Our next four years of cruising together!" He popped the cork right over the side. It bobbed gaily along with us for most of the long twilight.

We slogged through the doldrums for four days in almost unbearable heat. Topside, at least our dodger and canvas canopy protected us from the sun, but with no air moving at all it was stifling. Our constant need to brace against the swells that rolled us back and forth was wearing us down. We were in the Horse Latitudes. "These ought to be called the hobbyhorse latitudes," I said.

"It isn't because of the roll. These are called the Horse Latitudes because the old sailing vessels taking horses to the West Indies had to throw the animals overboard because of water shortages."

"Shush, Kelly—you're scaring Morris." Poor Morris suffered too, staring fixedly at us, silently begging for relief.

Kelly started the engine and powered for a little longer than the hour it took each day to charge the batteries. It gave us a brief illusion of progress, but its added heat in the cabin was hardly worth it. We'd done five miles that day. We barely welcomed night.

I awoke to the sound of water rushing along the hull, the thrumming of a loose halyard hitting against the mast. It was a familiar melody, singing the lyrics in a pure soprano voice. "The wind is up, the wind is up!" Naked, I went on deck to feel a breeze cooling my face and body. Kelly met me in an embrace. A motion that felt like heaven rocked us. "Wow, Kel, what happened?"

"It's the southeast trades at last. The trades the poets write about."

Time stopped somewhere in mid-ocean, perhaps the day the trades breathed into our sails and the boat began to surf the waves. The wind and the swells had shifted to our quarter.

The trades remained constant, blowing "force five," twenty knots. Each day eased into the next, our simple routines unaltered.

Each morning when the sun rose it touched the clouds with pale shades of lavender and pink, seeming now to almost race across the sky, blazing as it peaked midday, then dropping a scrim of gold for the magic hour of sunset. Together we would watch each day's end, transfixed until portieres of darkness mantled the last light, bringing on the night with its great company of stars.

The moon grew full, making jagged paths of silver through the swells. Our time was marked more vividly by its phases than the ship's bells that tolled our odyssey's inevitable end.

We spent all day on deck, never out of each other's sight, our bodies in a perfect harmony of contentment with the motion of wind and sea. "I was sorry about that bad part in the doldrums, Tom."

"Oh, Kelly, none of that mattered, we're in love. If only this could last forever…" In one swift glance, perception of this rapture brimmed in each other's eyes, as if we'd slipped together into immortality.

CHAPTER 5

Eternal Father, strong to save, whose arm hath bound the restless wave, Who bidd'st the mighty ocean deep its own appointed limits keep, O hear us when we cry to thee for those in peril on the sea.

—William Whiting, Navy Hymn

I T HAPPENED IN A SECOND. My body slowed its forward motion through the water. Confusion erupted into fright. My rope! I felt it go. I saw Kelly lunge toward me just as I grabbed the last rung of our swimming ladder before being swept perhaps irretrievably aft. Weak with terror, I could barely keep hold of it against the swift current that pulled at my body. Kelly kept a strong grip on my arm and helped me back up on board. His face looked stricken, then grim. "Sorry, Kel. Didn't mean to scare you. I must have tied a sloppy knot."

Dragging behind was one of our daily pleasures. We'd done it on passages back from Catalina and Santa Cruz over the years, so we were both comfortable with the idea, both loving the sensuous feel of saltwater caressing bare skin, the thrilling ride. In mid-ocean, it was more than a lark, we longed for and needed the refreshment. We hated to wear our suits, but the rope chaffed painfully around our waists if we were naked. As one of us dragged behind, the other stood shark watch. It was ominous to even think of dangling tantalizing white legs or worse to have them flutter kicking underwater like giant fishing lures. After about a week our anxiety level dropped to zero, but we still stood watch, eyes alert, scanning the sea.

Now, twice daily before lunch and dinner we dragged in the wake, a brief alleviation from the heat. The time my rope came loose reinforced my awareness that beyond six knots I didn't have the strength to pull against the boat's forward motion to grasp the swimming ladder. Often, when the wind gusted, Kelly had to reach down and pull me in. It was sexy to be rescued.

We argued some days when I thought we were making too many knots for him to pull himself back to the hanging ladder that bobbed partly underwater from our stern. He always went out farther on the tether than made me comfortable, extending his limits until the current was borderline too strong.

"Come on in now, Kel, the wind's freshening." I risked taking my eyes off him for a glance forward at the sails. "I don't like this. I don't think I could pull you in at…" I looked at the knot meter, "eight knots. Come *on* now. I mean it."

He laughed. Then I saw the pleasure on his face transformed into panic. I saw him slide aft so fast he was almost out of sight before I realized his rope had given way. "Kelly!" I screamed. I saw his wave, his smile, before a swell obscured his rapidly disappearing body. Even in my first moment of paralysis, I knew that he was thinking more of me than of himself, smiling to allay my terror, to reassure me, let me know he wasn't worried that I might not be able to rescue him.

Aghast, I threw over the life pole with its weighted float and pennant. I watched in horror as the orange flag caught on the metal clamps that secured the fish cleaning station, ripping through the Velcro with a sound like a scream. The pole and float went downwind in a second. The orange flag fluttered a moment on the waves. Bright against the blue, it flirted for a moment like a smile before it went under. Kelly was already out of sight.

My heart pounded like the onset of a heart attack. What do I do next? Our man overboard drill shrieked in my brain. Of course—the Lifesling! With a half-turn I reached the orange horseshoe. Struggling, I tried to release the toggles that secured it to our liferail. They were immovable from corrosion. I looked aft in despair, then bolted below for pliers. I knew Kelly kept the toolbox in the lazarette, under our bunk, where a morass of plastic bags protected toilet paper, paper towels, linens.

Everything I had to haul out I resented, impeding my access to the tool-box. It was too dark to see down there. I strained to drag the metal box topside. The smaller tools had shifted to the bottom. In desperation I dumped the contents on the cockpit sole. I grabbed the pliers and set them to the frozen toggles—thank God they released. I pitched the Lifesling overboard, throwing as far as I could. Kelly was out of sight—but only for a few minutes—I swiveled to the ship's chronometer. Dear God—not a few—twelve minutes already. *Now come about. What?* My mind blanked out.

Think, think. Our drills. Of course, you're trying to slow your forward motion. Come about maintaining maneuverability and retrace your course. Drop sail, drop sail, my memory dictated—but wait. Come about or gybe? I thought Kelly said it was quicker to gybe. The words of a manual I'd virtually memorized came to me. "This maneuver depends on no hang-ups from the sheets, guys, topping lift or sails, all hazards exacerbated in rough conditions. Should any of these go wrong the man's situation is much more dangerous…" The words pounded in my brain like bad rock 'n' roll. It would be less risky to tack. If I fouled something, my chances…*his chances* would be lost. We were sailing hard on the wind. The strategy would bring the boat far too windward of Kelly and I'd have to turn downwind to reach him, flying. I could likely miss him altogether.

Don't go there, I commanded my mind. *You'll see him the minute you come about.*

I roller reefed the jib, then leapt to the main. I uncleated the halyard and the mainsail dropped in a whoosh of canvas. I'd have to secure it soon in this wind, or it would blow all over the place, even overboard, maybe fouling the propeller.

If I lost use of the engine…

I rushed below again for the bungee cords, then tried to get control of the whipping canvas, a two-man job. Wrestling the sail, I furled it to the boom in a mess and tied down. More time lost. Sand running out of an hourglass. Everything in me yearned toward the ratlines and the binoculars. *You'll see him from up there*, hope caroled.

Wait—think now, think. Be methodical. Leave the mizzen sail up for steadying. Now disconnect the wind vane, start the engine.

Please, please don't stall, I prayed, realizing too late that I'd inadvertently skipped the priming step. The engine kicked on anyway. I threw over a white flotation cushion to try to mark my position, but the drift was so strong it was borne away in an instant. It was a foolish gesture. I knew the only sure way to get us back on a reciprocal course was by compass. I'd managed to come about but, with the main down, the boat rolled severely. The tools slammed back and forth on the cockpit sole, hurting my bare feet. It had been a mistake to dump them—no time. Time! I willed my eyes away from the chronometer and scanned the horizon instead. Nothing but big swells cresting into whitecaps, the rough seas further obscuring Kelly. Knowing my line of sight couldn't be more than half a mile at most, I swallowed hard, the taste of panic bitter in my mouth.

Okay now, the radio. No! First his jacket. My mind went everywhere at once. *How could you forget his jacket, the waterproof cylinder with his heart medication?*

I stumbled down to the hanging locker, hating to take my eyes from the sea for a moment. Vaulting back up in a rush I lost my footing among the tools and went down hard on my right knee, my open palm sliced by the hacksaw. Little droplets surfaced and swelled, lined up precisely like the saw's jagged metal teeth. Blood oozed. Anxiety anesthetized me from pain.

I threw the jacket overboard, hypnotized by the bright orange color as it crested, then sank out of sight in the troughs, surfaced, went under again. The whistle and strobe light attached to it would be my only chance at night—*his only chance, if he finds it.*

Twenty-five minutes overboard. Of course he'll find it; he even sees our mast now. He'll have the mirror too—to signal with the sun—he's looking right into it, blinded by its low dazzle. Shit! The sun. For God's sake, get a position. Shoot the evening sight.

I'd almost missed it. I reached below for the sextant. The horizon was clear but the roll prevented an accurate reading. The little green sun image reflected in the sextant's mirror pitched too wildly to kiss the horizon. I'd have to hoist the main again for steadying. No, too much time lost already. At worst I'd give Kelly's last log entry.

When had that been? Noon. Six hours ago. Way too far off. Still, with helicopters searching… Come on. Get real. Try the sight again.

As the *Vagabundita* rose she hovered for a moment on the top of the swell before she plunged. It was enough. I was ready with the sextant. The ball of the sun grazed the horizon and I pushed the button on my stopwatch. I'd got the fix. I checked the time on the chronometer, switched on the vane to free myself from steering, and descended carefully into the main cabin, favoring my knee, fearing to drop the delicate sextant. No shortcuts now. I put it back in its mahogany box and stowed it safely, wedged into its corner next to the books I needed—*the Nautical Almanac* and *Tables of Computed Altitude.*

Thank God I'd noted the exact time and logged the distance since Kelly'd gone overboard and when I'd first tacked. I marked small Xs on the chart at the appropriate places. I reconciled the time of my sight, "Apparent time" with Greenwich Mean Time, entered my sextant altitude and computed the latitude and longitude. My hands shook so hard I could barely work the calipers measuring my computations. Blood dripped on the chart. At last I was ready to give our position.

On the bulkhead above the radio, Kelly'd taped up instructions for sending an emergency distress call. He had thoroughly rehearsed me. At least I was sure of this vital procedure. I switched on the radio telephone, tuning it to the international emergency frequency 2182.

"Mayday, Mayday, Mayday! This is the sailing yacht *Vagabundita.* Position 1°25 South by 127°27 West." I had to take a deep steadying breath before putting into words what would make the crisis more irrevocably so.

"Man overboard! Man overboard! Require immediate help. Over."

Nothing but dead air.

Maybe the transmitter hadn't warmed up. A pulse beat in my throat louder than my voice when I broadcast again. Sweat poured down my face as I waited. Still nothing. I checked that the set was correctly switched on and tuned. With each passing minute our position would be invalidated.

"Please, God, help me!"

I tried over and over then switched to Channel 16. Maybe I'd pick up a merchant ship. How could there be nothing transmitting back to me—with the tremendous range of our single sideband? I might as well not have a radio. Suddenly I was screaming every bad word I knew. "This fucking useless radio! This whole fucking cruise!" Every impulse cried out for me to climb and watch from the ratlines. I couldn't stand it anymore. I'd find him myself. "To hell with you," I yelled at the radio, grabbing the binoculars, intending to run.

The pain and swelling of my knee slowed me to a limp. I climbed the ratlines awkwardly. The ropes had stretched since Kelly'd rigged them three weeks ago in Las Hadas. Now my weight pulled me out even further from the perceived security of proximity to the mast, exerting a horizontal as well as a perpendicular pull against my body. Every time I raised a foot to the next rung, I was thrown off center, wobbling. It was a grueling, painful ascent. With my swollen knee I should have at least worn a safety harness. Hooking an arm around one rope and under and up the next step to support myself, I raised the binoculars. This would be my last daylight sweep.

The emptiness of the surrounding seas drained me of hope. *"Please, God. This is all I've asked you for."* I spoke aloud the words of my new-moon wish. "Get us there—just get us there," I sobbed. The enormity of what was happening engulfed me. My chest cavity ached—extremities numb, as if my circulation had stopped. Was this feeling where Keats's poem came from? *"My heart ached and a drowsy numbness pained my sense."* Why did poetry come to mind? *"Abandon hope all ye who enter here."* Now Dante. Well, I would not abandon hope. I relived Kelly's last smile, his cheerful wave—he knew I'd find him. This was just another test the cruise threw at us. Tomorrow night we'd be laughing over it.

Kelly had a tiny compass on his watch. That and the position of the sun would be his only aids. But even if he saw me, what good would it do him unless I spotted him too? I imagined him yelling and waving as I slid by and sailed out of sight. I hoped he'd save his strength and wait for me to find him, not swim aimlessly.

I thought again of the sharks. We'd often seen them while scuba diving, but always in coastal waters. We talked a lot about the threat and decided there weren't any in mid-ocean. They had nothing to feed on. Same reason we hadn't caught any fish. Still, I knew Kelly had to be thinking about sharks. *Don't let him be afraid out there.* I glanced aft at the low sun, now under the yardarm.

A sick feeling rose in my stomach when I realized the errors of my early rescue procedures. All that stuff I'd thrown overboard. Time wasted getting the pliers. Time wasted on the Lifesling. It only had a range of about 150 feet. Since he hadn't gotten it right away, it presented a greater risk. If its line fouled in the propeller we'd be completely disabled. I resisted an impulse to climb down, haul it in—no, we were still making enough speed for safety. I had to look quickly away from the orange horseshoe that bobbed and tossed—a giant beach toy.

The sun set but the southeast trades did not die with it. Mares' tails whipped the sky. This streaky cirrus likely meant the warm front of a depression approaching, increasing wind, rain likely later. I welcomed night, knowing I'd see Kelly's strobe. I put my conviction in that hope, willing it to happen.

I'd worked out a twelve-mile grid course. Sailing under the mizzen alone, I made six knots. Knot speed divided into distance equaled two hours per tack. I set a timer to alert me to each new heading.

The wind freshened, then gusted. I glanced aft at the squall as it raced to overtake us, astonished as always by its blackness. I could hear a roar now, like a distant freeway at rush hour. Blustering gales preceded the squall's full-force hit. Adrenalin shot through my body—the implications of this! Thank God I'd already struck the main and jib. Now I'd have to douse even the mizzen storm sail I'd left up for steadying. I eased off the mizzen sheet and watched the canvas drop halfway. I slacked off, then babied the sheet, trying to free the sail—it bellied, abused by the wind, hung up on something. I wondered if I could save it. Time drummed at me, banging from the blocks and thrumming from the shrouds, a skeleton's orchestra.

"Clear the decks of all obstructions," I heard Kelly say. I made myself take time to throw the tools back into their box. It only took one minute. I crammed my feet into worn topsiders and yanked on my safety harness, clipping onto a backstay. Hand over hand I clawed along the wheelhouse grab rail, then thrashed the canvas loose from its entanglement with a wire rope cable snaking in the wind. I inched back blindly, head down, protecting my eyes. I dropped into the cockpit barely in time to dog both hatches to prevent flooding below.

The rain hit like a tidal wave, driven horizontal by the gale. Terrified by the sheer volume of water, I envisioned Kelly out there struggling in the monumental seas, struggling even to breathe, beaten underwater by the totality of the storm.

Howling wind tore through the naked rigging. I had no choice but to run before it. We were making eight, ten knots on bare poles. I could see nothing through the black gale. I flipped off the useless spreader lights that were draining our batteries. They could only serve to trigger Kelly's whistle response, which I would not be able to hear above the thunder of the breasting seas.

The gale, coming from the southeast, was heading into the normally peaceful following seas, with their broad, long swells. Now, hobbyhorsing, the *Vagabundita* bucked my hand at the wheel like a hard-mouthed horse with the bit in her teeth. I flogged her on. Knowing I lacked the skill of a seasoned helmsman, I agonized over my steering, longing for Kelly's sure hand at the helm in these wild, perilous seas.

Now I feared I could not keep ahead of the gigantic waves that were breaking over our stern faster than I could run before the wind. I estimated it at force seven. A mountain of water loomed up behind me, towering twenty, thirty feet above the cockpit. I braced against a pooping, a violent engulfment of water breaking over the stern. Somehow the

Vagabundita rose on the slope and the wave gushed under our hull, then I felt us fall with a crash into the following trough—dropping down to hell. How much could she take? She yawed and scooped up a hundred tons of water. My heart beat in my throat. My hands were paralyzed from gripping the wheel. I knew my faulty steering would bring a knockdown.

"Turn toward the wind to climb the wave; steer off when you reach the crest. Don't be afraid. Think of our boat as a little cork." Somehow Kelly's words resounded—sent to me like a Valentine.

All through that wild night we drove as squall after squall blustered through, the *Vagabundita* beating to windward on one tack, pounding into rampant seas, then hurtling before the wind on a course even more terrifying. Every time I came about in the dark I was afraid I'd swing too far around and gybe accidentally before adjusting to the new position. When the last squall stampeded through it left waves made hysterical by wind and rain, powerfully breaking cross-seas, going every which way. I thought of Kelly out there battling them.

He has no chance. No chance at all. I sobbed aloud, giving in to my terror. I gulped air, two big breaths. I cried out to the Lord and sat still, listening for a sign, waiting for my heart to slow.

All right, now what? Are you going to fall apart or are you going to figure out the next best step?

As the seas diminished the southeast trades stepped shyly up, assuming their accustomed steady velocity. I'd been running the engine too long, but at least I'd charged the batteries. I'd have to get under sail again. The thought of hoisting the main was overwhelming, exhaustion overtaking me. Twice I'd found myself staring at the same area of black water rather than maintaining a visual sweep. I reached into the cockpit cubbyhole for the tin box of hard candy we kept on hand to forestall sleepiness on watch. A little jab to raise blood sugar.

Morris, alerted by the crinkle of the cellophane wrapping, crept out from his shelter to join me, shaking first one front paw and then the other, wet from the water puddled on the bare cockpit seats. *He must be starved.* The smell of the peppermint induced a wave of hunger and my stomach cramped. I went below, grabbed a jar of peanut butter and the heel of the two-day-old bread. I pulled off small pieces and dipped them in the jar, wolfing the food down. Morris crowded closer. I stuck my fingers in the peanut butter and held them out to him. I felt his rough tongue licking, heard his purr. "I'll get us both water, Morris. You're on watch for Kelly now."

Was I getting delusional? No, I trusted the telepathic communication between Kelly and his cat. I knew Morris had seen Kelly go, but would his mind grasp the situation? He'd been agitated, meowing, running back and forth, and peering overboard. Sure, he knew. He would alert me—he'd warned us of the rocks in Baja. The thought comforted me and I nestled into it drawing it around me like a warm cloak.

I slammed up on deck in a rage, cursing the *Vagabundita*, the necessity of manning her preventing focus on my search. "I wouldn't have cared if I'd lost *you*, if only I'd found *him*!" I burst into hopeless tears. "I haven't been able to climb the ratlines even once all night because of you." I felt the boat shudder beneath me, as if sharing my anguish. Now that the prevailing trade winds were in force the stress was off her. I could hoist sail now. I brought her up into the wind and gave the wheel to the vane, my reliable helmsman. I'd pulled in the Lifesling, coiled its line at the ready, tried the radio again to no avail. There was nothing of immediacy left for me to do. Impulsively I hoisted our house flag as another visual aid for Kelly—or maybe to raise my own spirits.

At last, I climbed again, painfully, but the knee worked. I had the sense to wear my flotation jacket and full safety harness, causing the frustration of clipping on at frequent points, the dangling binoculars and strobe light further impeding my progress up the ratlines. The pain of my cut palm against the coarse Manila line served to remind me of the roadblocks I'd thrown in my own path. I needed to focus, be detached.

Though the squalls had abated, the seas were in an extreme confusion of crossed wave directions. The combination of the heavy motion and my glasses with their blended lenses made me reel. Every step was a terror, clambering aloft twenty-five feet, hurled to port one minute, starboard the next. The decks below were lost in darkness. All I could see was white froth above a vast abyss of water. I closed my eyes and climbed. I felt the spreader before I saw it. Made brave by desperation, I lunged up and over with my bad leg, sat astride the yardarm, and clipped on. Despite the jacket, my legs were cold in the shorts I hadn't taken time to change. I shivered. It was the first time I'd felt cold in weeks.

How must it be for Kelly in the water now, dropped from its 90° daytime temperature to what? Maybe 80° after the squalls? If he hadn't found his jacket, how long could he sustain that chill, 18° below his normal body temperature?

I couldn't remember if the U.S. Coast Guard hypothermia tables took energy loss into account. Almost hoping I wouldn't find it, I slipped a hand into the breast pocket of my jacket, feeling for the waterproof card of the U.S. Coast Guard tables. Of course it was there. I'd never had to use the jacket.

Thrown about violently, I made alternate sweeps with the binoculars and the strobe as best I could. My mind belabored what now seemed the most vital factor of Kelly's survival. He'd been in the water eleven hours. I had to know. I clutched at the card, shining the light down, trying to steady my hand so I could read. With escalating fear I ran my eyes across the headings:

Water Temperature	Exhaustion or Unconsciousness	Expected Time of Survival
60° to 70°	2 to 7 hours	2 to 40 hours
70° to 80°	2 to 12 hours	3 hours to indefinite

Kelly had to be on the cusp of the 70° to 80° water temperature category, but what the hell did "three hours to indefinite" under Survival Time mean? How could there be such a broad range? I bit my lip so hard I tasted blood. Did it mean they hadn't been able to rescue many or that most had died so these were inaccurate tables?

My mind eased back to our Southern California summers when the Pacific warmed to the high sixties. We'd dive together for hours. Kelly in trunks and me in a bikini. He'd spent his life in the water—but he didn't have an ounce of fat on him now. He wouldn't have that extra layer women had, that always made me outlast him in cold water—but if he'd found his jacket—*he did find his jacket. Hold on to that conviction.* My concentration flagged again. I caught myself staring into space. Suddenly, every sense and perception alerted. I thought I saw a flash to starboard. My heart hammered. *Get a compass bearing, quick!* I unclipped my harness and half crashed down, heedless of caution, keeping my eyes on the spot where I thought I'd seen his light. I estimated a compass bearing, flipped off the vane, and altered course. I sailed far beyond what could have been a reasonable distance for the two-mile range of his strobe, straining my eyes to penetrate the darkness. I agonized over the likelihood of the boat cresting a wave just as Kelly and his light sunk in a trough. I didn't see the light again. Perhaps it was only the last glimpse of a falling star. Covered by such a vast canopy of night, we'd seen many plunge across the sky.

I dreaded dawn. In one sense daylight implied greater search visibility, but I'd so counted on his strobe. *That light I saw. If it had been Kelly, I'd better be ready to get him aboard. Or should I try the radio again?* Uncertainty confused me. Exhaustion was eroding the validity of my decisions. I glanced east at the faintest lightening along the horizon. Soon the sky's palette of ombréd grays would stroke away the night.

"Morris, I'm going to work. I'm putting you back on watch." He stared at me in silence, solemn as an owl, with night vision as keen, hearing too. He rotated his head as far as it would go in both directions, then peered overboard, pricking his ears. He might hear the whistle when I couldn't, but could he communicate that? Many times I'd seen the distinctive way cats had of turning one ear sideways when they heard an unfamiliar sound. A spurious hope rose in me. I went below, leaving Morris steadfast on his watch.

I knew just which book had the information I needed. Often to Kelly I'd praised *This Is Rough Cruising Weather* for its explicit step-by-step procedures and realistic illustrations. Now I mentally thanked its author, Erroll Bruce, for depicting a woman single-handedly accomplishing a man overboard recovery by means of the book's diagrams. I was desperate now to be prepared for the likelihood that Kelly would be too cold and exhausted to make any effort when I found him.

First I made ready to heave-to, bringing the boat up into the wind and switching on the vane. I was able to hoist the jib, then winched-up the mainsail. When I tacked, without letting go of the lee sheet, the jib effectively braked the boat. I adjusted the main until we were making almost no headway, then lashed the helm alee. Now we lay broadside to the sea and wind, rolling, sure, but at least we were nearly dead in the water and I had both hands free. Next I dug our genoa jib out of its sailbag and hanked it along the guardrail, lashing it down at each end. I put a halyard on the clew, making ready for the hoist. I bundled and secured the sail and tied down the halyard. I was ready. Spent, I went below to find a Coke, desperate for energy. Gagging, I made myself gulp the lukewarm, cloying soda.

Up on deck again I watched as minute by minute the sky lightened then erupted into an aurora borealis, aflame as fingers of light fanned out. Sunrise never moved me as sunset did. Still, it was the beginning of a new day. I whispered a prayer, "Dear Father, let this be the day you bring him safely back to me."

Morris tensed, staring out to sea, intent on something to starboard. My eyes burned. I blinked to moisten them, squinting to see what he was looking at. I caught a movement in the water. Yes! No—a chimera.

Serenely, a lone dolphin curved into sight, lilting through the quieting seas. I held my breath. My hand moved to the ivory dolphin I wore on a gold chain. My symbol. I watched him cross ahead of us, surprised that he didn't veer off to waltz around our bow. Suddenly, bursting from the water he sprang in one magnificent Nureyev leap, rainbows playing in his spray, body turned to gold. Somersaulting twice in the air, he jack-knifed back into the sea. On an impulse, fueled by intuition, I altered course and followed his rhythmic motion as he dove, then surfaced to breathe. Always in my sight he did not leap again, as steady on his course he drove. Morris was riveted to the sight. To follow the dolphin wasn't that much of a deviation from my grid, only about 10° northwest, downwind. That would make sense if I'd mistakenly computed Kelly's drift. I was already embracing a wild notion. All at once the dolphin leapt again. My heart skipped a beat and leapt with him. Tears came to my eyes.

I thought I saw a flutter of orange but the sky and sea were so bright with color that I told myself it was an illusion, born of hope. I'd seen our orange flag rip off from the pole and sink...then I saw it again! All hell broke loose in my brain. Morris jumped to the upper deck. I revved up our speed. Could it be someone else's pole and flag? As we drew closer, I saw flashes of orange in the water, surfacing and dropping out of sight in the swells. I grabbed the binoculars. The flag looked weird, not the right triangular shape. Blinded by the glare, I lost the pole, panicked, then spotted it again.

"Kelly!" I screamed. I turned a little out of the sun and there he was, fifty feet away, head flopped back against the orange jacket, facing the heavens. The "flag" was the orange trunks he'd been wearing when he was swept aft. I screamed his name again as a swell bore him up. I thought he raised his head slightly but I heard no answering shout, saw no wave of his hand.

I cut the engine and brought us up into the wind, then threw the Lifesling. It came within a couple feet of him. He didn't respond, didn't seem to know I was there. I shouted again and this time he raised his head, saw the horseshoe, and made a listless grab for it as it fanned out and away from him on its long floating line. Thank God the swells were propelling him in our direction. I yanked off the bungee that secured the swimming ladder and it crashed down against our transom.

"Kelly," I yelled, "you're alongside, when you drift back grab the swimming ladder." He seemed more alert now. He made a stab at the ladder and grasped the last rung. He worked one foot onto it and reached both hands to the grabrails, trying to pull himself up. He fell backward into the water and went under. I was appalled to see him weak. He surfaced choking, gasping for air. I lunged for the boat hook and got it through a loop on his jacket before he sank again. He didn't have a prayer to assist me with even a handhold.

"Float—just float, Kelly. Float!" I dragged him around midship and lowered a bight of the genoa overboard. Using the boat hook again, I worked him into the floating sail. His head lolled back, eyes closed, mouth half-open. His face wore a greenish gray pallor. Had he passed out from the effort of trying to pull himself aboard? A horrible fear clubbed at me. I pulled up hard on a stanchion to clear the rail for the length of his body, praying I'd be able to hoist him aboard. I forced my mind to the book, visualizing the drawing of the woman working on the winch, the victim's legs hanging out of the bight of sail.

Endowed with the superhuman strength of extremus, I began to hoist, putting my whole body weight into each turn of the winch. When the sail-sling reached guardrail level, I cleated the line down and rolled Kelly onto the deck. I didn't pause to check for a pulse, but rushed below and back up with the brandy bottle. Supporting his head, I poured a little into the cap so I wouldn't choke him and dribbled it into his open mouth, then once again. His eyes opened, he tried to smile. His voice was so faint I bent close to hear him.

"Pelorus Jack," he whispered.

"Yes, darling. Oh yes! The dolphin—I knew the moment I saw him. So did Morris."

"Me too," Kelly said and fell into a deep, deep sleep.

I could hardly keep Kelly down for the two days I insisted he rest. His dehydration was my greatest concern, but I fed him juices and made soup from canned chicken. I would have welcomed medical advice from George, but when Kelly tried to transmit there weren't even the occasional bursts of static I'd come to know. In his meticulous engineer's way, Kelly began to dismantle the radio. Early on he diagnosed dead batteries as the reason for its silent voice when I was attempting my desperate Mayday transmissions.

"Tom, I'm glad George couldn't transmit. We have to talk. I want you to promise me…" I couldn't understand the source of the concern I heard in his voice since we'd been spared the worst that could happen.

"What? What is it?"

"Promise you'll never tell anyone about our ordeal, that I was overboard for fourteen hours…"

"But it was an accident!"

"…that I had put you at risk—it was all I could think of out there." He tightened his grip on my shoulders.

"Kelly, we're both at risk all the time. This is what we decided we wanted to do. My God—the dolphin! The story has to be told." I looked up at him, full of the joy that in God's great mercy we had been given another chance, but Kelly wasn't with me in this. His face was solemn. He seemed far away, as if in his imagination he was lost in the enormity of what-might-have-been. It came clear to me then. "All right, Kelly, all right. I promise."

On day three of his recuperation, Kelly came up into the cockpit looking as fit and hardy as ever, dying to start fiddling with the weather FAX and the fish finder. I saw disappointment cloud his face as he reminded me that our GPS was out of commission.

"Tell me about it!" I said. "That thing's worthless. We should have saved the two thousand and relied on the sextant to begin with." I felt bad for him though. He'd so loved using the expensive little gadget. "Cheer up, Kel. It'll be fun to shoot star sights. I told you I've been playing with the star finder on my watches. I can recognize all the constellations already. I'll teach *you* for once."

I tried hard to put our crisis out of my thoughts but my mind dealt obsessively with every detail of Kelly's near fatality. I was frustrated that Kelly didn't want to talk about it. We'd always discussed everything in our marriage with great intimacy. I was having a struggle. At one point my thoughts degenerated into imagining that I had caused his man overboard disaster by my fears and visualizations of just such a thing happening on our first passage to San Diego. A self-fulfilling prophecy.

Next, I focused on destiny. Clearly, destiny played a major role in our lives. I'd always believed destiny guided my first husband, Bill, to reintroduce Kelly and me twenty-three years after we'd met and fallen in love at the yearly Christmas dances at the Huntington Hotel in Pasadena.

My God, here we are in the middle of the Pacific Ocean, down to the last of our water and provisions, wondering if we're going to make it, and where am I in my thoughts?

Dressed in a robin's-egg-blue satin gown. Christmastime. Pasadena, 1957.

CHAPTER 6

Sooner or late, love comes to all.

—William Henry Drummond

"KELLY, DO YOU remember our Christmas dances at the Huntington Hotel?" Old favorites from our courtship days throbbed from *Vagabundita's* tape deck.

I turned my head sideways to the mirror, attaching the pearl-drop earring and glimpsing the reflection of my new evening gown. Hearing Bill's voice calling to ask how my dressing was coming along, I jumped, smearing my eye shadow. Startled from my fantasy of wondering for the hundredth time if Kelly Spear would ask me to dance, I felt a stab of guilt. After all, Bill had sent all the way to Bloomingdale's for the dress as a surprise for me to wear to the dance. I was twenty-four. Bill and I had been married two years.

We arrived at the party. My robin's-egg-blue satin gown shimmered in the light coming from the elaborate sconces illuminating the damask walls of the Georgian Room. I cast a quick glance around the dance floor to see if Kelly was there, but the men in their tuxedos were practically indistinguishable one from another. The room was redolent with the perfume fragrances of the beautifully gowned women. Everything glittered.

We met friends and sipped champagne. Dinner was announced. Bill escorted me to our table, and as I sank into my chair, the glow and excitement of the party seemed to diminish. I hadn't seen Kelly.

As the band struck up "I Only Have Eyes for You," Bill swept me onto the dance floor and into a mellow fox-trot. We were laughing, turning, and swaying to the music. I felt Bill's body tense in response to a sudden tap on his shoulder. Kelly came out of nowhere, cutting in. My face flamed and I was in his arms. I didn't even see Bill go. Kelly held me out from him for a moment and we just looked at each other. Then he pulled me close and we moved to the music. I loved his size, his big dimpled smile, and whatever it was that compelled us to be together. He told me about how he'd just brought somebody's boat back up from Baja, beating hard into weather on some ghastly north passage when the fishing season was over down there. He was exciting and I couldn't get enough of his sea stories. There was something, something there that made me know with a sweet certainty that every year Kelly Spear would ask me to dance.

The *Vagabundita* swayed, almost as if she too were keeping time to the music, not wanting to be left out of our joy. Kelly's arm tightened around my waist. He pulled me closer then bent his head down to my cheek. We only had a very small space in the main cabin in which to dance, but Kelly guided me around, light on his feet with the grace that a big man often displays on the dance floor. I liked the feel of his beard against my face. He murmured into my ear, "Tomkat, do you think I could ever forget those dances? You were like a breath of spring. You must have known how I felt about you." I had been holding my breath as I listened. Now I let it out with a soft sigh.

"Oh yes. I did, but then how come we never did anything about it?" I looked up into his green eyes filled with a love that had not diminished in thirty-five years.

"Don't you remember? It was the fifties," he said. "Then I lost track of you. The talk was you had run away…"

"But still, didn't you dance me out through the French doors that year for a kiss? I remember moonlight. I know I remember..."

He laughed and whirled me around in a circle. The trades had freshened and the candles on our dinner table flared and rocked in their gimbaled holders dispelling the dimness beginning to invade the main cabin as the sun descended toward the horizon. "No, that must have been some fantasy you're remembering. It was December. There were no French doors open then. Believe me, I wouldn't have forgotten a kiss."

I felt the whole wonderful length of his body pressed against me. The tempo of the music increased. We swung a little apart and Kelly led me in a tricky little dance step then bent me back in an exaggerated Fred Astaire finale. "Now. This moment," he said.

"This is our first kiss." As if equalizing the pressure from a very deep dive, I surfaced slowly, barely in time to hear him say, "You're the love of my life." Moving now with the gentle rhythm I so loved, I felt the boat rise on the crest of a swell, pause a moment, then glide down into the trough.

"May I have the next dance, m'lady?" He made a little bow from the waist. He was all funny and romantic and we danced the tango around the narrow space surrounding the stationary table, laughing and bumping into things.

"I know why you called me Lady, Kelly. There's no mistake about that memory."

As Kenny Rogers's voice intoned the heartbreaking lyrics of our song, I went on with our game of remembering. "Do you remember when you used to say 'Let's stop by the Biltmore for just one dance' and when we'd walk in, Hank and Wayne would break off whatever they were playing and launch into 'Lady'?"

"For so many years I thought I'd never find you." Kelly began to sing softly, "You have come into my life and made me whole." We went on together in a slightly off-key duet. "I'll always want you near me. I've waited for you for so long..."

The music coming from our tape deck reached a crescendo. The ardent yearning in Kenny Rogers's voice made me feel like I wanted to reach out and hold him. I tightened my arms around Kelly. "You want to know something?" I said. "I've often thought it was sad we weren't together all those years, considering how we felt about each other. I wanted you to have that young girl instead of—well, what I am now. But I don't feel that way anymore. This, just this moment, is our time."

We were sailing along in that golden hour of twilight, and we looked out at the horizon ringed all around with impossibly white clouds, but it was not that magic lighting Kelly's face. He looked at me as he had on our wedding day, eyes brimming with the promise of our great adventure, radiating the joy we shared.

I leaned back against Kelly's chest, both his hands clasped in mine. "When you think about it—just imagine—here we are in the middle of the Pacific Ocean together, living this dream. What if we'd never met again," I said.

"I know. Both suddenly single at the same time, living a hundred miles apart."

"Not a hundred," I said.

"Seventy at least. We wouldn't have exactly run into each other at Vons. We have to give credit to old Bill for getting us together."

"Yes, weird though. Former husband finding me future husband." I turned my head back to look at him, laughing.

CHAPTER 7

I have no other but a woman's reason:
I think him so, because I think him so.

—William Shakespeare

I DIDN'T MEET KELLY, I re-met him.

Dashing across my torn-out kitchen floor, hopping from joist to joist, I tried to reach the phone before the fourth ring when the answering machine would kick on. My remodeling contractor, Ted, called every evening to discuss our progress and inform me of deliveries and subcontractors scheduled for the next morning.

Lifting the receiver, I heard a familiar voice. Here I'd risked breaking an ankle and it wasn't Ted, it was my ex-husband, Bill, launching into a long story about running into an old friend of ours. "Thanks for thinking of me Bill but the *last* thing I want in my life right now is a new man. I'm up to my neck in this house project, and I have my job at Country Life Interiors on top of it."

"But we really liked Kelly years ago. What's it been, twenty? Twenty-five?"

"At least. That's why I'm not really sure I want to meet him again after all these years. What if he's turned into some kind of weirdo?"

"Tommie, he hasn't turned into a weirdo or I wouldn't suggest you meet," Bill said in a tight voice. "He's very attractive."

"If he's so attractive how come he doesn't have a girlfriend?"

"For God's sake, Tommie. I didn't get his entire life history. I ran into him, we talked about his new boat and I mentioned you. End of story. Do you want me to give him your phone number or not?"

"Bill, I don't mean to be abrupt but I'm freezing to death. I'm in a gutted kitchen with no heat. California or no California, it feels like winter around here, but, to answer your question, I guess I should give him a try. Thanks." I was mildly interested, but gave it little thought until Kelly called me a day later, inviting me for dinner in downtown Los Angeles at the California Club. The sound of his voice brought back some feelings out of the past I couldn't quite identify, but I was intrigued enough to fuss some over a woman's eternal question: What should I wear?

The old brick building sat far back from the street, near the intersection of Sixth and Flower. It was an anomaly amid its contemporary neighbors. The entrance to the California Club bore no sign and the discreet driveway could be easily missed. I was glad I'd known the venerable men's club from the past when Bill was a member or I might have missed my way in the early November darkness.

The valet parkers stopped in their tracks when they saw the head of a Merry-Go-Round horse sticking out the rear window of my eight-year-old Camaro. His gaily painted head nodded a greeting as I drove up the parking ramp and the overhead lights flashed on his jeweled harness and gold bit. "Whose secretary are you?" inquired the valet, pad and pencil in hand.

"Secretary!" I said, "I'm not only *not* a secretary, I can't even type." That got a laugh and they explained it was Secretary's Day and many were being entertained at the club. They wanted to know which member was paying for my parking. "Oh, I'm a guest of Kellogg Spear."

"You bringing this horse to the party?" another young man asked.

"No way. I wouldn't *think* of unloading him. I could hardly get him safely in the car. He's a valuable antique. Please keep an eye on him for me." They teased me about how come I didn't have a horse trailer and promised to park my car in such a way that the carousel horse wouldn't be decapitated. I loved joking with Hispanic men and since they liked blondes almost as much as they liked Camaros we hit it off famously.

I entered the club in high spirits. In 1980, it still had the *ladies'* entrance and the *ladies'* elevator, in deference to members who might not want to encounter a woman in their sacrosanct haven. The women's movement had not quite escalated to the point of forcing them to accept female members.

The long hallway leading to the elevator was hung with oil paintings and carpeted with Kilim rugs. I loved the elegant, old-fashioned atmosphere. I stopped off in the Ladies' Annex, as the powder room was called, to touch up my hair and makeup and adjust my white knit dress and silk scarf. The six individual dressing rooms were still there and hadn't been redecorated in the past twenty years. The small rooms were furnished in mirror-topped, skirted dressing tables and damask chaise lounges where, I liked to think, tightly laced Victorian ladies had once reclined to recover from their fainting spells. Certainly no woman had ever spent the night in the California Club.

I wished Kelly had been a bit more explicit about where we'd meet. He'd said to look for him in the library outside the main dining salon. The paneled room was not brightly lit. My eyes were drawn to the wood fire blazing and crackling in the baronial fireplace. Heavy, fringed draperies dressed the French doors and a vaulted ceiling soared over the enormous room. I scanned the seating groups nearsightedly, not wanting Kelly's first impression of me to be a woman wearing glasses. There were gaggles of short-skirted secretaries more attractively dressed than the conservatively garbed wives, who appeared cut from the same cloth in their dark dinner suits and pearls. Some occupants of the deep leather chairs were invisible behind their *Wall Street Journals* and I began to have the uncomfortable feeling that I might not recognize Kelly.

Well, he'll recognize me. I haven't changed.

I advanced slowly into the room, then turned at the sound of a familiar voice. "Is it Tommie? It is really you?" he said. "I hardly recognized you. You're so skinny, and something's different..." He made a vague circular gesture toward my hair, now cut in bangs with a pageboy falling to my shoulders.

"Well, for heaven's sake, Kelly Spear! I am glad to see you. You're pretty skinny yourself."

"Yeah. Well, single people tend to *get* skinny." We clasped hands in greeting and I recognized the expression in his eyes and the same smile that flashed dimples, almost incongruous in his rugged face. He had a full head of silver hair. I remembered auburn. He had the same broad shoulders and powerful arms that made him look slightly stuffed into his double-breasted blue blazer. It hung perfectly flat over his slim middle.

"You look so nice and summery in that white dress," he said.

Summery! It was the middle of November—summery was the last thing I wanted to look.

"Thanks. But this is *winter* white. Winter. You know, like snow?" *Oh why hadn't I just worn black?*

He looked for a place to sit and led me to a pair of chairs flanking one of the window alcoves, which extended outward to a lighted balcony with pots of red and white cyclamen and a sparkling city view. The Art Deco Public Library building came to life illuminated in spotlights. I was transported back in time to an earlier era.

"Let's sit here and have a drink before we go in to dinner," Kelly said and signaled a passing waiter. We both ordered white wine. Kelly leaned back in his leather chair and crossed one loafer-clad foot over his knee. He was wearing one black and one navy blue sock and it made me somehow happy to see it. I wondered if he'd dressed in the dark or run out of clean laundry. I took a deep breath and leaned back into the comfort of my leather chair, eager to see what would come next.

"It was nice of Bill to call me," Kelly said. "The last I'd heard of you was that you'd run away." I smiled at the outmoded phrase. That's what it used to be called though, "Running away with another man."

"Well, I didn't exactly run away," I said. "I stuck out my marriage for twelve years. How about you?"

"Eighteen for me," he said. "I've been single for seventeen years now." The waiter came with our wine and a silver tray of hors d'oeuvres. My hand hesitated over the array, then I selected smoked salmon with a rosette of cream cheese. "They have caviar too," Kelly pointed out. "Do you like it?"

"Oh yes, I love all seafood. The fishier the better."

"I remember you'd taken up scuba diving back in the days when we didn't have to be certified." The conversation turned to diving and sailing and the ocean in general. During his phone call, we'd told each other where we lived, but I hadn't realized he was right on the beach in Malibu and had built the house he now lived in as a bachelor pad with extra guestrooms upstairs for when his kids visited. I told him about my cottage high in the Laguna hills and how I loved overlooking the ocean.

"I'm just starting to remodel the house. It's fifties' tacky, all full of dry rot, but it has a spectacular view of Emerald Bay. It's going to be my dream house to live in forever," I said. No hint of foreknowledge told me that I would never live in it and that my destiny sat there before me with a yellow bow tie askew beneath his pleasant face.

"We'll have lots to talk about during dinner," Kelly said. "We'd better go in now." As we got up I resisted the impulse to reach up and straighten his tie. He touched me, though, on my bare arm just inside the elbow, and it came over me in a flood of remembrance of how we used to dance together when we were young. I wondered why I hadn't remembered until this moment. Was it his touch or that mellow voice that brought it all back so vividly? I felt a little weak-kneed and was glad when he took my arm to escort me into the dining room.

During dinner we talked mostly about our children—his two sons and daughter and my two boys, all out on their own in various stages of early career struggles. We discussed our professions and where we worked. I told him how much I liked being with Country Life Interiors as a designer and how much I loved seeing my clients' faces light up when they saw their new décor. When Kelly said he was a stockbroker with a firm in Beverly Hills, I blurted, "A stockbroker, that doesn't fit! I'd have thought maybe a *yacht* broker."

"No, unfortunately not. I don't much like my work. I hate to call my clients when they've lost on investments I've suggested." His eyes dropped and he changed the subject abruptly. "So, you're in Laguna

Beach and I'm in Malibu. I guess that could be construed as geographically undesirable."

"Well, maybe." I wasn't exactly sure what he meant. "I drive from Laguna to the Pacific Design Center in West Hollywood twice a week and think nothing of it."

"Great!" he said. "Then Marina del Rey's even closer and the freeway's deserted on Saturdays. How would you feel about meeting me at the boat for a day-sail?"

I felt a flutter of excitement. "I'd love that."

When we got up from the table Kelly unselfconsciously looked me up and down. My knit dress fit snugly and I felt a blush heat up my face.

At the porte-cochere we waited for our cars. My valet parker buddies waved at me discreetly as they assisted couples into the front seats of Jaguars and Mercedeses. When Kelly's car turned out to be a shiny midnight-blue Eldorado, I felt some anxiety about the effect my old, weathered, gray Camaro would make, but when Kelly saw the carousel horse looking out of the rear window he broke into delighted laughter. "That's so great," he said. "I bet that's the first time anything like that ever hit this stuffy garage. Goodnight, Tommie. I'll call you soon."

I thought about him all the way back to Laguna and wondered what "soon" meant.

I was excited when I answered the phone and it was Kelly Spear. I knew in my heart he'd call. He'd said it would be soon, but what woman knows what that means when a man says it?

"I know it sounds, well, kind of soon to be asking you out on the boat for the weekend, but there's a big run of sea bass in the Catalina Channel. It's rare and we shouldn't miss it." I heard the excitement in his voice.

"Well," I said tentatively, my mind going a mile a minute. All the insecurities of being back in the dating scene...the anxiety of being separated from my car without even a phone...*What if he makes a pass and it feels uncomfortable? What if I don't like him after all and I'm stuck out on a boat for the whole weekend hating myself for saying I'd come?*

He interrupted my thoughts. "You'll have your own cabin, of course. I realize you haven't even seen the boat but, believe me, you'll have some privacy." I felt a rush thinking about his invitation. Well, thinking about *him* really. I didn't even ask any more questions, just accepted on the spot.

I shopped for a new duffel bag and a pair of topsiders on my lunch breaks that week. I even managed to unearth my old sailing jacket. I wanted to look salty when I came aboard.

It was my Saturday to work at Country Life Interiors but I'd traded days with another designer to be able to meet Kelly early that morning in Marina del Rey. His sailboat, the *Vagabundita*, was straining at her dock lines, as eager to be off as a racehorse at the starting gate.

Kelly had an easy way about him. I already felt comfortable voicing my inner thoughts. "This is exciting!" I said. "I was supposed to be working in the studio today, bored stiff because hardly anybody comes in on Saturdays. I feel like I'm playing hooky."

"Me too," he said, casting off. We powered most of the way to Catalina since the westerly didn't come up until around 2 p.m., but Kelly assured me we'd have a brisk sail back on Sunday. I wasn't disappointed that we weren't sailing. It had been years since I'd even been aboard a sailboat. I felt transported back into my element, just being on the water.

Kelly tried one technique after another on the sea bass. I imagined great schools of them swimming beneath our hull. We were trolling under power and he tried first speeding up and then slowing down, various kinds of bait, and experimented with a variety of depths, though he said they swam deep. Nothing worked. Kelly didn't get upset over it. He didn't curse and complain. We were enjoying the sea and the morning and the early-on excitement of a man and a woman together. We both called Santa Catalina "The Island," probably because it was the only island off the Southern California coast, below Ventura's Channel Islands and above San Diego. The configuration of Catalina's bays and points was still invisible in the heavy overcast that clung to the land, but as we approached the outline was gradually revealed. Bird Rock loomed suddenly out of nowhere, like a giant iceberg in the Arctic Sea. It was even shaped like an iceberg, and every bit as lethal. We were almost upon it.

"Here's old Bird Rock," Kelly said, unperturbed over its proximity. "Hasn't moved since the last time I was here." *He must know it drops straight down*, I thought, remembering this from my scuba diving days. I could have reached out and touched it. Kelly's navigation was right-on. Bird Rock, entirely white from seagull droppings, usually gleamed like a lighthouse, visible far out to sea. It was the landmark for our intended destination of Howlands Landing.

The anchor chain payed noisily out of the forepeak locker, a sound I would grow to love, evoking a feeling like coming home. Kelly backed down a bit to set the trusty Danford anchor in the good sand bottom. Then he launched the dinghy and rowed toward shore to put out a stern anchor as well. I was thrilled to be given a pair of heavy gloves and the job of paying out the stern line and cleating it down when Kelly waved and yelled, "Okay!" He pulled alongside in the dinghy and said to hand him down the fishing gear he'd laid out in the cockpit.

As the fog dissipated, the day grew warm and I was glad I'd had the sense to wear a bathing suit under my shorts and T-shirt. "We missed out on the sea bass," Kelly said, "but I've got another plan in mind. Something even better." He flashed his smile and said, "Hop in." One doesn't exactly "hop" into a wildly rocking dinghy off the side of a heaving sailboat, but I had a dim memory of centering my weight and putting myself down decisively right in the center of the boat. It worked. Kelly didn't even comment, he just shoved off and said we were going fishing for sand dabs in a secret place he knew.

He estimated its location by taking a bearing on the center of Bird Rock and the end of Howlands Point. The sandbar we sought lay where the imaginary lines intersected. Its exact location was a nebulous uncertainty. The dinghy drifted so much on the sea anchor Kelly'd dropped that one minute we'd be exactly opposite Bird Rock and then a short while later we'd be some distance fore or aft of it. I hoped for Kelly's sake his bearing was accurate and asked how long it had been since he'd tried to find the sandbar. "I haven't fished this spot in years." He went on to say that I was the first woman who'd been on board since he'd bought the *Vagabundita* a year ago.

"Well, I hope I won't bring bad luck. There's a superstition about women on ships."

"You won't bring me bad luck," he said. His attention was focused on baiting the hooks, but he looked at me intently for a moment as if he'd made up his mind about something.

The sandbar was deep. We had to put out 275 feet of line with seven or eight hooks on each leader and a lead weight to carry it down. When the line went slack, we knew we'd hit bottom. I liked the fishy smell of the sardines Kelly was cutting; the sun burning through the overcast felt hot on my bare back. Bolts of sunlight stabbed down through the green water, glinting off the pieces of silver bait as they spiraled down and down. I was impatient to see what would be on the line, if anything, and suggested reeling in.

"No, don't jump the gun on pulling up," Kelly said. "We have to give them a chance to take the bait." After what seemed an eternity, he said, "Okay, haul up." It was awkward and time-consuming to wind all that line around the grooved spindle, but I was careful to pay it on evenly. Finally, Kelly's line surfaced and he had a sand dab on every hook.

I peered down into the water at my line and then yellow specs became shapes. I yelled, "Kelly, Kelly, I got something big! Look, look quick! Maybe it's a sea bass! Oh, I've caught lots." Fish surfaced one by one. They were patterned in brown and sepia with tissue-paper fins, eyes popping from the unequalized pressure of their rapid ascent. "What are these weird looking things, Kelly? They're beautiful!"

"Rock fish. Not good eating. We sure lucked out on the sand dabs though. We've got plenty." His radiant smile was full of the joy of a successful catch. I watched the rhythmic movement of his brown, mus-cled arms as he rowed us back to the boat. He made short work of cleaning the fish, then put them on ice for our Sunday lunch. Next, he demonstrated the mechanism of the head. I was pleased that I had my own little bathroom adjacent to my cabin. In its compact thirty-seven feet the O-Day sailboat was well laid out for privacy, as Kelly had promised. Of center cockpit design, its outstanding feature was an aft master cabin, at once cozy and luxurious with a built-in queen-sized bunk, two hanging lockers paneled in rich mahogany, all romantically lit by brass hurricane oil lanterns. Kelly rummaged in the locker below the bunk and tossed up a down comforter. "I think you'll need this. It's going to be a cold one."

He went forward and emerged from the forepeak cabin carrying a strange-looking orange contraption of concentric circles. I watched with interest as he hung it off the end of the boom, then hoisted it partly out of the water at right angles to the hull. "This is a wobble-stopper," he said.

"A what?"

"It helps prevent the boat from rolling. Works like a baffle. Does the motion bother you too much?"

"Not really. Oh, if it keeps up all night it might get a little uncomfortable. I can't say I'm exactly used to it, haven't sailed in twenty years, since Bill and I had our boat, but back then the sea was like first love to me."

Kelly said we'd better get up on deck or we'd miss the sunset. *There is simply nothing like lying off alee shore, inhaling the chilly salt air, and drinking in a crimson sunset with an exciting new man*, I thought. Our eyes met as he handed me up a steaming mug, redolent of butter and rum.

It was a cold November night all right and I was glad I'd promised to bring a stew aboard for dinner. "I hope that stew tastes as good as it smells," Kelly said. The mingled aromas of garlic and onions simmering in the rich beef burgundy stock permeated the cabin. Kelly lit the gimbaled oil lanterns mounted all around the bulkheads. The wicks smoked a second, then flared, light reflecting on the mahogany paneling and casting shadows on the overhead. I ladled the stew into earthenware bowls and tucked a warm loaf of sourdough bread into a napkin as Kelly poured a Merlot to go with the dinner. His eyes gleamed in the candlelight and the mellow fruity taste of the wine caressed my mouth. Kelly took seconds on the stew and we sipped our wine slowly, savoring the meal and our conversation. After dinner I watched him whisk egg whites by hand in a copper bowl and, when they formed stiff peaks, fold them into ingredients he'd assembled for a chocolate soufflé.

"You're amazing," I said, as he produced the resulting impressive dessert that rose all crusty above its brown paper collar. "I'd have thought it would slosh all over the oven in this roll."

"No, the oven is on gimbals too," he explained. "I'm glad you appreciate the soufflé. So many of my land dates won't eat this and won't eat that. Most of 'em are on diets, won't touch dessert." I kept quiet, not admitting that my life had been one continuous diet for as long as I could remember. "It can be pretty discouraging," he went on. "My wife said it made her nervous to have me in the kitchen. After our divorce I took a bunch of cooking classes and the soufflé class was my favorite." I could see why. It was indeed a dramatic presentation, emerging tall and chocolaty-smelling from the tiny galley oven.

Kelly poured on Cognac and touched a match to it. Blue flames flared briefly. Amid bites of airy soufflé, Kelly outlined his plans for tomorrow's breakfast in the cockpit. I was so stuffed I didn't think I'd want another meal ever. "I think I'll do popovers and individual omelets..." He was interrupted by the sound of the dinghy slamming into the stern. "I'm going to have to get that dinghy back on board. I have a feeling this isn't going to let up." I stumbled around the galley trying to hold on with one hand while I made a stab at the dishes. The pitch and roll was bad now.

"Come on, I'll do that," Kelly said, done with his chore on deck. "We'll have some nice Colombian decaf and a nightcap." Holding hands in the warm, candlelit cabin with his other arm around my waist, it was getting to feel a little too intimate or maybe a little too good.

"Well, thanks for a fabulous dinner, Kelly. A totally fabulous day, I should say. I think I'll hit the sack. All this fresh air and good food has made me sleepy."

We did not snuggle together that night. We were too new for that, but his hand brushed my face as he wished me goodnight. We retired to separate bunks, fore and aft. I wondered if he imagined us together in the master cabin.

Soon disenchanted from my anticipation of bedding down cozily beneath the comforter and drifting off to sleep as one only can on a sailboat, I was almost thrown out of the bunk by the now prodigious pitch. I tried tucking the bedclothes in securely and then crawling back through a tight opening at the top, but with every muscle tensed against the motion it was impossible to relax. I felt like I was in a straitjacket. The last thing I wanted was to join the list of the dates who had bitched not about the food, but about the uncomfortable conditions aboard. I was proud of my iron gut and the fact that I had so far never been seasick, but I was desperate for sleep. I lay there rigid, literally holding on to keep from being thrown to the cabin sole. Thinking the motion might be less intense amidships and knowing Kelly slept in the forepeak, I decided to try sleeping on one of the long bunks in the main cabin.

I groped my way up the companionway, across the cockpit, and down into the pitch-dark salon. I felt my way along the galley counter, across the chart table, and, then, expecting the arm cushion, my hand landed on a human face. I stifled a shriek and fled back the way I'd come, terrified Kelly'd think I was getting fresh on our first night. He was either fast asleep or too much of a gentleman to react.

It was a rough storm-tossed night, during which I'd slept little. The sound of anchor chain dropping into the forepeak locker awakened me from a deep, second sleep. The noise certainly dispelled further rest. I got up feeling itchy from sleeping in my clothes, longing for a hot shower. I hoped I could sneak undetected into the galley for a cup of coffee. Pausing to listen before I crept below, I thought I heard Kelly up on deck.

"Hi Tom. I know better than to ask how you slept, though you look beautiful." *He calls me Tom.* I ran my hand through matted hair. "The barometer's up and the weather report's bad," he said. I could hear the marine operator's voice coming over the shortwave radio predicting winds gusting to forty knots. "We're getting out of here while we still can," Kelly said.

"Okay, let me throw on a turtleneck," I made a mock salute. "I'll be on hand to take orders."

"Oh, there's not much you can do." Kelly gave a slight shrug and then frowned a little as his face mirrored his next thought. "I feel so bad. I'd planned to fix you a special breakfast but we've really got to get underway. I'm sorry."

I watched him move effortlessly about the boat, testing tension on the back stays, securing the dinghy, and finally hoisting the main as we sailed off our mooring. The mainsail steadied us some in the huge swells. As we left the comparative protection of Howlands for the main channel, the full force of the gale hurled into us and Kelly leapt up to reef the main. The boat heeled over abruptly and I felt afraid when our starboard rail went under. I shifted my weight as far up to the port side as I dared, but when I glanced down into the churning water and saw our keel half exposed I slid back down into the cockpit. I looked up to where Kelly worked alone, one bare foot braced on the afterhatch, body leaning against the boom for support. He wasn't even holding on. Both hands worked to tie the reef points. "Don't worry," Kelly said as he jumped down into the cockpit. "We won't tip over."

"I thought it was called 'broach to'," I said.

"That's a word I try to steer away from."

"Bad pun, Kelly." Scared stiff, I was trying to make light of the situation. We were sailing close-hauled and I was huddled in a corner of the cockpit. There wasn't anyplace to sit where you wouldn't get drenched. The *Vagabundita* was headed right into the northerly, and every swell we met broke over our bow and splashed into the cockpit. Kelly outfitted us both in yellow slickers. He'd donned rubber boots and foul weather gear pants as well. I watched him move with the roll as he worked the wheel, glad it wasn't me trying to hold a course in these seas.

"This storm came out of nowhere," he said. "I wouldn't have brought you out if I'd known." I looked to weather and took water full in the face.

It trickled down the inside of my jacket and I zipped up over my chin. "Why don't you go below?" Kelly suggested. "Read."

"I wouldn't miss this for the world," I said. Then I told him about how Bill and I got clobbered in a big January noreaster the first year, well, month really, that we were married. He'd wanted to spend the last part of our honeymoon aboard his eight-meter sailboat, *Angelita*. I was all for it too. I'd gotten my wish about being in a storm all right, and the reality of it shut me up fast on that score. For all her sleek fifty-foot hull and Olympic gold medal, the *Angelita* labored painfully through the heavy seas trying to make the mainland. She didn't have a self-bailing cockpit. I was tied on to a stanchion and bailing for dear life, but when the water sloshed to our knees, Bill turned back to Catalina and anchored off the east end of the island. We were in close proximity to rocks, terrified we'd drag anchor. It was three days of sodden boredom and two nights of gut-wrenching fear. Everything below was wet and our provisions were down to the worst of the canned foods, like spam and corned beef hash. "War rations," I called them.

"Some honeymoon," Kelly said.

"Sad in a way. Bill was a real sailor. He'd trained aboard the yacht *Enchantress* as a teenager and he learned to navigate. Fearless too. But for some reason he never trusted his anchoring technique, afraid she'd go on the rocks."

Kelly seemed to be pleased with my sailing background, and we passed the time in conversation, shouting occasionally when the wind howled in the rigging. I made a cautious trip below to scrounge up something to eat. I handed up the last of the cold baguette and a couple of Cokes, which Kelly said happened to be a good seasick remedy. "Oh, I never get that," I said.

"I know, that's what Bill told me when he called arranging to fix us up. 'She's a real sailor,' he said. 'She never gets seasick.'"

"He did not," I said.

"Sure he did, why else do you think I called you?"

"Come on, Kelly. You mean that's all he said? He didn't say one other thing to recommend me?"

"Nope, not another word. But that was good enough for me." Our camaraderie was doused by another wave breaking over the port quarter. The
storm was moving around west. "We'll be out of this in a couple of hours,"
Kelly predicted, squinting up at the sky. "This is a bad introduction for you,
and I'm sorry," he said again. "I'll make it up to you with a sand dab lunch
when we get in." *The individual omelets were already past history*, I thought
with amusement. The sky was beginning to clear as we finally pulled into his
slip in Marina del Rey. I jumped off and grabbed a dockline to secure the
Vagabundita, proud that Kelly commented on my bowline knot.

"Why don't you get out of those wet clothes," he said, handing me a
big terry cloth robe. "I'll have hot water for you in twenty minutes." I
heard the generator kick on and relished the thought of a hot shower at
last. We got out the lunch things while we waited for the water to heat
up. Kelly shook the sand dabs in fine cornmeal and started to sauté thin
sliced potatoes in butter and olive oil. The fragrance filled the cabin and
my stomach rumbled. I slid my hand against my body. It felt thin and
cold under the robe I wore. The sun was trying to come out and shined
palely through the translucent gray sky.

"I think it's going to be nice," Kelly said. "Bundle up after your shower
though. Do you have dry clothes?"

He's a mother hen, I thought with a smile.

I stayed under the shower a long time, hoping I wasn't wasting too
much water. Kelly hadn't said anything about that. We hadn't even had a
shower aboard the *Angelita*. I thought back to my chilly sponge baths in our
eight meters' cramped head and luxuriated a little longer under the hot
water. When I dried off, I rummaged around in my duffel bag, glad I'd
brought a sweatshirt and pants. Kelly tossed me down a fleece-lined jacket
and mukluks. I peered into the mirror bolted onto the bulkhead. *Dear God,
you've never looked worse*. I ran a comb through my straight blond hair.

"Hurry up," Kelly yelled down, "I'm starting the sand dabs. Aren't
you starved?"

"Who me?" said ravenous me as I came up out of the after cabin
and down into the warmth and cheer of the main salon. Kelly handed
me a spatula.

"Keep the fish moving around a minute. I have a surprise for you." He leaned over and opened the built-in ice chest. I heard a cork pop, then Kelly was pouring champagne into crystal glasses etched with schooners under full sail. The wine foamed over the rims. I felt the sharp tingle of bubbles on my tongue.

"Wow," I said. "What are we celebrating? Survival?"

"No, silly," he bent to kiss me. "We're celebrating the beginning of us." I smiled up at him—this big, slightly shaggy man with the beaming face, with whom I was already half in love.

Our courtship took place entirely aboard the boat. We solved the problem of our geographical undesirability by both driving halfway and meeting at the marina on Saturday mornings for our island run. Once we became lovers, we met late Friday nights after the crushing freeway traffic abated.

Easter fell in early April that year of 1981, and since Kelly and I had no young children to hide eggs for it was just the two of us rocking at anchor in Avalon, west of the casino off the old St. Catherine Hotel beach. The hotel hadn't been standing for years. All that remained was a crumbling balustrade that graced the once-elegant terrace.

"I have a surprise for you, Tom." Kelly spoke with excitement; his eyes were filled with it too. He let go of my hand to slap the pockets of his sailing jacket, which gave off a musty smell in the warm cabin. He fumbled through the inside pockets, the look of concern on his face increasing with each empty exploration. He got up and faced me in stunned silence, hands dropped to his sides. He looked so crushed I wished I could help him. He moved fast then, nearly knocking over our champagne. He grabbed his duffel bag, rummaged, then dumped the contents out onto the bunk, his back to me. A moment passed, then he turned around, face triumphant, holding something behind his back. I half expected him to say, "Which hand?"

He held a gift-wrapped box. Its flat rectangular shape gave no hint of the contents, but it was the signature turquoise color of Tiffany's, tied with a crisp white grosgrain bow. My heart quickened. Kelly pulled me to him in a deep, deep kiss. "I hadn't wanted to break the magic," he said. "God, I thought I'd *lost* this. I've had it in so many secure places since I…"

"Please stop, sweetheart." I put my fingers on his lips. "Don't think that. You only increased the suspense and you're so funny." I suppressed a strong impulse to giggle.

"Come on, open it!" He almost took the box from me in his eagerness.

I untied the white ribbon, lifted off the top, and inside was another box of black velvet. I pushed the tiny button activating the spring. It snapped open and there, lying on a bed of white satin, was a gold heart pendant. It seemed to wink at me in the candlelight. I bent to read the engraving,

T & K

100

April 4, 1981

587643

"Kelly, this is romantic, what's the one hundred for?"

"The number of times we've been together."

"You mean, you mean you *counted*?

"Well, estimated."

"You engineer guys slay me," I said. "I'm almost afraid to ask what the long number's for."

"It's a serial number registering your name and address with Tiffany's, so I will never lose you."

"Is that for real? You mean if I'm found stranded on a desert island, memory lost in amnesia, all my rescuers will have to do is call Tiffany's?"

"That's the idea. Look on the other side. See, it says *Return to Tiffany's*. Don't forget to call them with a change of address when you move."

"Move? I have no plans…"

"In with me," Kelly said. "As soon as we set a date."

"Hurry up, sweetheart. We only have half an hour to get our marriage license before they close. How come you're so late?" Kelly rushed me into the car, screeching the tires as he backed out. "My God, what's that?!" he yelled. We were deafened by a loud scary noise coming from the engine of his normally sedate Eldorado. "It sounds like we're throwing a rod." He shot me a desperate glance, then tried shifting into a lower gear. The car crawled. I glanced at my watch and saw we had little time to spare.

"Kelly, I've heard of reluctant bridegrooms but never one who went to such lengths as this." I was trying to alleviate our stress by joking. "Seriously, Kel, if we don't make it there's no way Father John will marry us illegally without the license." Instead of talking out the problem as women do, Kelly clammed up. I knew he was working it out in his mind and so I waited patiently for his resolution.

"We'll just fly to Vegas and get married by a Justice of the Peace, then go through with a fake ceremony tomorrow. You'll still have your garden wedding, Tom," he patted my arm reassuringly.

"Get married in *Las Vegas*," I breathed. "Are you crazy? We have the rehearsal dinner an hour and a half from now. Father John has driven over from Phoenix, Ariz..."

"No problem at all," Kelly interrupted. "We'll take the midnight flight to Vegas and be back before anyone's even awake." My heart sank.

"Kellogg, I can't think of *anything* less romantic. Can you imagine the preacher's wife standing up as my matron of honor in her chenille bathrobe and pink curlers?" I suppressed a shudder. "And I wouldn't be able to *face* your mother. I'm supposed to be staying at her house tonight. She'll think we *slept* together!" The late afternoon sun turned his full head of hair to silver and lit up his green eyes as he turned to me.

"Tommie, I'm fifty-six years of age. You're forty-eight. Who cares what my mother thinks!"

"I do." I sank miserably down into my seat.

"Here we are! Run!" Kelly leapt from the car grabbing my hand as we rushed into the courthouse. We charged up a long flight of tiled stairs, arriving at the clerk's counter just as the young woman was sliding the doors shut with a click. "Hey, wait a minute," Kelly shouted, brandishing our blood tests. "It's only four-thirty."

"Yes sir. That's what time we close on Friday afternoons."

"You've got to be kidding! We have a hundred and fifty guests invited to a garden wedding at my mother's tomorrow afternoon. Our five children have flown in from all over." Kelly smiled winningly, putting an arm around me. It was probably the mention of the family or perhaps the advanced age of the bride and groom that melted the heart of the pretty young Hispanic girl.

"Oh all right. I'll open up for you. I'll have to change the time though. My boss knows we close at four-thirty Friday and he'd know it was a forgery." She winked and smiled and forged the time on the papers.

We continued to rush for the next hour, hurriedly changing clothes for the evening's festivities. Slightly harassed, we finally arrived at Kelly's mother, Pinky's, house, where our five children and the minister waited.

Father John stood very straight and tall. With his small beard and ascetic face, he resembled one of the disciples. I breathed a sigh of relief at the sight of him.

Over a glass of champagne Kelly humorously told the story of our stressful afternoon. He couldn't resist asking the minister. "What would you have done, Father John, if we'd showed up for the wedding with no marriage license?"

"Oh, for heaven's sake, Kelly! I've known you and Tommie for forty years. I would have married you anyway."

CHAPTER 8

The ever-whirling wheel of change,

the which all mortal things doth sway.

—Edmund Spenser

THE WIND TORE at my hair and drove the rain in a horizontal torrent. The intensity of the tropical squall lacked only the element of cold. Close to the equator now, coolness was what we most longed for. Wearing my daily costume of a bikini, I glanced at the prone body of Morris, where he lay on the bare teak deck below. His tongue was out and his sides heaved with every breath. I pitied him his fur coat in this equatorial heat. "Kelly, poor Morris. He's terrified now over the sound of the gale. I'm going to carry him aft to our bunk."

I heard the concern in Kelly's voice as he answered, "I've finally decided after all this that bringing Morris cruising could be construed as cruelty to animals. Here, hold my jacket over him."

Carrying Morris, his wriggling body draped in Kelly's foul weather gear up one steep companionway, across the slippery cockpit, and down another steep little flight of steps without being able to spare a hand to hold on for myself was risky business. Kelly and I both knew the threat of a broken limb at sea.

Now, despite our reliance on radio contact with the outside world, the truth was we were many, many hours, even days, out of range of any kind of emergency help. Certainly no helicopter could reach us 2,000 miles out to sea. The only hope would be a passing vessel large enough to carry a doctor, but we purposely charted our course to avoid the shipping lanes. With a chill, I remembered the young crew member of a cruise ship we met over a beer in some seedy, dockside bar. He described his ship's crew complement, plus 2,000 passengers, frockling their way around the Caribbean, and how the crew had to stuff the bodies of stroke victims into the huge galley freezers. "Totally gross!" Kelly and I had said, not really taking it in.

"My biggest surprise is that we haven't even seen so much as one plane or a single vessel in over two weeks," I said. Our mutual vulnerability strengthened the bond of intimacy between us. Like disdainful adolescents, we believed we were somehow immune to danger. In our denial of the possibility of loss, one from the other, we calmly discussed how our five-year odyssey might likely end. We could both handle going down with the ship together off some treacherous lee shore. If we didn't make it to our final landfall, it would be a fitting finale, since neither could contemplate life without the other.

Prior to departure from Santa Barbara, we had signed up for every available course, laughing and joking together in the Red Cross classroom where we practiced mouth-to-mouth resuscitation and set each other's pretend broken bones. It had been fun, like playing doctor. I had even teased that I knew Kelly was a frustrated surgeon and could hardly wait to perform emergency procedures at sea. Heaven help me. Now I was trying to reassure Morris, stroking his soft gray striped coat. No wonder he was afraid.

The *Vagabundita* shuddered against the impact of the sea and each time we fell down into the trough I thought for sure the hull would split into pieces as the next wall of water slammed into us. I heard a sickening crash from below. I knew Kelly couldn't leave his station in the cockpit in such a gale. I thanked God it was he and not I at the helm this time. One false turn of the wheel in such seas and we'd broach.

I made my way below with as much speed as I dared muster through the blinding sheets of water descending into the cockpit. Our self-bailing pumps couldn't keep up with the deluge and now water poured below, flooding the main cabin. I shouted up through the deafening wind, "Kelly! Our medical locker gave way." Its door hung drunkenly from one hinge. All of our carefully prescribed drugs and medications in their plastic cylinders were now floating among packets of gauze and bandages. I was bewildered for a moment to see hundreds of little white tablets strewn in the mess. Then my heart almost stopped. "Kelly, it's your heart medicine! You left the cap open!" I rushed topside and was confronting him now face-to-face in the storm. I was already soaked from waves breaking over our bow and the drenching rain of the tropical squall.

"How could you have been so careless?"

"Don't scold me," he said.

"Don't *scold* you!" The salt covering my face now was from my own tears. "How dare you say that! Do you have any idea what it's like for me to cross the Pacific Ocean with a sixty-five-year-old man with a heart condition?" The wind rose and howled in the silence between us. I raised my voice another decibel. "We're not going to survive this. Do you know that? We're going to die out here!" I was screaming the words and couldn't stop myself. "You are a careless man, careless! Careless of your life. Careless of me."

I saw him flinch at that, but he just stared ahead, his powerfully muscled arms working the helm. I tore away from him and almost fell on the slippery steps of the companionway in my urgency to salvage the pills. Cotton had worked its way into the head's drain, plugging it. Oblivious to the water, I dropped to my knees. A hundred or more pills floated there. As I reached out to gather them up, one by one they disintegrated in my fingers. Nothing but dispersing white powder remained.

"Dear God, Kelly. Three months' supply of your Amioderone, nothing left." I was stammering in desperation as I flung back up on deck.

"Don't scold me. I mean it!" He hadn't raised his voice, but it sounded somehow ominous. There was something I didn't know. It seemed bizarre that he was wearing nothing more than trunks in this onslaught. We both ducked to avoid another engulfment of water.

"Scold you, for God's sake! Is that all you think this is? A scolding?" I glimpsed his bleak face. I felt the anger and tension drain out of my body and stretched my arms around him. I stared out at the gray, violent seas. "Kelly, you are my life." I swallowed hard to stop the shaking in my voice. "Why do you think I put my hand on your chest every morning when I am hardly half awake?" I raised a hand now to touch the yellow day-glow cylinder, hanging from a black cord around my neck. "Do you really not notice when I grab your heart medicine in case we have to abandon ship?" He just stared ahead, working the helm. "Yes, I'm out here with you," I went on—"because I love you." I felt my chest tighten up and my voice go out of control again. "But this is insanity. Insanity, I tell you!"

A noise like the crack of a rifle shot assaulted me. My mind could not shift focus to identify the sound. Kelly's shout of, "Get on the helm!" shattered my bewilderment. Horrified, I saw the source of his panic. Our storm jib had blown out. The torn canvas snapped and cracked in the gale. It could put out an eye. "You take the wheel," Kelly ordered as he leapt to the top deck.

"No, Kelly, no! Don't go forward. You're not even clipped onto your lifeline. You'll be washed overboard. I can't handle the helm in these seas. I'm afraid, Kelly. I'm afraid!" His form disappeared from my sight into the storm and my voice was carried away on the wind.

Two hours later Kelly, Morris, and I were recovering in the cockpit—Morris over a can of sardines, and Kelly and I over a glass of wine. The sea itself was like glass and the mutable sky, almost black during the squall, arched above us like a great blue bowl. The white clouds of evening were just beginning to form around the horizon. The memory of the tropical storm was like a half-forgotten nightmare.

"I can't believe how fast that squall passed over," I said. "Two hours ago I thought we were going to die out here."

"Oh, I knew the boat could weather the storm. It was you at the helm that had me worried." His impish smile teased. I heard no lingering resentment in his tone.

"What? Well, thanks a lot, Kel. I guess I should know by now that you only put me on the wheel under the most desperate conditions. That's because you want *me* to be the one to broach the boat instead of you." I turned my face to him for a kiss, tasting the salt on his lips.

"Seriously, though, remember how we used to talk about bringing extra crew for this Pacific passage?" Kelly asked. "Do you ever regret that we didn't?" I knew how crucial my reply was to him.

"Not for a minute. We wouldn't have been—you know."

His smile reached all the way into his eyes. The low sun caught them and they flashed—*maybe the only green flash I'd ever see.* Kelly stroked Morris. "It's bad enough having you on our bed all the time, Morris." He rubbed his hand under the cat's white chin.

"By the way," I said, "in all the turmoil of the storm I didn't tell you something really weird about Morris. He won't eat off the floor anymore. Just flat-out refuses food. The minute I put his bowl on the table, he jumps right up and eats. He's such a kick."

"I'm not at all surprised to hear that," Kelly said, "considering how we two humans botched things during the storm. Now *he* wants to be captain." We both laughed at Morris, imaging him in that role as he sat there with half-closed eyes.

"That's great by me, Kel. I'm perfectly happy being first mate and chief cook and cabin steward. We can demote you to chief engineer and navigator and make Morris captain. Then next time, you can put *him* at the helm." *All this teasing banter. This was the other me. The for-she's-a-jolly-good-fellow me.* I surreptitiously fingered the container of pills hanging under my windbreaker, waiting until I could make an excuse to go below and count how many were left. I'd tried hard to hide the persistent fear I felt below the surface of my cheerful demeanor—an albatross around my neck.

To Kelly, the worst aftermath of the storm was our blown-out jib, ripped from top to bottom. I knew I could repair the damage on my sail-maker's sewing machine and told him so. But I could think of nothing but the ruined heart medication. "Kelly, I'm going below to mop up the water in the head." Almost immobilized by fear, I had to struggle to make my hands work to get the top off the waterproof container from around my neck. I dumped the contents of the cylinder onto the bunk. My hands shook so hard I had to count the pills twice. Only six. *How many more days to landfall?*

"Kelly," I called up, carefully modulating my voice, "when George calls tonight, I want to talk to him. It's sort of a surprise, something I want him to send to us in the Marquesas, okay?"

"Sure, Tom. I'm expecting him to come through any minute."

"I want to be able to tell him how many more days to landfall—about."

"Let's see, I estimate about ten, eleven days, depending on wind."

It was always the high point of our day when George called, our only link to the outside world, but sometimes interference rendered the call almost unintelligible or he didn't get through at all. This time when he came in with his usual greeting of "Hi, old man," my excitement diminished because of anxiety. I studied Kelly's face as he talked. Not a trace of concern crept into his voice or shadowed his cheerful expression—he seemed unaware of the heart medication disaster, as though he didn't care. Suddenly I was so angry I had to bite the inside of my mouth. I let Kelly chat a while then shooed him topside, out of earshot.

"George," I said, "this is serious. I don't want Kelly to hear. I don't want him to know how terrified I am over this. Do you read me? Over." I was accustomed to the slight time lag before hearing a response.

"No, you're breaking up..."

"George, please, please—this is crucial. I only have *half* enough of

Kelly's heart medication to get us there." I could hardly hear his voice through the static.

"I'm unable to read you," very faint now.

"Dear God, George—try another frequency. I'm desperate. Over." There was more crackling, hurting my ear, then George's voice again, sounding very indistinct. "Did you hear that about the heart medication?" I was almost shouting. I curled my hand around the mouthpiece like a megaphone so my voice wouldn't carry up into the cockpit.

"Yes, barely. It's Amioderone, right? What about the Coumadin? Over."

"I've got the blood thinner. How much risk is it without enough pills?" Seconds dragged by. I dug my nails into my palm. George wasn't answering. It was as though I heard another voice through the static. The voice of Kelly's Santa Barbara doctor, Tom De Berry, when he'd initially leveled with me, saying, *"The danger is, in Kelly's case, if it goes too long between heartbeats the heart is apt to stop—premature ventricular contraction—but Amioderone regulates it. He'll be fine. He can live forever as long as he takes this."* I thought I heard George's voice again, barely.

"Give him one pill every other day. At worst it won't be as much shock to the heart as cutting off completely." I fought against a contraction in my throat, unable to talk for a minute, hoping George wouldn't think he'd lost the connection. Suddenly I could read him loud and clear. "What's Kelly's attitude on this?"

"He's not even worried. I can't believe it. It's making me crazy, but I don't want to add to his stress by freaking out when there's nothing I can do."

"He's in denial. He can't face that it's possibly lethal for both of you—that he might not get *you* there." My mind brushed that aside.

"I want you to order a prescription out of Papeete," I said. "Find a hospital. A prescription pharmacy. I want it there when we arrive. Same mailing, c/o Frank Courser, Keikahanui Inn, Nuku Hiva, Marqueses, French Polynesia. Marie knows the zip code...George! George, please..." He was fading out again. "George, please hear me..." The static took over completely, ending further conversation. I stood there with the

useless radio telephone in my hand. I closed my eyes and prayed to God
that George had heard me.

Awakening to my husband's caress in the early morning swelter, I
pulled away and rolled over. I saw his disappointment and a pang of
remorse knifed through me like a broken promise. "Oh Kelly, I'm so hot
and sticky." I hesitated a moment but it was too late. The physical discomfort of the equatorial heat and my itching, salt-encrusted skin were too
much of a deterrent to lovemaking. I dragged my aching body toward the
galley in search of hot tea. It had been a night of rough seas. We'd had to
brace our legs against the bulkhead to keep from rolling out of the bunk.
I watched Kelly walk stiffly up into the cockpit. *He must have a sore back
too.* During our morning chores, I stole little glances at Kelly. I felt terrible. Rejection of any kind had never been part of our marriage.

Our long Pacific passage was on countdown now. We were preparing
to make landfall within the next few days. At one point I plowed through
the aft cabin's underbunk storage compartment. This necessitated holding up the mattress with my head while digging through the contents of
a year's stowage. The locker was always an abyss, crammed with plastic
bags that shifted around whenever we dug anything out. Finally, I found
what I was after—our bolt of mosquito netting, mercifully not sopping
wet with bilge water. We had been told by other cruising yachtsmen to
anticipate an offshore infestation of no-see-ums.

Kelly reminded me of last December's cruise up into the Sea of Cortez.
We lay at anchor in the lee of the sheer rock cliffs of Isla Espiritu Santo,
enjoying a golden sunset. Suddenly, we were inundated by a cloud of
swarming insects. Futilely slapping ourselves all over, we stared helplessly
at each other, well aware that this influx had wrought ruination to our
idyllic anchorage. We had neglected to replenish the insect repellent. It
was a grave error we would not repeat.

Now, forewarned, Kelly helped me rig the fine white gauze over our
bunk, leaving plenty of overlap along the entry slit. Pleased to have

accomplished this in advance of the need, we admired the exotic effect it lent our cozy teak cabin with its brass oil lanterns and luxurious bed.

After a lunch of sardine-and-onion sandwiches, Kelly fell to his navigational computations. He raised a smiling face from the chart table, sun crinkles at the corners of his eyes. "I make it one and a half, maybe two days away from landfall now. As of tomorrow we'll be on island watch." I gave a shriek of elation. "And I have a surprise for you," he went on with a droll smile. "Since we can refill our tanks as soon as we get to the Marquesas, I think we can afford to splurge on water. How about a sun shower?" He laughed to see my delight over his suggestion.

I dashed down to rummage through the head locker and managed to produce a brand-new tube of bath gel. Brandishing it, I shed my bikini on the way to the upper deck. Aloft swung the solar shower, the plastic bag full of warm water. "Let's start with a shampoo," I said, "then we can wash with the runoff." I was already afraid we'd run out of water before the soap was rinsed out of my hair. "I'm so excited. This is as salt-free as I'm ever going to be, Kel."

We sighed with pleasure as the freshwater coursed down over our parched skin. The luxurious Georgio shower gel we were using enveloped us in a cloud of fragrance. We took turns soaping each other's bodies, swinging out on the mizzen shroud to let the other rinse off under the warm water. It was not easy to keep a footing on the soapy deck, hold on, and wash each other simultaneously. We were heeled over on a port tack with scuppers awash. It was a life-threatening shower. One sudden lurch could easily pitch either of us overboard and a wet head would disappear in an instant beneath the huge swells.

"Kelly, you're so tan you look like you're wearing white trunks." He squirted out another generous dollop of gel, hands lathering it over my naked body. We let go the salty lines and clung together, slippery as seals, laughing danger in the face. The trade winds blowing against our bare skin neither warmed nor cooled, they felt like a gentle caress ephemeral as a butterfly kiss. The Georgio fragrance hung only a moment in the air before it wafted away. We rinsed again in the last trickle of the precious water. "Kelly, I haven't felt so refreshed in weeks. Let's go below for a nap."

As he protectively guided me down into the cabin from our slippery perch, I heard the good-natured humor in his voice. "You do realize that what you call a nap is going to totally negate the benefits of this shower, don't you, sweetheart?" He reached up to turn on the fan he had installed to keep the humid air at least moving around the cabin. It fluttered the white gauze we had draped from the low overhead. As I sank back against the exotically patterned cushions made of old Batik fabrics, the afternoon sun filtered through the open ports. I felt transported to some enchanted love tent, with "magic casements opening on the foam of perilous seas in fairy lands forlorn."

When we awoke some two hours later, surfeited with love and sleep, it was with a lingering poignancy that we parted, barely able to step back into our world of ship and sea and sky. Kelly got up and went forward to alter sail.

I felt suddenly overwhelmed with a profound sadness that brought tears to my eyes.

CHAPTER 9

What seas what shores what gray rocks and what islands

What water lapping the bow…what images return.

—T.S. Eliot

THAT NIGHT KELLY made contact with the Pacific Maritime Net. It was a thrill to hear the now familiar voice say, "Will the yacht *Vagabundita* come in, please? What is your position?" This Net was a dedicated group of hams who unofficially kept track through nightly radio contacts with all of the cruising boats crossing the Pacific at any given time. The day we left Mexico there were seventeen boats ahead of us. Now we were first to be called since we were the next estimated to make landfall. Four nights earlier we had cheered to hear that *Summerwind*, Cindy and Tim Adams' boat, had reached Nuku Hiva in the Marquesas. We hadn't met the couple, but had felt a strong affinity while following their progress. Their boat was an unbelievable nineteen feet in length, manned by a young couple who had sold every material thing they possessed to go cruising. Jim and Janice's *Loki Lani* had made landfall a week ago. Their last call was eerie. They were completely surrounded by whales.

Lying in the cockpit that night on watch, gazing up at the stars pavéd across the heavens, we imagined sighting land the next day. How would that feel? Something stirred in my heart.

It was the part of me that hoped our long Pacific crossing would never end. Though I usually dozed, it was hard to sleep at all that night. We had to keep especially vigilant watches, since we had sighted the first vessel in twenty-seven days. It appeared to be a huge fishing trawler and we experienced an odd camaraderie with it.

In the late afternoon Kelly climbed the ratlines to hoist the French tricolor. It was exciting to see it flying, and I wondered how long we'd technically been in French Polynesian waters. Many weeks earlier I'd made the red-white-and-blue flag on my sailmaker's sewing machine. We carried all the colors of tough nylon fabrics aboard for the purpose of making flags to comply with international marine regulations—flying the flags of the foreign ports we entered. I watched with some concern as Kelly climbed high above the deck to secure the burgee to the first spreader. How well I knew the hazards of trying to hang on with course Manila lines cutting into hands, feet feeling for the next narrow rung. I shuddered, remembering. Holding my breath, I watched Kelly's careful hand-by-hand descent for a few rungs, binoculars swinging with the boat's roll.

Suddenly I was stunned by a shout of sheer joy.

"Land ho!" Kelly sang out. Before I even strained my eyes toward where he pointed, I thrilled to realize this moment. "Kelly, Kelly, you're incredible! That tiny island is exactly where you knew it would be." He had sailed us over 3,500 miles of Pacific Ocean and the island of Hiva Oa was a mere spec among the Marquesan cluster.

Kelly descended, his long tan legs set off by his now famous orange phosphorescent trunks that made my blood run cold. He could hardly wait to hand me the binoculars, bracing me from behind to steady my view, pointing me in the direction of a barely perceived island outline hugging the horizon. "Is it...do you think it's Nuku Hiva?" I was stammering in excitement and turned my face to his glowing one.

"No, I think it's Hiva Oa. Say, if I'm not mistaken, I'm entitled to an extra measure of rum for sighting land."

"What! Is that really a custom out of ancient sailing lore or did you just make that up?" Overflowing with elation, he gave me an impulsive kiss.

"And you, my laughing fellow rover, get one too!" I was glad he viewed me as such.

"I'll look at the chart in a minute," Kelly said. "This is too special. Let's go forward and watch from the bowsprit." Bare legs swinging amid the spray of the bow wave, I had to hang on tight. Kelly was making his way forward slowly from the cockpit. He was carrying two little glasses. I could see that he had no hand for the ship. A sudden lurch flung a stream of amber liquid over the side and I saw Kelly stagger. I felt a stab of fear as I rose to meet him. Kelly's frustration vented in humor as usual. "I've *spilled* more rum than I've drunk on this passage."

"Never mind, Kel. Tomorrow we'll be drinking Chardonnay. Please come forward and get settled with the binocs. I'll bring your drink." I made myself slip into my worn moccasin topsiders for the hand-over-hand trip back along the narrow deck, holding on whenever I could and calling back to Kelly, "It doesn't matter if we run out of rum now. It doesn't matter if we run out of *anything*, sweetheart. We're here!"

A moment later we were clinking glasses, no plastics for this ceremony. Our legs swung over the side, doused with salt spray flung up from the bow-wave. We shrieked in unison at the sight of a lone dolphin, dorsal fin knifing the water, sharing our joy as it dove and leapt about the bow, whistling its song of welcome.

We'd sighted land at 4:49 p.m. As soon as Kelly consulted the charts he easily identified the emerging island as Hiva Oa, one of the larger in the fourteen-island chain of the Marquesas. We were bound for Taiohae Bay on Nuku Hiva, where we were required by the French government to check in. To obtain a two-month visa, we had to produce elaborate documentation and post a cash sum equivalent to our combined return airfares, a hefty $3,500, refundable upon our departure providing everything was in order. The French weren't about to have any indigent yachties cluttering up their waters.

The islands of the Marquesas lie along the southeast/northeast line of the trades. They form a cluster 1,250 kilometers northeast of Tahiti beyond the Tuamotu atolls. The Marquesas are considered to be the most remotely situated islands in the world, the farthest from any major land-mass. On the map, they seem to lie on the crossroads of the earth's greatest ocean, between Cape Horn and Canton, Panama, and Sydney, Australia. They have never been easily reached.

Kelly told me we would be coming in on a triangle course to avoid the danger of a night landfall in an unfamiliar bay. I was accustomed to the wisdom of his decisions, but to wait hours until daylight seemed anticli-mactic now that we had finally sighted this tiny island. I'd imagined us hand in hand, splashing ashore together, reaching the white sand beach. Well, it wasn't going to happen that way.

"Kelly, I'm so excited! I'll make something special."

"Sounds great. Shall we have a little wine?"

"Sure, but I don't know how much we have left. There's that case of Chardonnay stowed forward, but it's probably buried. Look under here first." I pointed to the compartment under the bunk. One of my double-duty small efficiencies was to cover each wine bottle in a heavy sock to prevent the annoyance of clinking sounds as the boat rolled. We'd learned, the hard way, to select the dinner fixings while it was still light, otherwise we would be rooting around on our hands and knees, pawing through a dark storage compartment. Once, after such scrounging, Kelly had ceremoniously uncorked a bottle bearing an ornate European label. Surprised when I turned down a second glass, he remarked that, "Out of all those wonderful wines we've stocked, this one's not too palatable."

"Yes," I agreed. "Let's try to remember not to get this one again." I noticed he didn't replenish his glass either. It wasn't until I was stowing things the next morning that I realized we'd been toasting each other with balsamic vinegar.

The frequent deprivations of our Spartan life made even small luxuries seem exciting. Now, on this night of nights, I decided to surprise Kelly. "I don't want you to peek, Kelly. I'm going to splurge on dinner." His face lit up. I loved to see him smile.

"What are you fixing?" His green eyes fairly sparkled.

"No, don't even ask or it won't be a surprise." I shooed him up to the cockpit. "Entertain Morris a while."

I set the table with my best yellow batik placements, which enlivened the dim, teak cabin—like a patch of buttercups springing up in a brown field. I selected one of the little canned hams I knew Kelly liked and made a pungent marinade from poupon mustard thinned with Madeira wine, garnished with dried apricots, which would cook down soft. I glanced at the stowage hammock and saw about half a dozen onions left, already gone bad through their outer layers. By now I was accustomed to salvaging half-rotted produce. Feeling prodigal in my use of so many, I trimmed, sliced, and sautéed what was left of three onions in a little canned butter. To round out the menu I lavishly opened two more cans and mixed pineapple chunks into mashed yams.

Our festive dinner was punctuated by alternating trips to the cockpit to share reports on the island's growing proximity. It was still little more than a chimera hanging gray on the horizon—the humped back of a distant whale.

Kelly doubled-reefed the main and struck the jib to slow our speed, setting a triangle course for a morning landfall. As the sky grew dark, Venus trembled in the twilight, heralding the night. Kelly made a thrilling suggestion. "Let's stay up all night and watch these islands emerge by starlight."

Morris caught our excitement and snuggled with us in the cockpit.

Kelly and I were hardly able to tolerate clothes and wore our swimsuits even at night. We lay half-propped against canvas flotation cushions, Kelly holding me against him, I in turn cradling Morris, though

I did not need his added warmth. Holding him against my bare midriff felt like a cummerbund of fur.

Kelly got up abruptly and went below. I heard him rummaging around in the head for a few minutes before I called to ask what he was looking for.

"Do we have any Rolaids?" he called back.

"How come? What's wrong?" I rushed below. Kelly was massaging a hand over his bare chest.

"Just sort of a tightness. I kind of wolfed down my dinner. It's the excitement." A spasm of pain distorted his face.

"Kelly, I'm worried. What is it?" Fear snaked through me. I didn't voice what I was thinking. *Chest pain.*

"It's nothing, just indigestion. I'll be all right."

"Oh sweetheart." I put my arms around his bare, muscled shoulders. "Come on. I want you to lie down." He reached out for me. His hands felt rough and reassuring as he stroked my bare back.

"I'm sorry about our star watch. I've suddenly had it. I'm going to try and sleep." I went with him to our cabin. I took off my bikini and lay next to his naked back, massaging his neck and shoulders, loving the feel, the salt smell of his skin, and the size of his body. I heard the water swishing along the hull—the sound we loved—whispered secrets between boat and sea. When his breathing became regular, I carefully removed myself and returned to my watch.

It had grown too dark to distinguish island silhouettes. I was relieved that after a careful charting of our new course, Kelly'd set the automatic pilot. He made his usual, meticulous notation in the ship's log, indicating the estimated time when the next radical change of course would occur.

Doubly charged as I was with concern for Kelly, and in anticipation of final landfall, it was easy to keep an alert watch, but sailing at good speed through a moonless night in such close proximity to the Marquesas had me worried. With Kelly asleep below, I made frequent checks on the radar screen.

At about 4 a.m., Kelly came topside to relieve me. My antennae sought danger signs. There were none. He exuded his usual vitality. "I feel

so refreshed. It *was* indigestion. So much for your special dinner, Tomkat."
A wink and a smile. His sense of humor was back. I exhaled my anxiety
in a deep breath, then eased gratefully below.

A couple of hours later I awoke to hear Kelly on the radio telephone
speaking to George. I heard the elation in his voice announcing our
landfall. Kelly had made the last course change as I slept, and it seemed
strange to see the sun coming up off our starboard quarter now, instead
of directly astern. I joined him in the cockpit, thrilled to see Nuku Hiva
rising massive and green in the bright morning sun. A wilder, more
romantic island would be beyond imagining. It was anything but a
palm-lined shore. There was no beach. The lofty cliffs dropped sheer
into the sea. Land never looked so good. "Smell it, Tommie? Can you
smell the land?" Even Morris seemed mesmerized. He stretched up on
hind legs, gazing toward shore, ears pricked forward, tail twitching. I
dashed below and whipped up a batch of corn muffins to go with our
breakfast coffee.

Dolphins appeared out of nowhere. Some thirty strong, they escorted
us along the coast on our approach to Taiohae Bay. Perhaps they were trying to tell us something in their droll squeaky voices, but Kelly and I knew
they'd come to share in the excitement of our accomplishment. Gaily
they vaulted three abreast from the sea in perfect synchronization while
others streaked beneath, barely clearing the acrobats' crash—a choreo-
graphed ballet. We couldn't contain our delight. Hugging each other, we
shouted greetings to them, then, laughing, switched to French. Rainbows
arched in their every splash—with each joyous leap, the last of my fear
evaporating like the spindrift blown from our wake.

My new moon wish played in my heart—a tinkling refrain. I wrote in
the log: *May 4, 1991. We have great joy and elation. Nothing can ever take this
from us. We've had it all.*

Even without the verification of the charts, we would have recognized Taiohae Bay from Melville's description. We had been reading
aloud to each other from *Typee*, his book about his adventures with the
cannibals of Nuku Hiva. He described the bay of Nukuheva, as it was
called then:

An expanse of water not unlike in figure the space included within the limits of a horseshoe. You approach it from the sea by a narrow entrance...from the verge of the water the land rises uniformly on all sides, with green and sloping acclivities, until from gently rolling hillsides and moderate elevations, it insensibly swells into lofty and majestic heights...

And so it appeared to us. "Tomkat, we're going to come in under sail just as Melville did," Kelly said. (Our usual approach to any unknown anchorage was to drop sail well out, then come in under power for increased maneuverability.) I was thrilled—his choice was appropriate to our momentous landfall and his romantic spirit. We would make a slow perusal through the bay, then drop anchor where Kelly's expertise determined.

We passed the binoculars back and forth in a fever of excitement. There was little we could pick out on shore, so dense was the tropical vegetation. "Look at that...up on the hillside, Kel. It looks like something Gauguin might have painted; it might even be the Keikahanui Inn."

"I bet you're right. I can hardly wait to go there for a martini and a hamburger tonight. And look at that church with the twin red spires. Exotic!" He dropped the hook in water so transparent we could easily see where the anchor took hold in the sand bottom.

"Kelly, it's going to be a snap to spot the coral reefs from the ratlines. I've never seen such clear water." We were about a ten-minute swim from a little palm-fringed beach. To port and extending for about a mile all the way across the bay lay a considerably large and varied fleet of sailboats. I commented with surprise to see so many. Kelly was studying them through our twelve high-powered glasses.

"It's the Euro '92 race boats; that's what they are. See that burgee they're all flying?" We had been following the progress of their two-year circumnavigation as best we could, with no T.V. or newspapers. I knew Kelly was elated at the prospect of meeting other blue-water sailors from all over the world and swapping sea stories. It was the frosting on the cake for him, and it made me happy to see his face.

An orange inflatable powered by an outboard approached. It held four people, and someone was waving a long loaf of bread. Of course it had to be Jim and Janice welcoming us with a baguette. Congratulatory greetings were shouted across water, and then they pulled up alongside. I was not quite prepared for people, so long had I been in sole company with my husband and our cat. I felt their presence as a little intrusive, but how could they know I wanted to experience this peak moment alone with Kelly? It was somehow too profound to share amid the jokes and laughter of others. Of course we asked them aboard and they introduced the other couple, Cindy and Tim, whose landfall we'd heard announced over the Net. Morris was warmly greeted and he responded with much serpentining against their bare, tan legs. Not in a biting mood, he was a far more gracious host than I.

Our friends filled us in on the check-in procedure here in these French islands. Kelly had carefully assembled our papers in advance. "Don't even bother to try to check in with the Gendarme—that's what they call the Port Captain. On Fridays they close early, everything's laid back here." Having arrived about a week ahead of us, Jim and Janice knew the ropes. Though our reunion was a thrill, I thought Kelly seemed preoccupied and I was glad when they left. The tropical heat was staggering—far more so than when we had been at sea, with the trades cooling us a little every day. "I just feel so totally had-out," Kelly said.

"I know, sweetheart. It's the excitement. Here's some water. I'd have been glad if we hadn't had to entertain right away. Come on, let's go for a swim." I knew this suggestion always made him smile, and it did. We dove in together, feeling a new freedom, untethered to our lifeline. When we surfaced, we exchanged glances. Kelly said, "I can't believe this water! It's not even refreshing to dive in. It must be exactly the same temperature as the air." I agreed, but I didn't want Kelly to be disappointed over anything now.

"Maybe it's just an especially hot day, or are we in the lee of the island? I don't know anything yet!" This was true and as we learned from cruising in Mexico, no matter how much one read, each new location was full of surprises.

"Since we can't check in and you seem so tired," I said, "why don't we just lay low and rest this afternoon?" Kelly was moving toward our outboard motor, secured to the aft liferail stanchion. Jim had helped him launch our Achilles. I watched with concern as Kelly heaved the heavy engine up and over the side. It seemed to cause him great effort.

"I can hardly wait to go ashore," Kelly said. "Let's walk up to the Keikahanui Inn and get our mail packet and make a dinner reservation. I want that martini and hamburger."

I burst into delighted laughter. "Kelly, it just seems so bizarre to be talking about dinner reservations clear out here."

There was such a crush of dinghies and inflatables tied up around the flight of concrete steps leading from the water up to the quay that Kelly deemed it safer to tie up further in toward shore. Now the quay was far above my head. As I glanced around perplexed, a powerfully built Marquesan reached down to give me a hand and a smile of welcome.

Our feet touched dry land. Kelly took my arm. Speechless, with eyes full of amazement at all we saw, we slowly made our way along. The combined fragrances of many flowers hung sweetly in the air. The intense green almost hurt our ocean-oriented eyes. A park all filled with ancient-looking stone sculpture ran right along the beach, bordered by low European-style walls made of carefully fitted rocks. We came upon several brightly painted, meticulously varnished outrigger canoes. Kelly broke our silence. "Look, Tom, we'll see these go out this evening. There is no more beautiful sight at sunset."

I squeezed his hand, thinking of all that lay ahead of us, now that the challenge of the long passage was over. His next words dropped in my heart like a stone.

"I don't know why, but I feel so dizzy." He staggered slightly. "I'm going to sit down here on the grass a minute. You go on up to the Inn."

"No, Kelly, I'm not going to leave you. I'll sit here with you. You just don't have your land legs yet. I feel like I'm rocking a bit too." He looked as tan and ruddy as usual, but an alarm was sounding just below the level of my consciousness. I had to finally ask the question that always hung there. "Kelly, your heart. Are you all right?"

"Sure, I told you. I feel fine. Just a little dizzy. Now, really, go and get our mail. I'll walk to meet you when this passes." He hated me to play mother hen, so I reluctantly got to my feet. The structure we had seen on the hillside *was* the Inn, but the walk was a lot farther than I expected. I spotted the Keikahanui Inn sign hanging out in front, but the place did not seem like a going concern. It had a strangely deserted air. I knocked ineffectively at one door and then another. Finally a woman appeared through a half-opened door, clutching a pareau around her. Clearly I had interrupted her nap.

"Hello, I'm Rose Courser."

"Thank God! I'm desperate for a prescription sent here from Papeete—I'm Tommie Spear off the yacht *Vagabundita*—did it get here?" She looked blank. In my urgency I grasped her arm. "Do you know if it came?!" She pulled away from me, uneasy.

"Frank keeps the mail locked up. He's not here..."

"Not here! For God's sake—it's my husband's heart medication. We had a terrible accident. I have to have it now. Can't you get the key yourself?"

"No, it's on my husband's key chain. He should be back. When he gets back I'll have him drive it down to the quay and get a boy to row it out..."

"No! Have him call me when he leaves here and I'll row in and meet him..." I scribbled Kelly's call sign on a scrap of paper from my purse and thrust it at her. "We can't lose any time. Kelly may have something wrong already. I'm so afraid!"

"I'm truly sorry," Rose made a helpless gesture. "Try not to worry. Frank will know what to do." She smiled tentatively and shut the door.

I started back, running now. Once I was clear of the dense growth covering their hillside and passed the little tumble-down cemetery, I had an unobstructed view of the dirt road bordering the beach. I strained my eyes to watch for Kelly coming to meet me. I knew I'd recognize him by his walk, even from a long distance away. He slumped a little more than I wished, but he moved athletically with his shoulders.

There was no one on the road. I had an eerie sense of being the only living soul on the island, so alone was I.

It was a good half-hour walk before I reached the few small concrete structures housing the shops. I could see Kelly's silver hair gleaming in the sunshine now. He sat on the grass but not where I had left him. He'd gotten up and walked a little further. I took it as a good sign. Across the street quite a few people were standing around drinking beer and socializing. There were some jeeps and pickup trucks parked nearby.

"Kelly, I'm going to get us a ride back to the quay and you're going to sleep until it's time to come back for dinner. Okay?" I didn't say I'd forgotten to make the reservation. A nice-looking young man detached himself from the group and came toward me.

"Hello, my name is Guido. Can I be of any help? I speak four languages. Is this your husband sitting here on the grass?"

"Yes, thank you. He feels a little off the weather. Could someone give us a ride back to our dinghy?" Just then an elderly gentleman approached speaking in French.

"No, no, Madame. Do not take him back to your boat. Take him to the clinic, where they will check him out." Within minutes we were underway in a pickup truck offered by a beautiful Polynesian girl with a hibiscus in her long, dark hair. Keeping a careful eye on Kelly, I saw how he climbed effortlessly into the open back with Guido.

We drove along for only a few minutes, the town was so small. The only thing of note we passed was the post office.

My heart sank when I saw the clinic. It was a depressing-looking, shabby little one-story structure. We could hardly see the way in. I took Kelly's arm and murmured a question to him as we went up an overgrown dirt path. It was as though he didn't hear me and he seemed suddenly vague. A familiar fear clutched my heart.

CHAPTER 10

Oh Captain! My Captain! Our fearful trip is done;
The ship has weathered every rack, the prize we sought is won.

—Walt Whitman

B LACK SPOTS AND FLASHES OF LIGHT, like the quick action of a camera shutter, blurred my vision. A fine perspiration broke out on my forehead. "Janice, I'm going to pass out." I slid my body down the wall of the clinic and put my head down between my knees. The temptation to sink into oblivion was strong. *No, I won't betray my watch…Kelly always trusted me standing watch, as long as I stand watch nothing bad can happen…*

Janice's voice cut through my semi-consciousness. A sheer effort of will revived me from the fainting spell. I raised my head, blinking my eyes. "Tommie, you've got to eat something. Cindy and Tim brought cold beer and dinner." She indicated a cooler. I'd forgotten they'd come, offering to relieve Janice who'd been with me for over eight hours. I remembered with a chill that Cindy had suggested we go into Kelly's room and pray.

"No, I don't want to pray," I'd said, though I was in constant inner prayer, my faith steadfast. Someone else praying with me seemed somehow inappropriate—still, *"When two or more are gathered together in my name…"* A sudden body-awareness cut the thought short. "Janice, do they have a bathroom in this God-forsaken place?"

"Yes," she said, helping me stand. "It's at the far end. I'll go with you."

Funny they'd put the bathroom on the ocean view side, I thought, my mind registering even insignificant details. We looked out on the end of the day, outriggers silhouetted against a red sky. *Kelly's hand was in mine. I rubbed my thumb against the bump at the base of his ring finger—recalling his joy when we'd come ashore—remembering his words—"Tonight—when we see them go out—there's no more beautiful sight."* Janice took my arm, guiding me, pulling me back to reality. I felt very confused. "How did you know to come here?" I asked her.

"It's all over the island—about Kelly. Even broadcast on the Pacific Marine Net. Cindy and Tim heard them announce the *Vagabundita* making landfall, then about Kelly being in the hospital with a heart attack—they called this a hospital."

I was barely conscious of what she was saying as I glanced around at the primitive room. One lightbulb hung from a cord festooned in webs, coated with dust. Words started pouring out of me.

"Janice, all of a sudden his eyes rolled up—I screamed—and all hell broke loose. They started pumping on his chest—a huge man doing it—finally the man gave up. I screamed again, 'No—don't stop!' Then they started electric shock. There were a lot of men—maybe doctors. I saw an electrocardiogram making patterns on a graph. One doctor told me to leave. Guido, this young sailor, took me outside—we talked and talked—it seemed like hours. I couldn't be in that room where he lay unconscious—*I couldn't!* Do you understand?" I heard the hysteria in my own voice.

Janice led me to the sink and turned on the cold water. I splashed my face, then groped for a towel. There was nothing but a dirty rag hanging from a hook. When I pulled it down a spider the size of my hand dropped onto my bare, sandaled foot. I screamed, trying to kick it off, its furred legs clinging to me. Janice grabbed a broom from a dim corner and swiped it off. I watched it walk slowly, tottering obscenely on its arched legs to gain the darkness. My body shook uncontrollably.

We went back out into the corridor, approaching the closed door to the room where they'd moved Kelly. Someone in a wheelchair was propelling himself toward us. He stopped and, speaking in a heavy French accent, addressed me. "Madame, everyone on Nuku Hiva has heard about your husband, the American navigator. I am deeply sorry. What I thought was my careless accident of a broken foot I now see is God's providence bringing me here. I will be able to administer the last rites for your husband." He lifted a bony hand to the cross hanging from his neck and extended the other to touch my arm. Recoiling, I lunged to bar the entrance to Kelly's room and extended my outstretched arms across the door.

"No! You are not to go in that room, Father. I don't want my husband disturbed." I heard the violence in my own voice, saw the priest's startled face.

"In the name of God, Madame." His eyes pleaded. "It would bring peace to his soul." We stared at each other. I was aware of the sound of chickens scratching around the dirt yard of the clinic. I spoke slowly and with patience now, as if explaining to a child. "Those French doctors wouldn't have left if they didn't feel that Kelly was stabilized. They got his heart started again. He just needs to rest."

Janice came up and acknowledged the priest with a respectful gesture. She put a protective arm around me. "Tommie, do you want us both to go in and pray with you?"

"No, Janice!" I pulled away. "I don't *need* anyone to pray. I know God won't let Kelly die." I was gripping her shoulders now and shouting, "He's not going to die! Do you hear me?" I leaned against the wall to steady myself, running my fingers over my throbbing temples, through my hair. "It's the not *knowing*. Why can't those doctors tell me something?" I searched her face. Her eyes dropped.

"Well, they hardly speak any English for one thing, except for the woman doctor. She told me he only has a…a ten-percent chance."

I cut across her stammer. "Yes, so you see he isn't going to die. He's strong as a horse, Janice. You saw him before he went down. He's six-foot-three. Standing our night watches, he never took more than a couple hours of sleep. He just needs to rest a while." My voice echoed into the emptiness of the corridor.

Janice faced me, moved closer, and took a deep breath. I noticed her tanned young skin. "This is a terrible shock for you, Tommie. Twenty-seven days at sea and then the very hour you step ashore…" Her voice trailed off. "Tommie, Father Picot and I are just trying to prepare you in case…" Again she couldn't go on. I heard her intake of breath. "You must realize that Kelly probably won't ever regain consciousness."

At that moment the French Polynesian nurse, Celestine, who had been monitoring Kelly, came silently on bare feet out of his room. Her pareau made a bright splash of color against the bungalow's corrugated tin walls. In this time of anguish, trust had developed quickly between us. I had seen the tears in her solemn eyes and watched her gentle hands move to aid Kelly. Now her expression was impassive. She shook her head and shrugged slightly, palms turned up. I bolted to my feet.

"I think Celestine is trying to tell me Kelly is revived. I'm going in there." I ran down the corridor to his room, then stopped short before entering. I felt a rush of relief to see one of the French doctors examining him. Kelly laid perfectly still, face dropped to one side. His hair gleamed in the light coming from the EKG screen. I longed to hold him. As I hung in the doorway, the doctor turned abruptly toward me.

"Madame, this is not the first heart attack of your husband." He spoke in such broken English I was not sure I had understood him. Instantly, my mind flew back to the storm. Kelly'd said, "Don't scold me." *Had he already…?* "What do you mean?"

"We can tell by this." He indicated the needle, making barely perceptible fluctuations on the EKG. I grasped the doctor's arm.

"Are you taking him into surgery, or what?" My question hung in the silence—as though poised on the edge of a great chasm. The doctor dragged his eyes away from my face before he answered.

"Madame, we have no operating room here."

I turned back out into the night. The humidity enveloped me like a shroud. There was the priest again. He sat hunched in his black robes, staring at me like a great bird of prey, watching, waiting. I turned away with a shudder. *Maybe I should have let him go in to Kelly…no!* I slammed the door shut on that thought but the echo followed me down the corridor—a white scream.

"Please, a beer now," I said to Janice. Anything for some alleviation of the tension that gripped like a vise. A tall, gaunt-faced man stood speaking with her. He turned at my approach.

"Hello, Tommie, I'm Frank Courser. I run the Keikahanui Inn here on the island." He had the voice of a man with no illusions left. "I brought your mail packet, and this prescription came from the hospital in Papeete." He looked at me as if expecting a reaction of gratitude or maybe relief. "If you need a radio telephone, we have the only one available at night."

"Thank God, finally someone who speaks English. Of course I've heard of you. All the yachtsmen know you, Frank." My words came out in a rush of urgency. "We've got to get Kelly to Papeete to a hospital. I don't even know if he needs heart surgery." For a moment Frank didn't move, just stared at me.

"I don't think you realize how remote we are here in the Marquesas." He spoke quietly and with great compassion. "We're eight hundred and sixty *miles* from Papeete, straight across water. Six days by boat, if you're lucky. We only get two flights a week in here. Little prop planes. Our landing strip is on the other side of the island, a two-hour jeep trip over a rutted dirt road. Man, that road." The memory of it seemed to almost make him sick. He paused to wipe his sweating face. "The last person we tried to move outta here...why the I.V. tube jounced out on that road. The patient died." Embarrassed, Frank stopped talking. No one spoke. My heart pounded in the silence. He turned to Janice. "What's the latest word from the doctors?" His voice sounded harsh.

"Frank, I haven't seen or spoken to anyone except the nurse since early evening. It's as though they don't..." She didn't finish the sentence, just shook her head slightly at Frank.

"I see. I'll stick around a while." He bent his head to light a cigarette. I saw his jaw muscle tense in the flare of the match.

The southeast trades had come up and carried Celestine's voice softly to us. I thought she said, "He's awake," and saw her beckon. Though I ran, it seemed an interminable distance down the corridor to Kelly's room. He lay motionless as before. One hand hung over the edge of the bed now. The light from the EKG shone on his gold wedding band. I bent to hold him. They had cut his aloha shirt open with scissors and I slipped my hand next to his bare chest. I trusted the feel of that heartbeat more than its mechanical counterpart on the graph. I felt his familiar warmth. I put my face against his cheek and whispered, "You just sleep, darling, and you'll be fine. Oh, Kellogg, I love you so." I raised my eyes only as high as his face. I saw no eyelids flutter open. I heard no wakening sounds, only Celestine's voice above the pounding in my ears.

"Madame, now it is time to say goodbye."

"No! Kelly is not going to die." My head flung back and a great wrenching cry tore out of me. "No, God! Now it is time for the miracle." I dropped to my knees on the concrete floor. I kissed his fingers one by one then pressed my lips into the palm of that hand I knew so well. An intense coldness crept into my body. Before I raised my eyes to the EKG I knew. The jagged graph had quieted to a small straight line. The nurse reached over and turned off the switch.

There was no more light.

I clung to him in a last embrace. "Fair winds, my navigator. Oh, Kelly, my love, you and I will never say goodbye."

"Would you like a drink?" Frank's voice sounded hoarse. It was 4 a.m. and we had just left Kelly's deathbed. Now we stood on either side of the little bar at Frank's place.

"Yes, anything." Lifeless eyes met lifeless eyes. The dim light from brass oil lanterns cast deep shadows on Frank's gaunt face and shrouded the room's corners in gloom. He poured amber liquid. Brandy, I thought, or perhaps rum. No question of ice or water. I gulped it down, shuddering at the taste but welcoming the feeling of fire spreading through my chest. My heart pounded so intensely that for the one insane moment I thought I too was dying. "Thank you, God," I breathed. It was a momentary hope as I realized what I felt was only the rush of the alcohol.

Frank stubbed out his cigarette and came from behind the bar. A few hours ago he had been a stranger. Now, he touched my shoulder with the intimacy born of a shared catastrophe. "Okay, Kiddo. Let's hit the road." His harsh voice turned gentle. "They have a twenty-four-hour burial law here, Tommie. You know, primitive place, the tropics." What he said only half registered but I followed along docilely, insulated by shock.

Moving with a great weariness, we descended the stone steps of the Inn. Frank helped me into his rusted jeep. As we drove down the steep hill, the wheels churned up the smell of dirt. The night sky was black velvet and I raised my eyes to pick out the constellations Kelly and I had so studied during our twenty-seven days at sea. We jounced along in silence, too exhausted to talk. As we passed Taiohae Bay, the stars paled one by one. The bay was turning to dull gray. It seemed dawn broke as rapidly as dusk descended here in the middle of the South Pacific. I began what was to become a compulsive counting of the hours since Kelly had been gone. "It was about one-thirty, wasn't it Frank?" He knew what I meant.

"Yes, Tommie, and now it's five-thirty. Everything will be ready, trust me." I couldn't remember what we had done in the four hours since Kelly died. I counted up the hours yet again on my fingers. I vaguely recalled that Frank had rowed me back and forth to the *Vagabundita* in a futile effort to use the boat's radio telephone to inform our five children of the tragedy.

Now, as he drove through the simple stone arch to the cemetery, horses and goats raised placid faces, mildly disturbed from their grazing amid the fallen gravestones of an earlier century. I was astonished to see two gravediggers already waiting, shovels in hand. I caught a flash of their dark liquid eyes before they averted their gaze from my stricken face. Frank spoke to them in French, then translated for me. "Tommie, you have permission from the French governor to pick any spot you want." I didn't have to deliberate long. I glanced back over my shoulder and there, glimpsed through a gap in the palm trees, was the yacht *Vagabundita*, white hull gleaming in the early morning sun. I looked back toward where the men stood waiting and saw that there was a frangipani tree

dropping its fragrant blossoms on what was to become Kelly's grave. I gestured with my hand. The men started to dig.

I was back alone on the boat at last. I had forgotten about Morris
and felt a wave of compassion for his loss too. Jim and Janice had
dropped me off with their outboard dinghy. As we came alongside the
boat, I was ashamed to see how bad our hull looked. We always kept it
immaculate.

Kelly had changed the oil just after we sighted land. Ever vigilant of
conservation, he had carefully planned to be well out at sea to avoid the
possibility of an oil spill where we anticipated making our landfall. The
boat had lurched in the heavy roll at just the wrong moment and the contents of the oil can flung back against the white topsides. At the time, I
was terribly, irrationally disturbed about coming into port bearing that
ominous black mark. Kelly didn't seem perturbed over it at all, focused as
he was on the final navigating and chart work for our arrival.

The *Vagabundita* bore the black mark of death.

I shivered despite the heat. I had lost track of the passage of time. The
activities of the past hours seemed to be the most important of my life
and the smallest detail was etched indelibly on my heart. I was exhausted
from the decisions and efforts of preparing for the funeral, but my whole
fragile perception shrank from the thought of Kelly's beloved *Vagabundita*
marred with the oil stain on his day of farewell. Before dressing, I put on
swim fins and a rubber strap fitted with a suction cup for one hand. It
effectively held me high against the hull to scrub for about a minute
before letting loose and dropping me back down into the water. It was
tough, tiring work. I had to scrub the surface many times before I was satisfied. Finally, I threw the equipment back on board and swam around the
boat hoping to find a cooler current in the warm sea before it was time to

dress for the funeral. There was just a little water left in our sun-shower bag, suspended from where Kelly had rigged it. I washed my hair and rinsed off the salt.

Below in our master cabin I rummaged through our hanging locker to find the skirt, an ankle-length black one printed in a subtle design of large tropical green leaves interspersed with a few pomegranate-colored blossoms. I had jokingly hinted to a friend that I would need it, saying "What a stunning skirt, Janet. I should have that for my cruise to the South Seas." We'd laughed at the idea of me dressing for dinner on my kind of cruise. Months later when Kelly flew to Santa Barbara for his mother's funeral, Janet gave the skirt to him to bring back for me. He had pulled it all crumpled from his duffel bag and carelessly thrown it on the bunk as if it had no importance. Now, I wondered which of us three had sensed that I would need it.

Next I put on a sleeveless, black, scoop-necked T-shirt. Kelly's wedding ring was now on a long gold chain hanging from my neck. My hair had not dried since my shower, nor would it quite ever in this intense humidity. After a year of cruising, it hung below my shoulders. Relieved to get the damp strands off my neck, I tied it up with a black grosgrain ribbon. There were oil stains under my short fingernails. I didn't really care. I only wanted to be dressed suitably and look nice for Kelly's ceremony. As nice, I thought, as I had for our wedding. My mind flashed back to Pinky's garden in Santa Barbara, nine years ago.

I stood beneath the garlanded arbor in my ecru lace dress, hearing Father John speak the words, "Will you take this woman..." I stopped listening as Kelly, beaming down into my face, slipped the wide gold band on my finger.

Time took on a strange dimension. Suddenly desperate to know exactly how many days we had shared in marriage together, I rubbed my thumb over my wedding band and counted nine years, one month, and how many days? I was possessed to know. "Thirty days hath September..." I murmured, intoning the child's rhyme. We celebrated our anniversary in Manzanillo on March twenty-first, just prior to our departure. Kelly gave me the pavé heart diamond bracelet, mistakenly thinking it was our tenth anniversary. I went on with my compulsive computations. *Let's see.*

Thirty days in April. He died May fourth. That makes exactly nine years, one month, and thirteen days.

I was startled from my reverie by the arrival of Jim and Janice, coming to take me to the funeral. They pulled alongside and Jim extended a hand to help me aboard. I cast a glance back at Morris. He stood alone at the bow, bereft to see us go.

The graveside scene swam before my eyes. I stumbled in dizziness, nearly blinded by my incessant tears. Insulated in a cocoon of aloneness, I felt bewildered by the crowd of mourners. I looked carefully around, surprised to see the women so gaily clad in colorful pareaus, wearing leis and flowers in their hair. The local men arrived bare-chested, either because of the heat or to show off their elaborate tattoos, but as the funeral began, they donned aloha shirts. I felt an incongruous surge of joy to see these beautiful people dressed as if for a celebration instead of a funeral.

My perceptions were acutely rendered by the enormity of the moment, each detail cut by an exacto knife. I heard music playing somewhere but didn't take my eyes from the grave to determine its source. The dominant sound was the rippling of the waves as they advanced and retreated from the stone-strewn beach, their impact made gentle by the deep bay.

Frank had been right. Everything was ready. The French Catholic father stood robed in white, flanked by two young Marquesan boys swinging containers of incense while chanting a prayer. There were some yachtsmen and their wives as well, come in from their boats to mourn a fellow sailor. *Mostly strangers at Kelly's funeral.*

Kelly lay in a handmade wooden box in the pit of a deep grave. The coffin was already strewn with leis, strung in the night by unknown hands. The same two gravediggers I had met at dawn leaned on their spades, heads bowed, shedding tears for a man they had never met. I marveled at how many had come to grieve with me. It seemed that the whole town turned out for the funeral.

Someone passed me a shovel and I looked around perplexed. It was the custom for the widow to cast the first spade of earth into the grave. I did so, recoiling, hearing the sound of a hollow echo as the clods struck Kelly's wooden coffin.

I knew he was not there.

Janice came to my side. I was in such deep concentration that she had to squeeze my arm, hard. Then I remembered and handed her a small, leather bound book of poetry. She opened to a page marked by a slender blue ribbon. It was John Masefield's "Sea Fever," Kelly's favorite poem. He had selected it unknowingly for his own funeral a few months before. We lay on a Baja beach passing the book back and forth and laughing in the sun. I remembered how he'd said, *"If anything ever happens to me..."*

Janice tried to read the haunting words but her voice broke and she passed the book to Cindy, who began again with,

> "I must go down to the sea again, to the
> lonely sea and the sky
> And all I ask is a tall ship and a star to steer her by."

Her words kept cadence with the sound of the clods thudding onto Kelly's coffin. The cloying scent of ginger and pikaki could not quite mask the smell of dirt. I turned away to wipe the sweat and tears from my face. Then I looked out to the bay and saw the *Vagabundita*. She turned and turned on her anchor rode. I thought it strange because I felt no wind.

I smiled then, looking up to where gulls circled against the brilliant azure sky. Kelly's radiant face shimmered down at me through the intense heat. He spoke only my name, but it was suffused with a profound joy. I saluted his spirit, then flung the armful of leis I had been given into his grave—my final symbolic gift to the man I loved. I remembered with a surge of joy that the lei is the symbol of reunion and return. *But when, my Captain? Oh when?* I felt the blood rush into my head and then the agony of my loss. Frank reached out his arms to catch me before I fell to the ground. It seemed from very far away now that I heard Janice's voice intoning the last stanza of the poem.

> "And all I ask is a merry yarn from a laughing fellow rover,
> And a quiet sleep and sweet dream when the long trick's over."

Someone had fetched my dinghy. I waved off the people pressing around me. I needed to be alone and wanted to row back by myself in the stillness of evening. The tropical sky was the color of sapphire and so very clear that Jupiter and Venus trembling there almost eclipsed the light of the early risen new moon.

As I approached the *Vagabundita*, I saw Morris standing his patient watch on the foredeck. He ran to greet me as I climbed aboard. I cradled his warm body and we stared into each other's faces. Mine streamed with tears, his seemed all great golden eyes lit up in solemn knowing. "He's gone, Morris. Our Kelly is gone." I raised my face to the sky, searching and listening in the silence. Hanging there was that lying sliver of a crescent moon in which I had put such impossible faith.

On the eve of our departure for the Marquesas I remembered how Kelly and I last wished on it, laughing together in the dusk of Manzanillo. I'd put my hands on his shoulders and turned him around, his face so tan, eyes smiling into mine. "Kelly, you have to look at it over your *left* shoulder when you wish. And be careful what you wish for. You may get it." I well remembered what I'd wished for. It had been my only and unvarying wish on each new moon the year we had been at sea. "Get us there. Just get us there."

We'd gotten there all right. It had taken exactly twenty-seven days, so of course here was that new moon again, its pale light illuminating the neon orange color of Kelly's trunks hanging from the liferail. He wore them on our first swim in Taiohae Bay. *Dear God, when had that been?* I counted back. Fourteen hours ago. Fourteen hours since we set foot on our island landfall and walked along the quay, exalting over this paradise. Fourteen hours in which he then lay in a coma, died, and was buried. Now I stretched out a hand to take down the trunks, and felt them still wet from our last swim together.

Morris slid silently into my lap, and as I hugged him to me I thought how valiantly he stood the night watches with us, even though he was in such terror of the sight and sound of the sea as it churned and foamed by the hull. Our night watches! The half-remembered couplet of a poem drifted through my memory and I spoke it aloud to Kelly and the star-strewn sky.

> "Now I a long night's watch shall keep
> And you shall sleep, and you shall sleep."

I heard a sound like the rush of birds' wings. It was a school of flying fish, bursting from the black water like a rain of silver coins flung in the moonlight. Was it a message or a passing dream?

CHAPTER 11

...for many a time

I have been half in love with Easeful Death,

Call'd him soft names in many a mused rhyme,

To take into the air my quiet breath;

Now more than ever seems it rich to die...

—John Keats

I
T WAS A SLOW, SWEET AWAKENING. I half opened my eyes. Sunshine
streamed through the hatchway. Kelly always left it open for fresh air.
A breeze wafted in. Then a half-remembered nightmare brushed my
consciousness. I stretched out a hand to feel Kelly's warmth. Then I
remembered. And then I remembered again.

Alone all day, I felt abandoned by my sailing friends, until I realized
they were trying to give me the gift of self-sufficiency. I'd spent the day
trying to sort through Kelly's clothes. Confused in my perception of time,
the hours had alternately dragged and flown, and now it was almost dark.
I needed to get back to the Keikahanui Inn and try again to reach the
boys. The urgency of Kelly's funeral had prevented any further attempts
to telephone.

I'd lost my address book somewhere in the disruption of the boat's lockers, so I didn't even have phone numbers for Kelly's children. I thought Kenny was staying in his brother's beach trailer, where I knew there was no phone. Reaching Billy was my only hope.

As I climbed down into the rubber dinghy, I realized it was too far to row across the bay. I wasn't sure I could start the outboard. The new motor we'd bought in Mexico worked hard. When Kelly tried to check me out on it, I usually failed to get it started. Now I heard his voice. *"Tommie, put your whole body into it."* I grasped the starter cord, and throwing my weight into the pull heard the motor sputter into life on my first try. I opened her up and sped recklessly across the bay. Knowing I would have to make a beach landing, I slowed the engine to think how I could accomplish this all alone in the dark. I could hear the waves breaking with some force on the steeply sloping beach.

"Pull up the outboard before you get into shallow water so the prop won't hit bottom," I heard Kelly say. *"Row if you have to."*

I jumped out at the last minute and grabbed the painter line, splashing ashore just before a wave crashed. I knew Kelly was proud I'd done it right.

The trees grew thick and dark along the beach. There was only a branch to tie up to. I made secure as best I could with a bowline knot. The dinghy was my only way back to the *Vagabundita* and I was afraid it would be stolen for its valuable engine.

It was pitch-dark, the beach deserted. At high tide there was only a narrow strip of sand to cross before I reached thick vines that snaked down through the tropical growth. As I pushed through them, something made a quick scuttle underfoot. I'd forgotten to bring a flashlight.

A brief, violent squall had blown in that afternoon. The downpour was enough to turn the steep incline leading up to Frank's place into a mudslide. My topsiders carried two or three inches of mud on each foot. I began to slip and fall to my knees, covering my legs with the thick clay. I nearly screamed as I felt something live brush against my face in the darkness. Now that I'd made the sharp turn I remembered from Frank's jeep trip, I figured I had about a mile to go. It felt like an overwhelming distance.

I sensed Kelly's presence trudging along with me, holding my hand, the empty space beside me filled with his energy.

Then I saw the light shining through the big bay window of the Inn.

Frank must have heard me trying to clean off my shoes on the porch. He came out to greet me. "Tommie, you shouldn't have come without a flashlight. All sorts of things come out at night in the tropics. The road's dangerous enough."

"Frank, I know it's a God-awful time for me to come. I tried to time it when you and Rose were done serving dinner."

"It's okay. You know we'll do anything we can." He handed me a drink. I needed it.

"Frank, our children...they all know, don't they?" He reminded me that he'd radioed George in Santa Barbara. Apparently he and our secretary, Marie, had placed the painful calls.

"I've never talked directly to anybody," I said. "I'm desperate to reach my sons. Billy's is the only number I have."

"Someone else called, very anxious to talk to you. Barry Mc-something. He left the number."

"Oh my God, my college boyfriend. He must have heard somehow. Yes, yes, he would call. I'll try him later. Billy first."

"With the four-hour time change this should be good." Frank placed the call to California on his radio telephone. He got through and I heard him explain the procedure of saying "over" then waiting a few seconds for the time lapse. He handed me the phone. I heard my son's voice at last.

"Thank God, Mom. We've all tried so hard to call you. We couldn't even spell the name of the island or the Inn. George was so distraught he couldn't tell us much, only that Kelly died of a massive heart attack." He broke off for a moment. "Oh, Mom, I'm so sorry."

"Billy, someone has to come." It was all I could manage.

"Mom, why don't you just get on a plane and come home? It seems to me..."

"Billy, I need someone."

"It seems to me, considering the expense and the hassle, it'd be better if you just came home."

"I have to have someone come, help me build Kelly's grave." That was all that mattered now. "I don't even have any money." I took a gulp of the drink.

"We could arrange to have somebody bring the boat back later," he said, trying to work it out.

"No, no. This is beyond my endurance. I need somebody else to be strong." I took a deep breath, summoning the strength to go on, and said, "I'm not going to survive this. I don't want to survive it." There was a pause. For a minute I thought we'd been disconnected.

"Which one of us do you want to come?"

"Whichever one of you can."

"Kenny or me, Mom?"

"You, Billy. You always know what to do—but your work—well...I need someone from the family. Send Robin if you have to."

"Robin is having a tough pregnancy. Terrible morning sickness. I'm afraid she might miscarry. Mother, I feel so torn..."

"Don't, darling. Send Kenny then, but I know he's at loose ends now. No money. Maybe not even a job..."

"Don't worry. I'll get Kenny on the first available plane. It will take a little time. Passport and stuff. I've got about five thousand dollars saved up. Count on me, Mother." I heard his voice break, then, "I love you." There was a click and the line went dead.

Out in the middle of Taiohae Bay, I was finally far enough away from shore so no one could hear me. Alone now, I started to scream. I was screaming at God, screaming, screaming—an animal sound, filled with rage and despair. In desolation, I looked down into the black water— thoughts of oblivion.

We had a gun on board. I hadn't thought of it in months. It was care-fully hidden in the engine room, concealed in a waterproof pouch. Kelly hadn't wanted to bring it, concerned over regulations barring transport of guns into certain ports. I'd prevailed upon him, afraid we'd be boarded by pirates some moonless night.

I remembered another gun I'd owned. Kelly'd bought me a tiny pearl-handled revolver to carry in my purse when I had to drive alone at night. He'd helped me practice shooting it at targets he threw overboard, but when he saw how I'd squeeze my eyes shut and cringe before I pulled the trigger, he decided it was more of a hazard than a precaution. I wished I had it now.

My heart thumped. In sudden excitement I turned the dinghy back in the direction of the *Vagabundita*. I revved up the engine, then thought of the noise and decelerated to a purr, moving with the stealth of one about to commit a crime. Earlier when I left it was dusk, the sky darkening fast as I crossed the broad bay. I'd been too distraught to take a bearing. Now, some internal compass kicked on, and I easily found my way, although forced to carefully serpentine through the anchor lines of the many sailboats. The boat looked ghostly in the cold, faint light of the new moon.

I tied up and leapt aboard. I unhooked the companionway steps that blocked the entrance to the engine room, then removed the entry panel. Where in hell was the light? Stooped over in the dark I felt around behind the engine. Unerringly my hand touched the pouch, exactly where I'd hidden it a year ago. In my haste I didn't replace the panel and steps. Energized with strength, I grasped the safety handle mounted on the bulkhead and pulled my body up into the cockpit by one hand. I let myself carefully back down into the dinghy. My mind worked with clarity, as if following step-by-step instructions.

I'd have to go pretty far out to sea. Sound carries across water. How far though? There is the muffle of the crashing surf...well, why does it really matter? I'd probably wash ashore eventually anyway. Too bad. Better if it looked like an accident.

I cut the engine and carefully undid the waxed-tie on the gun pouch. I felt a thrill—like opening a birthday gift. And there it was, the dim light of the new moon illuminating the mellow steel. The rich gleam made me think of grandmother's pewter plates. I ran my finger along the barrel, feeling its length, its smoothness. I felt a tightening deep down in my belly. I weighed the gun in my hand—substantial.

A lot easier to aim than that little pearl-handled number...

I gasped and struck my hand to my mouth, momentarily panicked. Then I remembered that we kept the gun loaded—of course—for emergencies like this. I flicked the safety on and off, then raised the barrel to my face. There was a faint smell of gunpowder lingering there. It triggered a powerful memory.

I was thirteen when I found him—my father's body splayed on the concrete floor of the garage, the small red hole in his white shirt, the flung revolver... I pressed the barrel to my head, feeling the cold steel against my temple. *Would it make only a small charred circle or would it blow my brains out?* An ugly phrase. *The head or the heart?* Some people, *lots* of people missed— then went brain-dead. No wonder Dad picked the heart shot. Still, easy to miss there too. I imagined him placing his hand on the left side of his chest to feel the beat. I did it now, moving my hand around—I could barely feel anything, much less take aim where it would be fatal.

Dad, Dad, how could you pull the trigger? It was not the first time I'd thought my father brave. *I understand better about you now, Dad.* The hopelessness. Devastation beyond despair. The going mad. With sudden clarity, I knew. People take their lives with little thought if the means comes easily to hand. My father's way lent an odd permission. I laughed aloud remembering Billy's black humor, saying suicide was an old tradition in our family. All four of his grandparents died by their own hand if you counted Mother, dead at forty-nine, driven to alcoholism by the emotional havoc created by my father's suicide.

I fiddled with the gun, holding my life in my hands. I spun the cylinder and clicked the safety. I thought of how my brother Pete and I used to pretend to play Russian roulette. If he hadn't already done himself in with booze he would have played it with me now—a risk-taker, like me. My family...I envisioned them as a row of identical paper dolls, hand-in-hand. Me on the end.

My mind went to memories of my beautiful mother and the town of Pasadena, where I grew up. Driving in from Los Angeles, its most prominent landmark was a graceful bridge, spanning a dry riverbed, linking the old Vista del Arroyo Hotel with the exclusive San Rafael residential area. I remembered how Mother and I used to discuss the frequent suicides...the *Star News* headlines blaring, "Unidentified Woman Found..." and "Student Jumps from Colorado Street Bridge."

Obsessed with suicide in my teenage years, I used to ride my bike to the bridge. I'd peer over the balustrades and wonder how they dared to jump. It never looked quite high enough to be reliably lethal with the soft-looking sandy river bottom below. Better off a building, into the street. Briefly, I mourned the sad bridge jumpers—maybe with time to think on their way down. Well, there were no bridges or tall buildings to jump from here. Then I raised my eyes to the Aakapa, dark cliffs that fell sharply into the sea. I guessed their jagged peaks rose 2,000 feet. High enough to die. I shuddered and looked away. I hated heights, glad when I didn't have to ski anymore since Kelly was a sailor. I held the gun motionless in my lap. My thoughts turned back to the water. I let the dinghy drift, trailing my hand in the warm sea. The words of a favorite poem lapped at my memory.

"I will go back to the great sweet mother
Mother and lover of men, the sea."

Yes, it would be the water I loved and did not fear. I activated the outboard and turned the dinghy out to sea. The blood pounded in my ears and I felt some relief knowing the pain was about to end, that it would look like an accident—distraught after Kelly's funeral, losing my way. A thought fluttered.

It would be so much quicker in the icy Atlantic. Here in the warm water of the Marquesas I would never hypothermiate. What then? Just finally pass out and drown? Still, it would look like an accident. The boys would never think their mother had...the boys! I glimpsed my fine, laughing sons—the men left to me. They would blame themselves. *If only we'd come sooner, if only she hadn't been left alone...*

On sudden impulse, I flung my arm back and threw the gun as hard as I could. I heard the finality of its splash. That small sound. *Even men need their mothers.*

Drained of energy I steered the Achilles back in the direction of the yacht. The trade winds picked up. The only light came from the forward lanterns, bobbing like fireflies from the bows of the many sailboats. I couldn't see the *Vagabundita*. My internal compass wasn't working this time. Nothing was. I was lost. Lost. I didn't care.

As I slowed the outboard to thread my way through the anchor lines, I heard a faint meow. I hadn't even thought of Morris. He must have been asleep when I boarded earlier. I followed the sound and sure enough it was him. Now I glimpsed his white belly in the moonlight, front paws stretched up to the lifeline, standing watch for me. I tied up the dinghy and stepped aboard, feeling the heat from the still warm deck radiating into my bare feet. "Oh, my faithful Morris." I hugged him to my face, tangling my long hair in his extended claws. I held him a little away and met his silent, golden stare.

Morning.

I dove off the sailboat and made for the narrow rocky beach lying below the cemetery. The water was so transparent I could see down to the sandy bottom where our anchor lay half-buried. Tropical fish bright as neon signs darted in and out of the coral formations. Some coral heads almost broke the water's surface. I had to be careful not to cut myself as I swam above them.

The mild surf tumbled me in the trough cut by the receding waves. I relaxed into the movement of the water and allowed it to wash me up onto the beach, the sand coarse against my body. Coral shards lay thick on the beach, so sharp against the soles of my feet that I had to watch for smooth rocks and pick my way from one to the next until I reached the path leading up to the hillside cemetery. It was deserted.

There was an elaborate memorial under construction. I remembered hearing snatches of conversation about it at Kelly's wake. It was for the young mayor, whose little prop plane crash-landed on the island's airstrip, killing him and three others. He'd left a wife and two small children, and his loss was considered a great tragedy on the island.

"Too many deaths," one young Marquesan woman said to me in an ominous tone, shaking her head, as if some God of the island had been angered.

Many of the flowers with which the villagers had adorned Kelly's grave were beginning to droop despite the water in their glass jars. There was a plastic milk carton stuffed with tendrils of the tiare flower, still fresh, but its fragrance was overwhelmed by the leis gone rank overnight. I was startled to see a newly turned patch of dirt where there had been weeds the day before. It was only about three feet long. It must be for a child, or maybe a dog. No, they wouldn't bury a pet here. The villagers were all Catholic. This must be hallowed ground.

Turning at the puttering sound of an engine, I recognized one of the Frenchmen I'd met at Kelly's funeral. His motor scooter bounced over the uneven weedy grass. He greeted me by name. "Bonjour, Tomee. I thought I might find you here. I came up to check on the grave. Sometimes after a rain there is settling and we need to add more soil." In the blur of the funeral weekend, I couldn't remember his name.

"Thank you. It looks all right. What is this other grave next to Kelly's?"

"I heard it is a one-day-old baby boy," he replied. "It's very sad. He died the same night as Kelly."

"What about the parents?"

"Nobody seems to know anything much. They came from another island."

"How terrible for them to have it all happen so fast," I said, wondering if the priest got to the baby in time.

"Here, Tomee," he patted the passenger seat, "I'll give you a ride back to the quay."

"Thanks, but I swam over," I said, suddenly feeling embarrassed standing in the cemetery in my wet bikini. "I think I'll stay here a while and then swim back to the boat. If you hear anything more about the baby, I'd like to know." His broad French face looked solemn as he nodded.

"Stop by the bank later. Marceline and I'll help you any way we can."
That was it—Bernard. Bernard and Marceline. He took off with a wave, the
childish-looking scooter dwarfed by his impressive size. I watched him
bump down the hill, passing beneath the cemetery's stone archway. Its
cross gleamed white in the morning sun. I was still watching as he gained
the dirt road that ran along the sea past the French governor's house. Just
as I lost sight of him I had a flash of foreknowledge, sudden and inexplicable as déjà vu. *This man would figure prominently in my life—who was he?*

I turned back to the graves, one so laden with flowers, the other nothing but a small patch of barren soil. The smell of the dirt induced a wave
of nausea and the memory of Kelly's funeral washed over me. Its colors
and smells and sounds all jumbled together—images in a kaleidoscope.

It was sad, shocking even, that the baby's grave bore not even one
flower, not a cross or a balloon. I was possessed to know more about his
short life and his parents and why no one seemed to care. I walked back
down to the beach to look for something to put on his grave. There were
very few shells. Those I found were so abraded by the sand they were all
chipped and nearly colorless. Then I saw a piece of coral shaped like an
animal. Long body with four legs, head with horns, and a stub tail. It had
the look of a Pre-Columbian piece, even a slightly droll quality. It was a
treasure. I thought it would make the baby laugh. I searched for another,
larger piece of coral with which to disguise the ugly milk carton, then
ascended the path again. After I picked the dead flowers off Kelly's grave
I gathered fallen frangipani blossoms to make a heart for the baby's burial plot. The pink flowers seemed out of place against the dirt and the
animal looked small and lonely.

I sat on the low wall of the monument next to Kelly's grave. It was
made of concrete, like they all were, and decorated with what must have
been the best the family could find—yellow and green glazed tile probably left over from a bath or kitchen job. Shells stuck into the gray surface
were the only part I liked. I shuddered to see the framed photograph of
an emaciated old man. At least his death was not untimely. My mind
went back to the baby lying under his blanket of black earth. Had the
mother, anticipating complications, put her faith in Nuku Hiva's clinic to

ensure a safe birth? Had she needed a Caesarean at the last minute? If there had been an operating room on the island, might her son have lived? Might Kelly have? Intuiting that it was not an unwanted baby, I thought of the young parents waiting out the nine months then hearing their son's first cry. I thought of them now. Isolated even from each other in the agony of their loss. Then leaving for their own island, unable to bury their child. And what about the baby's grief?

After his brutal birth, snatched from the safety of his mother's body and then cast out into what void? Would not the pain of separation that so agonized the mother be equally felt by the one who died? I raised a hand to wipe the sweat from my forehead and felt my face wet with tears.

"Janice, you and Jim have already delayed by five days to stay and help me. Just go—please—I'll be okay." The trade winds had come up and I was relieved to feel them cooling my damp face and body. We were walking along the quay six days after Kelly's death. Six days since I had sailed into beautiful Taiohae Bay.

Janice smiled as she reached over to remove a strand of hair glued to my neck. "Tommie, I'm touched to see you put those little white tiare flowers in your hair to meet your son but, dear, you don't even know if he'll be on that plane. I hate to see you make a two-hour passage on that old tub and then the dusty bus trip in this heat. The road to the airport is torturous. Please don't go. You'll be so disappointed if he isn't there."

"Janice, he has to be on that plane. They only have two flights a week out of Papeete. I'll have to wait another four days if he doesn't make it." I turned away to hide my face, and she reached out to hold me. I knew she felt my whole body tremble and she hugged me tighter.

"Now you're crying again. Don't worry. Your gut feeling is right. Kenny will be on that plane." We watched for a moment as the gigantic Marquesan stevedores, massive arms tattooed from shoulder to wrist, lifted passengers and luggage across some two feet of water from the quay to the wildly pitching *Aranui*, the supply ship I was about to board. "We'll be here when you get back," Janice said. "Bring Kenny aboard this evening." She smiled reassuringly.

The *Aranui* cast off and I was surprised at the speed she made despite her ponderous roll. I stood on deck and watched Janice's form grow tiny as the ship made way through the anchored fleet of cruising sailboats.

Janice was easily the most intimate friend of my life. Not from years of sharing good times but from what we knew together now of sorrow and pain in these last few tragic days. I picked out Jim and Janice's sloop, *Loki Lani*, and then our own *Vagabundita*. Both sailboats had crossed the Pacific from Manzanillo to these islands. Both women alone with their mates. Now only Jim and Janice would be going on with the cruise. It was the first time I had been powerfully struck by that reality. The prophetic words I had spoken to Kelly the day we left Manzanillo came back to me with a grim reality. "Kelly, I feel like I'm going on the cruise by myself."

The two hours aboard the *Aranui* with its pitch and roll seemed interminable and the stench of vomit from the seasick passengers finally started to turn the iron stomach I prided myself on. I held one of Kelly's big linen handkerchiefs over my nose to keep from retching.

Everyone crowded off the boat at once, disembarking onto a dangerous wooden dock so rickety I feared it would not bear our weight. We boarded an open-sided vehicle with hard wooden benches running lengthwise along both sides. It looked like it had been made from scrap materials in someone's backyard. Barely a quarter-mile inland we'd already left the trades behind and the heat was staggering, the humidity so intense it was like trying to breathe in a steam bath. I wished for many things—insect repellant, a long-sleeved gauze shirt, most of all a hat, but my mind had been focused entirely on the likelihood of Kenny's arrival. The narrow dirt road was severely rutted, this part of the island far too remote for anything like a tractor to get to. Every time our wagon wheels hit a pothole a spasm cramped my back, exacerbating the pain of the sciatic nerve I'd pinched when I heaved the outboard motor back up on deck.

An American, seemingly elated over his departure, tried to make light of the insects that whined around our faces and bare necks. "Are these the no-nos or the no-see-ums?"

"Probably the no-nos," someone else said, "but the joke here on the island is that you can't see them either."

Indeed I could see nothing alighting on my arms, but red welts erupted before my eyes and I had to exercise an act of will to keep from tearing into them with my fingernails.

We jounced into the airport parking lot an hour later. Most everyone mobbed the bar for an icy Hinano. Trying to clean up in the unisex restroom, where there were no paper towels or even a door on the stall, I washed with toilet paper, ruining the makeup I'd so carefully applied in an effort to disguise my drawn face. I pulled the brown wilted tiare flowers out of my hair and threw them into the trash. Smoothing my hair with a weary gesture, I looked in the mirror. I'd aged ten years.

Unintelligible French, full of static, erupted over the loudspeaker and I followed the locals outside to scan the sky. I heard the propellers before I saw the little Air Tahiti plane land in a shimmer—an image appearing in a distant mirage. It was some 200 yards away. The passengers were beginning to descend the ladder onto the dirt landing strip. I couldn't see clearly with the sun in my eyes, but the fourth one I thought was Kenny—his size and the youthful way he skipped down the steep boarding ladder with no hands on the rails. I stopped just short of throwing myself into his arms when I saw that it was a stranger who, except for height, bore no resemblance to my son at all. I turned away in disappointment so intense that I lost my last hope about Kenny being on the plane. Concentrating on calling Frank, I'd almost reached the waiting room when I thought I heard a voice call, "Mom!" I whirled as a sprinting figure ran toward me. Close enough to see the crinkly eyes now, close enough to see the grin. Dropping his beat-up duffel bag, Kenny enveloped me in a hug. My arms went around him and we held each other until he pulled back to scan my face.

Kenny was full of talk about how he and Billy had struggled to work out the vital details of his abrupt trip. How he'd slept on the concrete floor of Faaa Airport last night, afraid he'd miss his early flight. "I'm so glad to finally be here, Mom," he said. "Oh, I don't mean *glad*, I mean..." I saw that he, at a loss, was unprepared for the enormity of my devastation. Nor was I capable of talking about what had happened. It was all to come out eventually in little unconnected rivulets.

On the return passage he sat quietly with his arm around me, making occasional comments on the stark beauty of the island. I sat in silence, twisting and twisting my wedding ring. Finally, I found myself telling him, "Kelly was overboard for hours and hours—all night. I was alone and he was out there in the sea. It was a miracle. Morris and a dolphin found him—wait, I know, I know." I held up a hand to forestall the flood of questions that I knew would follow his initial speechless incredulity. "The thing is, he made me promise never to tell anyone."

I heard Kenny catch his breath, then he threw his head back, eyes closed, lips moving as if he were whispering a prayer. "He got you here, Mom. By God, that's Kelly. He got you here." The intensity in his voice matched that of his expression.

"I feel like I'm betraying a solemn pledge."

"No, Mother. That was when he was alive, and for whatever reasons he had then. Now he's gone. That's a story the world needs to hear. A miracle."

Two hours later we steamed back into Taiohae Bay. I saw for the second time and Kenny for the first, the lush green jagged cliffs rising sheer from the sea. Flamboyant trees abloom in vibrant red and gold were startling against the tropical sky. "It's a paradise, Mom, this place you and Kelly sailed into." His arm was around me again and I looked into his face. I wondered if it was the sky or the sea reflecting in those blue eyes filled with sudden comprehension. I watched him as he envisioned Kelly's and my landfall and saw its meteoric descent from zenith to nadir.

Kenny and I disembarked and stepped onto the quay. I recognized many familiar faces, including those of Bernard and Marceline. The crowd pushed forward, all wanting to meet the American widow's son. News of his arrival at the airport had preceded us and the whole town turned out to get a look. Evidently his appearance, California surfer sun-bleached hair, coupled with his height of six-foot-four and his ready smile, did not disappoint. Groups of young women huddled together giggling, playing eye games when he glanced in their direction. Young men his age and younger came forward to shake his hand and introduce themselves.

Finally, Bernard and Marceline rescued us from the crowd. Their shining faces, his French and hers Polynesian, beamed in welcome. My T-shirt was damp from the humidity and I tried to wipe my face before being greeted with quick kisses on both cheeks, the "French salute" in the manner adopted by the Marquesans. "Tomee, you must bring your son to our home for dinner this evening."

"Thank you, Bernard. That would be very nice." I glanced at Kenny, seeing his eager nod. "It's been such a long day. We have to freshen up and leave Kenny's luggage aboard the boat." Someone had considerately moved our dinghy to the quay.

"I had no idea it would be so hot!" Kenny said, stripping off his shirt.

"Well, we're practically on the equator. Go for a swim. It won't be very refreshing, but it's a quick way to bathe. I'm going to wash my face and change and look for a special bottle of wine to bring our hosts. Kenny, I hadn't meant to involve you in a social situation the minute you got here, but these people have taken me under their wings."

The Au Maitres' house was right out of Somerset Maugham. It was fronted by a wide, covered veranda that could accommodate two rows of tables and chairs or provide a romantic refuge during tropical squalls.

Vines crept all the way to the roof, entangling themselves in the thatch, creating a filigree of sun and shadow, the bay sparkling beyond.

Bernard and Marceline held important positions on the island. He was head of the Westpac Bank and she ran the only travel agency, as well as the entire airport operation. In addition, at noontime their home was transformed into a restaurant, serving lunch daily and dinner by reservation some nights. This evening it was just the four of us.

Their large central room was furnished with comfortable sofas and a T.V. A tiny, four-stooled bar stood at the opposite end. An indoor waterfall added its tinkle to the music Bernard selected from his large collection of CDs. "Tomee, I see already you have a very fine son, a man really, though I think still with the heart of a boy."

"You are right, Bernard. I have been blessed with two wonderful sons and my husband. I only wish you could have met Kelly—seen what a fine and handsome man he was…"

"But I thought you knew," Bernard said. "I came that night. The nurse Celestine told me the American navigator was dying, that there was a wife."

I'd been unaware of his visit during my vigil, but from the little I knew of him, I sensed that Bernard was the eyes and ears of the island. "Oh Bernard, I didn't know. So you came to the clinic…that place that kills people." I added under my breath.

Bernard heard me. He reached over and squeezed my arm, "It is all we have." He shook his head and cast his eyes down. "Celestine took me into Kelly's room. I saw him lying there. As you say, a fine, big man. Too young to die. It made me very sad. I spoke aloud to him and made a promise that I would look after his wife. They say people have a perception of sound through their comas, that the sense of hearing is the last to go."

"I knew none of this. Thank you, Bernard. It must have eased Kelly's death to know there was someone. Even if he didn't hear you at the end, he would know it now." The Frenchman's face was serious. Our eyes met and held.

With French gallantry, Bernard broke the solemnity by saying, "I did not even know you were a pretty woman when I made that promise, so you see my heart is put in the right place." He chuckled and risked a flirtatious glance. I had to smile at the pleasure he took in his little joke. Bernard excused himself to go to the kitchen, then came rushing back, eager to resume our conversation. "Tomee, after the grave is built will you and your son return to Californie on the boat?"

"Oh no. I don't have the heart to make that passage again without Kelly, and Kenny doesn't have the skills. He doesn't know navigation. Frank said nobody else here does either. We'll go soon to Papeete to interview whomever we can find. Probably run an ad for delivery skippers."

"I must warn you to take great care. There will be many who try to rob you of the boat. It carries much things of value, no?"

"No is right. I mean *yes*. We have state-of-the-art electronics on board." I remembered how proud Kelly was of me when I'd been able to buy the $2,000 Global Positioning System out of my interior design earnings—how excitedly his engineer's mind anticipated using the sophisticated new gadget.

"It is as I thought. You will have to pay the skipper who returns your boat very much money in advance, no?"

"Right," I said. "Frank filled me in on that too. About twenty-five thousand dollars, maybe more. Half up front and the rest on delivery. No matter what the condition of the boat on arrival. That's the biggie."

"So, when you pay him one-half there is nothing to prevent his taking your boat to one of our many islands to conduct a grand garage sale." The way he rolled his R's made a sound halfway between a gargle and a growl.

"I appreciate your advice," I said, "go on."

Bernard gave a modest shrug. A lock of hair fell across his forehead, giving him a boyish look. "He could even abandon the boat, and after selling everything still become rich."

"It's a good point you make Bernard..."

Kenny came over with his canvas bag. "Mom, I think it's time for our gift." Marceline had been showing him the house while Bernard dashed back and forth to the kitchen, from which the unmistakable fragrance of hot fresh bread emerged. He said dinner was about to be served. Kenny's timing was perfect. There was deep silence as our hosts bent low over the bottle of red wine, examining its label in the dim candlelight. Château Lafitte Rothschild, it read. Kelly had raved about its impressive vintage when his wine-enthusiast friend Joe Coberly presented it specifically for our landfall in the Marquesas.

Bernard drew the cork. They passed it back and forth, inhaling the aroma with great sensuality. Then the first sip was poured, swirled in the glass, inhaled again, and finally tasted. Bernard's eyes closed in ecstasy and Marceline moaned aloud. Kenny laughed and said watching the performance was akin to voyeurism.

"Kelly would have loved this," I said, sad and angry that he was missing the special wine. I blurted out that he'd saved it to have on my birthday. The plan was to celebrate in Papeete, exploring the island together. I talked as though it was yet to come to fruition. There was an uncomfortable silence. I jumped up from the table. My wine glass shattered against the first thing I encountered—the fountain.

"My God, Mom—you're bleeding!" Kenny was by my side examining my hand, looking shocked and scared. "I'll get some ice..." Everyone was up now, in a commotion.

"I'm so sorry—it was an accident." I glanced at Kenny and saw by his face that he knew I'd gone out of control.

CHAPTER 12

I returned and saw under the sun, that the race is

not to the swift, nor the battle to the strong neither yet

bread to the wise, nor yet riches to men of understanding, nor

yet favor to men of skill, but time and chance happeneth to them all.

—Ecclesiastes 9:12

KELLY'S OVERSEAS DEATH ENTANGLED US in a mesh of red tape that extended from the Marquesas to the U.S., spanning the ocean we had crossed with such high expectations. His burial had followed so hard upon the heels of his demise that there had not even been a coroner's report. U.S. regulations would not accept the death certificate (all in French, no less) without one. Every day we called at three offices—the mayor's, the gendarme's, and the governor's—attempting to procure paperwork. They didn't have the forms we needed. We were always treated with courtesy, even compassion, but our efforts to comply with the demands of the U.S. attorneys led to dead ends. Each communication took days, since there were no faxes at that time from the Marquesas.

With my heart in my throat, I visited the clinic with Kelly's Primary Health Insurance and Medicare Cards, which I'd found in his worn brown wallet, curved to the shape of his body. The head man of the clinic was not there and I was told to come back the next day. When we met he barely glanced at the cards, and explained that of course there would be no charge since the patient had died. I couldn't help but think what the cost would have been at home, with four doctors in attendance for nine hours.

Compassion for my widowhood also extended to the situation of our boat, stranded in French waters. The Port Captain waived the fee of $3,500 required as guarantee of payment for our two return airfares after a maximum stay of eight weeks. Conversely, as a widow in a French Protectorate, I now fell under the regulations of the Code de Napoleon, allowing no rights in my own name. Even my ownership of the *Vagabundita* was in question and no corroboration of legalities was forthcoming from the U.S. attorneys until their documentary requirements were met.

The governor's office presented another stumbling block. In the head man's absence (he was vacationing in Paris), they employed a skeleton staff. No one had the power to make decisions on the anomalous situation of Kelly's death. Ironically, in a hand-delivered letter emblazoned with the governor's title and crest, I was informed that as the first American to die on the island Kelly was to be honored. His gravesite was a gift from the French government and would be maintained in perpetuity. Despite these courteous generosities, we were in an impasse situation that would have seemed ludicrous were it not tinged with tragedy. Eventually, we obtained a death certificate without a coroner's report. Finally, with some embarrassment they admitted there wasn't a form for such a document, the implication being, "Who cared anyway?" Everyone knew Kelly had died of a heart attack almost upon arrival. The whole town had attended the funeral.

No one worked in bronze or marble on Nuku Hiva. Our plans for Kelly's memorial took shape from the meager materials available on the island. Frank suggested enlisting the help of a village boy he had employed from time to time. Nakeaeiou, or Theo, as he went by, came out to the boat on his surfboard to meet us and discuss the project. At first the two young men just stared. Each must have thought the other equally exotic—the small tattooed Marquesan boy and my tall blue-eyed son. They talked about surfing, and Theo admired Kenny's diving watch and

worn Nikes as he fingered his own shark-tooth necklace. They drank a
Hinano together, then went diving for lobsters with Theo's handmade
spear.

The setting sun stained the sea with coral tones and when the boys
came back to the boat they had a squirming gunnysack. Elated over their
catch and hungry, Kenny called down to the galley, "Put the lobster pot
on boil, Mom." They laughed and joked like a couple of old fishing buddies, barely mentioning the construction project. I figured it would be a
sort of by-the-seat-of-the-pants operation. Theo caught sight of Morris
down in the main salon, dozing on a sun-warmed cushion.

"Hey, Kenny," he said as he reached into the sack, laughing a little in
anticipation, "watch what happens." He set a lobster down on the cabin
sole and grabbed Morris, still all warm and stupid with sleep, and plunked
him down on the sole too. The lobster was the more aggressive of the two,
advancing slowly on his spiny legs with first one and then another pin-
cer held aloft. Theo laughed to see the terrified cat's quiet retreat, one paw
placed silently behind the other until he deemed it safe to turn tail and
run. I thought it was cruel to frighten Morris and chided them, but it
made me happy to see the boys having such a good time and for a
moment...I forgot. The boys agreed to meet at the cemetery next morning and shook on it as if formalizing a gentlemen's agreement. When he
left, Theo was wearing the diving watch.

There was nothing even remotely approaching a hardware or home
improvement store on the island. Even a hose was impossible to buy. The
Chinese couple who ran the most prosperous of the little dungeon-like
shops explained to me in English that since it rained every day, there'd be
no call for such a thing. They also said my only hope of getting cement
mix was through a local contractor and I'd better start asking around. The
only thing on my list that they had was a flat trowel, already gone to rust.
Looking around the store, I saw big empty spaces on the shelves and
noted that their sparse stock consisted mainly of the most basic staples,

such as sacks of flour and rice, a few canned foods, and case after case of Hinano stacked floor to ceiling. I wondered again how the villagers could afford the vast quantities of beer everyone consumed.

It was a long walk to meet the boys at the cemetery and already so hot I dreaded noon. Who could I possibly ask about the cement, not even knowing the word for it in French? I began to think we were on a futile course. It made me sick at heart to think of leaving Kelly in an unmarked grave, a grave as dismal as the baby's.

A blister burned on my foot where my sandal strap rubbed against my heel, so I was glad to accept Frank's offer of a ride. He'd pulled up in his jeep that looked like it had been left over from World War II. He brought us a wheelbarrow, so now at least we had that and a trowel, but no construction materials. I questioned Frank about the scarcity of supplies and he confirmed what the Chinese shopkeepers had said. "If there's a big construction job going on they order things like cement from Papeete. Otherwise, it's just not available. I don't know what to tell you."

When we arrived at the cemetery Kenny and Theo were hard at work hauling volcanic rocks almost larger than they could manage. They carried them in backpacks one by one with grueling effort up the steep slippery path from the beach. I saw the sweat glistening on their young bodies as they toiled in the tropical heat. "Kenny, I wish you wouldn't work barefoot. Frank said there's risk of infection from the coral."

"I know, Mom." Kenny carried a rock in each hand in addition to the boulder in his backpack. He gestured with his head in Theo's direction. Theo was now wearing the Nikes. I just shook my head and sighed. "The thing is," Kenny said, "they just come right out and ask for things and they won't take money for working on a grave. I asked Frank what we should pay Theo and he said to just buy him a few beers."

"They're superstitious. Something like if they take money for it, maybe they'll be next," I said. "The gravediggers wouldn't take anything either. Not even the carpenter who made the coffin. He hardly let me reimburse him for the lumber."

Theo went over to talk to the crew, who showed up about mid-morning to work on the mayor's monument. After much discussion and glancing in our direction and then all of them walking over to view Kelly's grave, Theo came back, walking with a slight swagger in his new shoes. He explained the gist of the deal he'd made, though he didn't call it that.

His friends offered to give us the cement we needed in exchange for Madame, that was me, bringing a pique-nique to the cemetery. Baguettes with butter and French cheeses, he suggested. "And plenty of beer," Kenny mouthed.

I hoped it was the French government rather than the mayor's family who was going to pay for the little under-the-counter deal of the cement. When Kenny saw I was about to say something, he wagged his finger in front of his lips. Apparently larceny bred like mold on brie in Nuku Hiva. We were beginning to get the picture of how things got done on the island.

I was glad to be given a job that made me feel I was contributing to Kelly's grave project. My heel blister was so painful now I left my sandals and walked barefoot on the dirt road that ran along by the sea. I passed the governor's estate. Stone obelisks flanked the long curved driveway leading to the French colonial home. The tri-color flew from a tall flag-pole and a deserted pique-nique table and chairs looked small set out on the sweeping lawn.

Despite Theo's rough map I became disoriented and wandered for some time through a park filled with ancient-looking sculpture. Grim-faced tikis stood amid granite obelisks. There were many war canoes crowded with stone occupants, some rowing and many holding spears, and face after massive face, most worn almost smooth. There were no houses or shops along this stretch of oceanfront. It was eerie to be the only living soul in the midst of all these gray stone people. I looked around for someone to ask my way but there was only silence. Walking further I saw thatched huts and modest tin-roofed dwellings standing on higher ground up lanes all overgrown with twisting vines. Coconut palms rose in clusters, their moving fronds shimmering in the noonday sun.

Lavish gardens bloomed with sprays of orchids, tiare, and exotic spiky flowers I could not name. Trees heavy with mango and papaya flourished everywhere. The ground was covered with fallen fruit, the air mumerous with the sound of swarming bees. A rotten smell mingled with the pungent scent of ginger and I turned away, half sick.

Finally I glimpsed the cheese shop, tucked into a grove of bamboo. Its screen door banged behind me and the proprietor scowled to see that flies accompanied my entrance. He was an unsmiling Frenchman, no doubt rendered cynical by customers unable to afford his costly imports. The sight of me in my shabby cutoffs and bare feet did not seem to cheer him. I couldn't imagine the islanders or the semi-indigent yachties buying such things as tinned escargots and Bar-le-duc, a tart sweet jam made of currants, imported from Paris. I bought the last three baguettes he had and was glad I could at least identify Camembert and Roquefort among his array of cheeses. The grocer made no effort to hide his contempt over my pronunciations and he let me struggle along trying to order in French before he addressed me in perfect English. He suggested a Montresat cheese unknown to me and volunteered that the imported Chevre cheese was much prized by the islanders, since their own goats only gave enough milk to feed their own kids. I'd seen small herds of white goats everywhere.

The grocer cut portions with a more lavish hand than I indicated and I suspected he weighed my selections with his thumb on the scale as well. Despite worrying about how much all this was going to cost—I was down to less than $200—I increased my order with several lengths of sausage and two jars of the Bar-le-duc. I wasn't about to buy the beer from this expensive shop, planning to get it at the last store on my return route. I wondered how I'd manage to carry everything back. I needn't have worried. As I came out with my purchases individually wrapped in white butcher paper, a red pickup truck braked in my path, splattering my legs with mud. I recognized one of Kelly's pallbearers, the handsomest Marquesan man I'd seen on the island. He had the unforgettable name of Leonardo da Vinci.

One of the nastier little slaps the French leveled against the Marquesan culture was to require everyone to take a French name to be used on all official documents. They could keep their Marquesan names, sort of, and the diehards introduced themselves to Kenny and me as such. We thought the names they selected seemed to mock the French, but Frank said no, they just wanted to be named after famous people. Theo's father was called Voltaire and we were eventually driven to the airport by none other than Marie Antoinette. There were lots of Napoleon Bonapartes and Coco Chanels, clad not in chic Parisian suits with ropes of pearls, but in long pareaus with jewelry made of shell and shark tooth. How Leonardo's Italian name sneaked by I never discovered, but I was enormously grateful for his help and invited him to join us for lunch at the cemetery. We stopped for a case of Hinano beer, complemented by a generous chunk of ice, a luxury on the island.

When the grave workers saw Leonardo and the rich American lady unloading the pique-nique they threw down their tools and plunged en masse into the sea to rinse off before lunch. Someone spread a large canvas for us to sit on. The young men popped beers and, leaning on their elbows, began to question Kenny about Californie. They wanted to know how the surfing was since they shared opposite sides of the same ocean. They asked the inevitable questions about Disneyland. Even the grown men seemed lured by its glitter. I hoped nothing would tempt them to leave their island. Not a one of them had ever been off Nuku Hiva and they marveled that Kenny had flown so many hours and been on a jet and then the Air Tahiti prop plane. One young man asked Kenny if he hadn't been afraid his plane would drop out of the sky like their mayor's had. I could tell they considered flying far more hazardous than Kelly's and my near-month at sea, sailing across the Pacific in our small boat.

Kenny wanted to know about their tattoos and if maybe he could get one. He turned to me and asked, "You too, Mom?"

"Yes," I said. "I'd like to commemorate this."

"Maybe a dolphin on your shoulder or an anklet of tiare flowers?" Kenny said. He watched me like a hawk these days trying to read my mood fluctuations, hoping to see me smile.

"That's easy," Theo said. "We got an artist right here on the island." Being young he had only a modest ankle design and a coiled snake, ready to strike, on one bicep. An older fellow, who introduced himself as Hakaui, got up to show off traditional tiki faces he had tattooed on his knees. He demonstrated how the eyes and mouths pulled down into a grimace as he flexed his legs in deep knee bends.

"That's how we feel about the French, using our islands for nuclear tests," he said. A roar went up from the young men, accompanied by aggressive arm punches. They hated the French. The group fell into a moment of sullen silence, punctuated by the sound of dynamite blasting in the distance. Kenny tried to lift the pall with his cheerful voice as I unwrapped the food.

"This looks great, Mom. We're all starved." He sliced the sausage with his Swiss Army knife. It passed from hand to hand, every blade pulled out and tested and the miniature scissors tried. Kenny's eyes met mine and I smiled slightly and shrugged. Laughter and talk escalated in tandem with the consumption of beer. My habitual numbness was intensified by drinking a Hinano on an empty stomach. Grateful for the anesthetized feeling, I walked around distributing the food. The ground seemed littered with brown tattooed legs in attitudes of relaxation. Suddenly an image familiar as the feel of my own body jolted me out of my lethargy. The image of Kelly's legs swam through my memory—his inner thighs imprinted with twin birthmarks shaped like little brown hands. I used to touch first one and then the other with my finger and laugh and say, "See, these prove you came out of a mold," and he'd laugh too and reach for me. Suddenly I was cast into an emptiness so acute that I staggered and reached out a hand to steady myself against the insubstantial air. Kenny couldn't see my face. I walked blindly toward the nearby herd of white goats. I had a piece of a baguette spread with brie in my hand. The goats had decided on a safety belt perimeter beyond which they dared not venture, but they watched my approach eagerly from their tight semicircle. I extended my hand and they crowded one another to get at the bread and cheese, tails twitching with excitement. One mother, either with triplets or wet-nursing an orphan, had three kids quarrelling over her two teats. I felt the touch of her velvety lips still nibbling at my palm when the bread was gone.

After paying for the pique-nique, I was almost out of cash. We were stuck with no money, 3,000 miles from home, and living on a sailboat needing maintenance. Marceline was the only Polynesian we met who held a position of importance—running the airport—probably because her husband was French and the local banker. She extended us credit on two round-trips to Tahiti at a hefty $1,600 apiece and wrangled a cheap room rate at the old Hotel Tahiti.

There we began each day with breakfast in the open-air palapa-roofed dining room that overlooked the water. Kenny was popular with the Tahitian waitresses and along with our café au lait they always served him two halved papaya and two croissants, though the continental breakfast called for only one of each. I was surprised I could enjoy food, though I was never hungry and ate little the rest of the day.

The young waitresses wore red or yellow hibiscus in their dark hair. Cascading over their bare shoulders, it fell thick as a horse's tail to the waist. Clad in long pareaus, the women swayed as gracefully as the tall haari trees, whose fronds moved constantly in the trades. Kenny said he hardly knew where to look. Bare-breasted young French girls sunbathed unselfconsciously on the end of the hotel's pier. The scene was enlivened by the comings and goings of outriggers and small boat craft. Asians skilled in fishing pulled impossible-looking creatures from the abundant sea.

After two days Kenny told me he'd learned not to stare and could handle the women's semi-nudity with French savoir faire. Still, the exotic women of the South Seas seemed to be served up and offered as graciously as the lush platters of tropical fruit laid out for the picking, clearly the stuff of male fantasy.

The hotel was located six miles from town. On our second day we caught Le Truck into Papeete. Flamboyantly painted, the droll vehicles (spelled "Le Truc" in French) were the islands' mainstay of transportation. Armed with my letter of credit from a Santa Barbara bank, Kenny and I confidently went in search of the Bank of Tahiti. The letter of credit introduced Mr. and Mrs. Kellogg Spear and guaranteed funds to be released from our joint account at home. Since the manager was away, we attempted to do business with a woman teller who had never seen or heard of a letter of credit and spoke little English, saying we'd have to come back after the two-hour lunch break. Kenny wanted to explore the town and we agreed to meet back in front of the fountain.

I was crossing a street when a new awareness stabbed into my consciousness with the finality of a sentence. *Widow. You're a widow now.* The judge's gavel pounded out the word. *Widow. Widow. Widow.* "No, I don't want to be a widow!" The stares of the people I passed told me I had cried out. When Kenny met me I was dimly aware of his concern in perceiving my nearly catatonic state. I didn't try to explain it to him nor would I have known how.

"Come on, Mom. You need something to eat." With his talent for unearthing the best the world had to offer he'd found the ultimate café. Though no train existed in Papeete, the tiny Café de la Gare could have been a station restaurant right out of Paris. It had only three marble-topped tables with ornate wrought-iron chairs. The bar had four tall stools and an impressive brass footrest, its mirrored wall reflecting a plethora of fine French wines and brandies. The waiter looked Parisian in his formal black trousers and white apron. Kenny watched me expectantly for my reaction, proud of his restaurant "find." I tried to smile but my heart was in the grave. This was to have been Kelly's and my island.

I could tell from Kenny's air of suppressed excitement that he had another surprise for me after lunch. He led me next door to a boutique for French baby clothes. I felt a sudden thrill, my grieving subsided for a moment, eclipsed by the thought of my next expected grandchild. Perhaps because my concentration was so entirely focused on the present, no detail escaped me. Years later I could describe every garment that hung in that exquisite shop.

The saleslady exuded the taste many French women have. We spoke about our respective grandchildren, both girls. She advised me on selections and sizes for Kenny's two-year-old daughter, Kendal, and pointed out "unisex" infant wear for impending births of unknown gender. For Kendal we finally settled on a jumpsuit of finest French cotton with an all-over strawberry print and a white puff-sleeved blouse with strawberries appliquéd on the red piped Peter Pan collar. "The Baby's" outfit, for Robin and Billy's expected child, was an impossibly sweet pale-blue romper embroidered with ducks. "It better be a girl," Kenny said when he saw it.

"Oh no, monsieur," the saleslady protested. "This is appropriate for boy or girl. It's after all a petit bebe!"

The transaction was made in francs. Fortunately I didn't pay any attention to the exchange rate or I'd probably have fainted. As Kenny predicted, no one balked at Kelly's gold Visa card and I signed it with the unpleasant thought that I'd be met at the Los Angeles airport, handcuffed, and thrown into jail for illegal use of a credit card. My name was not even on it. Kenny tried to explain there was no way they could call for verification and with the billing time a month away, I could safely use it for the duration of our stay.

In compulsive repetition, I told everyone we met I was newly widowed and my husband was buried on Nuku Hiva. The Tahiti newspaper had screamed out in inch-high red headlines, "U.S. Yachtsman Dead at the End of His Dream." The story was a masterpiece of error. The journalist transposed Kelly's age with the length of the boat and reduced our Pacific passage to one of impossibly short duration. There were pictures of the funeral and of me laying flowers on his grave. None but the French so love a romantic tragedy. Kenny and I became overnight celebrities; recognized everywhere, we were the recipients of great interest and special treatment.

But not at the bank.

The manager of the Banque de Tahiti indulged in such an exaggerated Gallic shrug it made me want to hit him. Shaking his head, lips pouting, and palms thrust up, he mimed his inability to help us. He made short shrift of our letter of credit, explaining that as a widow in a French protectorate I now fell under the civil laws of the Code Napoléon. I also did not have proof that I was executrix of Kelly's estate, as I knew I was according to the terms of the wills we had drawn with an attorney in California before we sailed.

The manager did go so far as to call our banker in Santa Barbara and was informed that both accounts, our joint and the one in Kelly's name, were frozen until proper legal documentation was presented. Kenny and I looked blankly at each other when asked to produce a death certificate. It seemed I was subject to Napoléonic Law in California as well. I was not even permitted to cosign on Kelly's $1,000 worth of traveler's checks, which we carried for emergencies.

Kenny turned just short of rude and then motioned me to the lounge area, where we held a mumbled conversation. "It'll be okay, Mom. All we really need is petty cash for things like Le Truc and tips. I still have a couple hundred in dollars left over from the travel money Billy gave me."

"I hate using Kelly's credit card. It makes me feel like a crook."

"We're fine with it at the hotel, and the shops and restaurants haven't batted an eye." He was trying to reassure me, not realizing I didn't really care. Life's frustrations had ceased to be of concern.

Kenny spent most afternoons interviewing the cartoon characters who presented themselves as potential delivery skippers for the *Vagabundita's* return trip to California. Frank and Rose had been in that profession for many years and advised us of the pitfalls, the most serious being the traditional financial arrangement whereby the skippers were paid half the going rate of $25,000 for a Pacific passage up front in cash, the balance due upon delivery of the boat in California. Though the sailboat was of modest size and ten years old, as noted she carried thousands of dollars worth of the latest state-of-the-art electronic equipment. What was to prevent someone from holding a "grand garage sale" as Bernard had put it, of her contents?

Only a few of the seedy applicants held official-looking professional skipper licenses. We checked with the Papeete Harbor Master and he advised caution. Forgery of licenses was common, as was theft, and if a yacht was of foreign registry, well, (another Gallic shrug) little could be done since the French would not extradite in their own waters.

Dashing across the street just as the light changed, Kenny was about one body-width ahead of the onslaught of taxis, motor scooters, and "Le

Trucs." The lively green-and-orange color scheme of the small bus seemed an appropriate reflection of the gaiety of its Friday-afternoon passengers. Clad only in trunks or pareaus, many were whooping it up and drinking from pint bottles concealed in paper bags. One gorgeous Polynesian girl leaned dangerously out of Le Truc's open side, pareau aflutter and long hair streaming, to wave and shout at Kenny. "Hey! Hi! You are a beautiful man!" He cast her a look poignant with missed opportunity as Le Truc careened around the corner.

As usual, I had hesitated a second too long, afraid to run across the street against the surge of traffic and, failing to grasp Kenny's outstretched hand, watched the charming scene from the opposite curb. Kenny's lingering grin was mixed with exasperated body language. He shook his head and called, "Mom, you're chicken. One of these days you're going to get us both killed." I knew he just wanted me to trust him.

Kenny and I exchanged a glance of relief when we finally spotted the garden shop. "Kenny, what are we looking for here? Ready-mix concrete?" I experienced frequent memory lapses, but our efforts to complete Kelly's grave were paramount in my mind.

"No, Mom," he answered gently. "That's all arranged. It would be too heavy to take back on the plane to Nuku Hiva anyway." He glanced around the garden shop. "Look, bare-root roses! Here in Papeete of all places!" He so hoped to cheer me. The gunnysack-wrapped bushes were already sprouting dark red leaves. *Here in the South Pacific nothing stays bare-root for long*, I thought. Examining their tags, I saw that they were romantically named after famous French personalities. General Charles de Gaulle—a stalwart yellow. Princess of Monaco—a pristine white with pink, ruffled edges. The Edith Piaf rose was scarlet, conjuring up a memory from my college days—sitting in some dim bistro hand in hand with a boyfriend—hearing that passionate voice wail out "La Vie en Rose."

We were joined by the young French Polynesian salesman. "Will these roses do well in the Marquesas?" I asked. "It's very important to me. You see we are taking them there to plant on my husband's grave. There is so little to work with on Nuku Hiva. No fertilizer, not even a hose. He was buried the very day we arrived..." I saw I had said too much.

The young man looked away from my desolate face, seeking an avenue of escape. When he saw none, he changed the subject. "These come from France, Madame. The cost is, well, very dear. I suggest you buy some time-release rose food. They will of course also have to be inspected at the French Agricultural Department to get customs clearance. I have to warn you, customs may not allow this transport." I stared at him. The conditions he outlined seemed overwhelming. We paid an astronomical $120 (on the credit card, of course) for our purchases.

"Mom, we have an eight a.m. plane to Nuka Hiva tomorrow. There's no way we can get clearance on the rosebushes through all those French officials. I'm stuffing them into my backpack." Kenny didn't fuss too much over regulations. He did what he had to do, accomplishing things in an expedient manner. They went into the overhead compartment of the small prop plane, which served an unexpectedly elaborate breakfast accompanied by beer and wine at 7 a.m. I leaned my head against the window and looked down at the vast, empty expanse of blue water over which I now flew.

Again, Bernard and Marceline met us at the dock, pressing us to join them for dinner, this time with some of the other cruising sailors. Kenny was struggling to shrug off his heavy backpack. "Bernard, could you please drive us to the cemetery first? I need to get these rosebushes into the fresh air before they die." I'd explained that tomorrow was Mother's Day at home and I wondered if it was observed here as well. "Oh yes, here too," Marceline said. "We'll all meet at church tomorrow."

"Good. Then we can plant these after the service when there's time to do it right," Kenny said.

Awakening in an already sweltering early morning, I remembered that Kenny had hauled freshwater out to the boat and replenished the solar shower. With relief I rinsed off the stickiness of the tropical night. It felt good to be back on board. Kenny and I took turns washing and felt at least slightly refreshed to face the Mother's Day church service ashore. I wondered how it would feel to be back in the same churchyard where Kelly's coffin lay for the first part of his funeral before being transported to the cemetery.

After the service, we gathered in the cobbled courtyard. There were none of the yachtsmen we had known so briefly, so we walked up to pay respects to Kelly's grave. Kenny and I and the Au Maitres and their assorted Polynesian relatives and little barefoot children trailed along the dirt sea road together to the cemetery I now so loved.

Goats stared out of their odd pupils, disturbed in mid-bite from their grazing, and a couple of untethered horses galloped noisily off a few feet from our intrusion. Headstones and tumbling crosses were almost enveloped in the vines that crept everywhere. Kelly's grave was still nothing but a dreary patch of dirt. It did not even bear his name.

The frangipani tree, dropping its blossoms, tried to adorn his grave, imparting a sweet, heavy fragrance to the air. Our friends crowded around the rose bushes, an exotic rarity unknown on the island. Kenny put a finger to his lips and spoke softly in shocked disbelief. "Mom, there are only four now. We brought six." Hearing, the Marquesans fell silent in mortification. I had to suppress hysterical laughter. It seemed so outrageous that anyone would dare steal off a grave—a grave as famous now as that of the American navigator who had crossed the Pacific from Manzanillo, Mexico, with only his wife and cat as crew.

Swallowing hard, I put an arm around Marceline. "Please don't be concerned. I think it's rather sweet. Someone was just overcome with the chance to give his mother a magnificent gift. They must have thought it providence. Look how they carefully left us one of each color and only took the extra red and white." She smiled at my tolerance.

A week later, the four rosebushes planted, Kenny and I were again in

Papeete interviewing potential delivery skippers.

A charming call came through from Bernard. "Ken-nee! I have discovered ze robber of ze rosebushes!" His voice was exultant. "They had the courage to plant them right in the front yard. Can you imagine? Of course it was not on our main street, but I discovered, nevertheless." I had a vision of the robust Frenchman cruising slowly along on his motor scooter peering into overgrown gardens. I took the phone. "Bernard, it's all right about the stolen rosebushes. Just leave it be. Kenny and I like to think we've helped to propagate French roses on Nuku Hiva." I paused, hoping to think of a way to further reassure him. "Bernard, we know that Kelly is laughing."

Monday, May twentieth, was a holiday and the bank and government offices we visited regularly were closed. Kenny suggested we spend the day on the neighboring island of Moorea. Le Truc transported us to the ferry landing adjacent to the quay where the majestic *Wind Song* and the motley Euro-92 race boats were moored. The *Wind Song's* crew was all a-bustle, readying her for the evening embarkation. We'd seen her from the hotel terrace sailing at sunset, white topsails flying against a pomegranate sky. The race boats might as well have been in dry dock. Not a soul stirred aboard a one of them. We spotted Guido's tacky *Marie-Louise* and Jay's state-of-the-art racing machine, *Excalibur*. Kenny had met them earlier and was fascinated by the two young men, one Belgian and the other a Brit, both having pledged two years to their sailing adventures. I suggested to Kenny that he bang on the hulls to rouse his friends. "No way, Mom. Everybody was partying 'til all hours last night. Papeete is their first big port since Honolulu."

"Well, they partied every night in Nuku Hiva, from what I saw."

"Not ashore with girls and bars," Kenny assured me in his sage thirty-year-old wisdom. "I'll catch 'em on the way back this evening."

The ferry was loaded to the gunnels, cars below and passengers crowding the upper decks. Once underway, two young Tahitian women approached Kenny, asking him to take their picture. They stood together at the rail, with a stage-set background of jagged peaks tearing through the clouds rising over Moorea. One wore her hair twisted on top of her head and the other's blew free in the wind. Their full lips and darkly fringed eyes needed no enhancement of makeup. They could have stepped off a Gauguin canvas. I thought their camera routine was a clever ploy to meet Kenny. He, of course, asked them to photograph us in return. Blond and dark heads leaned close as he demonstrated the camera's fill-in flash mechanism. We posed sitting on a life jacket locker, I in my short, lime-green skirt with the white palm tree print, and Kenny in shorts and sandals, sun-bleached hair growing scruffy down his neck. He went below to the snack bar and came back on deck, balancing four Cokes and bags of chips. The young people chatted for the rest of the crossing. Phone numbers were exchanged and plans made to meet back in Papeete.

Later, I wasn't surprised when Kenny told me the taller of the two young women was Miss Tahiti of 1990 and the other, equally gorgeous, Tara, was her cousin. Both natural beauties, they bore themselves with the dignity and grace that distinguished Polynesian women.

Kenny and I had about six hours ahead of us to explore the island. I climbed on the back of the rented motor scooter, and our adventure began. A road twisted above the beach and afforded glimpses of the sea on one side and modest houses on the other. Graciously situated on large jungley lots, most had broad front porches and tin roofs. Sherbet-colored churches with pointed spires and white Colonial gingerbread trim sprang up every few miles. No large hotels or resorts commercialized the landscape, and we saw only a few cottages for rent. With its discreet sign, we almost missed the fabled Moorea Club Med. The guard was polite but firm. He was sorry, we weren't allowed to tour, but we could book for as little as three nights. I saw Kenny mentally file this important information for future use. Next we came to Bali Hai, the resort made famous by the four Southern California men who, in the mid fifties, abandoned their predictable lives to "go native" as it was called then. They took Tahitian wives, set to work, and Bali Hai was born. It was too early for lunch though we were tempted by the open-air dining room set in a tropical garden with emerald lawns sloping to the sand.

If we'd been looking the other way around a bend in the road, we'd have missed the ultimate romantic restaurant where Kenny stopped, but he had a nose for such things. We walked across a rope-handled bridge to a sort of reconditioned tugboat. Though moored on the water, "Le Bateau" felt stationary underfoot—and a good thing too, considering all the bottles of wine set out on the highly varnished tables. Crystal and brass gleamed everywhere. We were greeted by a black-trousered waiter with an apron tied in the French manner. The first basket of bread disappeared quickly between the two of us. Then we ate langoustine accompanied by a French white Bordeaux and ordered a pear tart for dessert—a meal we should both have been sharing with lovers.

We planned to take the ferry back from the Sofitel Hotel, a new French resort on the island. The afternoon heat grew oppressive and nothing seemed more appealing than a swim. "Mom, that's the hotel boutique over there." Kenny indicated a palapa-roofed shop half hidden in the palms. "Why don't you buy a bikini and we can swim for an hour or so before we leave?" Robot-like, I acted on every suggestion he made.

Upon entering the shop, I closed my eyes for a moment and breathed in the mingled fragrances of the sea grass covering the floor and the pikaki lei worn by the proprietress. Fans hung from the bamboo ceiling, creating a breeze that cut the humidity a little and fluttered her long hair. She showed me around the exotic shop. I bought a book on the Marquesas I'd not seen before and, in sudden inspiration, nine big cowrie shells to set in the concrete on Kelly's grave, one for each year of our marriage. When I asked for something for my two-year-old granddaughter, the salesgirl held up a shirred bikini bottom, piped in pink with rows of ruffles along the derriere and around the tiny leg holes. It could only have been French. It made me laugh. When it came to a bathing suit for me, she indicated a tall basket filled with bright, tie-dyed hair scrunchies and bikini bottoms. "I have to have a top," I said.

"Oh no, Madame, here even grandmothers go topless. It is not so shocking."

"I've noticed the grandmothers," I said, "but you see, I'm recently widowed and the thought of calling attention to myself is…" I searched for a word that would convey the depth of my distaste for walking out on the beach semi-nude—"not possible."

"Oh, Madame," the young woman stretched out a hand and clasped my wrist. "I extend you my condolence." The tears in her eyes belied the formality of her words. "My husband died too. He was a pilot. We had a little girl. My mother said it took me five years to even begin to get over it."

"I am so sorry," I said, and when I looked into her face I saw that it would take her forever.

I came out on the beach to look for Kenny, self-conscious in my tiny yellow-and-green string bikini bottom with my white T-shirt on top. Full of the wonder of the chance encounter with the young Polynesian widow and the depth of our connection in that brief moment, I did not know that it was only the beginning of such encounters, and that lost souls with broken hearts were often cast in one another's path to be comforted by the profound intimacy that can occur in sharing their grief.

I met Christopher Bon Carre in the lobby of the unpretentious Hotel Tahiti. It was another stifling day. The heat was just slightly lessened by the trade winds, which made a tinkling sound in the chandeliers dripping long ribbons made of white shells. I was sitting in the open lobby in a big wicker chair, a book on which I couldn't concentrate open on my lap, waiting for Kenny to get back from town. He'd gone in to make arrangements for Morris to fly home.

The handsome young man had checked out of the hotel and was

waiting for his ride to the airport, keeping an eye on his luggage. "Well, you have a great tan. How long have you been in Tahiti?" Chris said, regarding me with a friendly smile. I noted his dark good looks and size and thought—*football player*. He didn't look quite like the average tourist.

"Six weeks so far," I replied, "but the tan isn't exactly from lying around on a beach." He looked at me quizzically, then went on to say, "Wow, that's a long time. Most people come over on a ten-day package. I've been here over a month too. Not exactly a vacation for me either. I came to help a woman who was like a mother to me. She had such a tragedy." His voice got husky and quiet. "Her husband was washed out to sea by a rogue wave. They never even recovered the body."

I felt cold chills come over me and stared at him in some kind of inexplicable recognition. "Well, we've both been here a long time for the same reason," I said. He signaled the smiling Polynesian barmaid, who was clad in a pareau done in the hotel's signature red-and-white hibiscus print.

"I'd like to buy you a drink. Sounds like we could both do with something cool and relaxing," he said.

"Thank you. I'll have whatever you're having." I drew a deep breath and went on, "My husband, Kelly, died of a massive heart attack the day we set foot onshore in the Marquesas. We'd sailed for twenty-seven days crossing the Pacific, been cruising for a year before that." I saw the pain and caring in his eyes. "So what happened to your friend?"

"Her name is Sarah Nance. She and her husband had a dream. They'd been cruising sailors like you and Kelly. Couldn't bear to go back home to Iowa. Iowa! Can you imagine that landlocked place after a couple of years of cruising around this paradise?" Our drinks arrived and we clinked glasses in a solemn toast. "They bought an old, run-down place on the atoll Rangiroa. Only thing it had going was its spectacular white-sand beach and a lot of palms needing attention. They didn't have much money and they worked hard for two years just to get it in bare shape for their first season."

Chris got up briefly to take a look out through the Porte Cochere for his airport transport van, then resettled himself in the open lobby. "So, here's what happened. Sarah's husband was standing no more than waist

deep in the lagoon, demonstrating snorkeling technique to a young honeymoon couple. Evidently they were all so intent they didn't see the
rogue wave coming. The woman, who wasn't much of a swimmer, was
washed up alive clear on the other side of the island." Christopher's voice
broke then. He closed his eyes and rubbed a hand across his brow. "The
two men were never even recovered. You can imagine poor Sarah. Of
course I had to come."

Kenny came back with the discouraging news that he would have to
take Morris daily to Faaa Airport, prepared to have the confused animal
fly spur-of-the-moment to L.A. whenever Air New Zealand could take
him. The upside of this inconvenience was that, surprisingly, no exami-
nations or shots were required on either shore.

"Go to Rangiroa, Mom. It's less than an hour's flight. You should meet
this other widow. I've got this cat hassle and I can hang out with Guido
and Jay at night."

I spent a lonely two days on Rangiroa, staying in a modest little cottage where the harsh light from a single bulb lit the room. I tried to read,
lying on a lumpy mattress on the floor. The bathroom was an outhouse.
I bathed in the sea.

Everyone I encountered knew Sarah and tried hard to help me track
her down. Word was she'd gone to another island for a few days.
Discouraged, I waited in the shabby airport for my return flight to
Papeete. The girl taxi driver who'd dropped me off seemed to be friends
with all the airport personnel and drifted off to chat. Suddenly she came
rushing back, pointing to a woman sitting across the room. "That's her!
She's back!" Sarah Nance and I finally met. I was saddened to see that she
was so young, mid-thirties, I guessed. Pretty, with her naturally curly dark
hair and petite figure. She hadn't done a thing to enhance that prettiness,

and I noted with dismay that she was thin and worn-looking.

We told our stories, then cried and held each other, arms clasping, rocking back and forth on the hard, white plastic airport seats. We looked up at the sound of a jet landing and Sarah met her arriving Iowa relatives. Her stout, middle-aged mother surveyed the airport with disapproval. "Sarah, is that a unisex bathroom?" she asked.

"I'm afraid so, Mother," Sarah replied. She brushed a strand of loose hair away from her face and seemed to slump down further into her seat. The mother's disapproval clearly extended to us two women, who had so carelessly lost our men out here in the South Pacific, sailing away to help them live out their dreams.

As my own plane landed and I prepared to bid farewell, Sarah gripped my shoulders and looked intently into my eyes. "Tommie, I went back to Iowa right after the tragedy. I took one look around the farm and knew I had to come back here to Rangiroa. Some days it seems as if nothing happened. Other days, I'm so overwhelmed." She made a helpless gesture and I clasped my valiant little friend-of-an-hour in one last hug. I turned and walked slowly toward my plane, wondering if I could live out our dream, alone out here in the South Pacific.

When we returned to Nuku Hiva, I was relieved to see that Theo and our helpers had followed Kenny's instructions to leave off working on the grave until we were back. Fortunately the plan was to pour the slab the next day. Everyone was impressed with the big cowries I'd bought at the Sofitel but I needed time to find enough shells to imbed in the wet concrete to spell out SPEAR.

I walked along the surf line, searching for the tiny cowrie shells I'd spotted earlier. Those I found were exquisite, about the size of a little fingernail with a miniature double row of teeth on their underside. I was disappointed to find only three. Theo'd said they were called Porcelaines, plentiful on the reef if I wanted to dive for them. It was low tide. I wouldn't need a scuba tank. My snorkel, mask, and fins would be adequate.

Drifting slowly, I discovered that the minute shells I sought came in identical pairs and that the mate was never further than a foot away, though to find it I sometimes had to go upside down to peer under a ledge or create a current with my hand to move the eel-grass, sinuous and flowing as mermaids' hair. The sun burned on my back and it felt good to dive down at intervals. The Porcelaines' colors ranged in a subtle spectrum from lavender to burnt sienna, with matched patterns laid out in infinitesimal dots. No two pairs were exactly alike. After each new find, I searched with great diligence, obsessed to locate the mate, for I did not want to leave the one without the other.

My hands were clumsy in their diving gloves and I dropped one shell, watching it fall and fall down through the clear water, rays of sun glinting off its white underside. I felt a deep pang of anguish, imagining the tiny creature moving at a snail's pace over the convolutions of the coral, like scaling mountains, searching endlessly for its companion. I marked its fall and took a bearing. When I found the mate, I disengaged it with great care, then cast it down at the spot where the first had fallen, longing to give them a chance to be together again.

Sometimes I felt no pain at all, so concentrated was I on an activity related to building Kelly's grave. The other cruising sailors, mostly the European and American race crews I met in the village, were embarrassed by my display of grief, averting their faces from mine or looking away, as if I symbolized a death-head. Not so the Polynesians. Women I barely recognized, perhaps had seen once in a shop or at church, would spontaneously enfold me in their arms and say, "Courage, courage, Madame!" They would look into my eyes with deep compassion, communicating their love. They were like big, soft mothers.

Frequently I passed the gravediggers who also worked on the quay as stevedores. Their eyes flashed me a solemn salute, honoring my mourning. When I hugged Morris it was like the comfort toddlers get when caressing a teddy bear or a threadbare blanket. There is something profound about the living pet of a person who has died. Morris became a kind of conduit, transmitting love back and forth between Kelly and me.

It was not entirely a milieu of love and spirituality. I saw Kenny's shock and fear when I railed at God. "Don't curse the Big Guy, Mom," he whispered, glancing nervously around as though he expected me to be struck down then and there or turned into a pillar of salt.

"What kind of God would have Kelly go through all this and then not let him have one day—*one day…*" My voice rose on a high, desperate note and I searched Kenny's face as if I could find an answer there. He put an arm around my shoulders as I burst into furious tears.

"Mom, you need someplace to put the anger. Some people put it on the person who died and left them, but, I see, you're not blaming Kelly— but it's not God to blame either. I don't think it is…" his voice trailed off, sad and stymied in his inability to bring me a word of comfort.

I was able to stop my diatribe before I went too far and told my son I wanted to die myself. I pleaded exhaustion and encouraged him to go out that night with Guido and Jay since the Euro '92 race boats were back in Taiohae Bay. Not that there was much for them to do onshore, but I wasn't fit company for Kenny that night.

My exhaustion was genuine. Grieving burns enormous amounts of energy. I dropped twenty pounds, my very flesh wasting away in the famine of my loss. I barely slept more than a few hours a night, nerves and concentration shot. Trying to read I'd turn the pages of a whole chapter and realize I didn't know what the book was about. My mind dealt obsessively with the tragedy, in compulsive repetition of its details. I wondered why I didn't get sick or die. *Maybe that's what happens to the lucky ones who bottle up their grief and can't even cry.*

"Mom, we're batting zero on this delivery skipper hassle."

"They've been a scroungy lot all right, but what are we going to do?"

"Let's call Alex. He's bound to know someone in Port Townsend."

"I'd so wanted to meet the skipper."

We were having dinner at Rose and Frank's place, as we did most nights. The food was good and more reasonable than buying from the expensive specialty shops. We usually ran into friends there and met other newly arrived sailors. Then, too, we could use Frank's phone. For once we got right through. "Thank God, Kenny," Alex said. "I must have taken the telephone number down wrong. Couldn't spell the name of the Inn..."

"Nobody can," Kenny put in.

"Elena and I've been worried. We know about your problems with Dad's grave. Now what's up?"

"We have no prospects for a delivery skipper. We should have relied on your contacts to begin with but Mom wanted to first meet whomever we hired. The boat is such a sentimental thing to her."

"Of course. To be expected. I think I know just the ones. They're a couple. Doris and Willie—both licensed delivery skippers. I saw them at the harbor yesterday—I'm re-doing a teak interior down there—they were just back from sailing a big yawl to Friday Harbor. Evidently they're trying to buy a house together. I think they'd jump at the chance for a major delivery passage."

"Sounds good, Alex," Kenny glanced at me with a thumbs-up gesture and I nodded. "See what you can do. We sure appreciate your help."

Now that the wheels of our departure had been set in motion, it seemed inconceivable to think of leaving the South Pacific, where by some inexplicable twist of fate the most profound occurrence of my life had taken place. We'd abandon the idea of returning the boat, live aboard, and start over I decided. Kenny shared my desire. Back home, in the face of protestations from his boss, he had virtually walked away from his hard-won job to help me, knowing it would not be there for him when he got back. Attracted to the idea of a new life, he interviewed with a local magazine, *The Tahiti Beach Press*, his appointment arranged by a young woman we'd met on the Moorea ferry who'd recognized and done a story on us.

Our fantasies of staying in Tahiti were soon dashed. Billy and Alex had put practical considerations into effect and before we knew it the delivery skippers had arrived and Billy'd airmailed our return tickets on Air New Zealand. Willie and Doris were a tall, handsome couple. The minute I saw them I realized that we'd be very cramped on the boat with four good-sized adults sharing space. The Keikahanui Inn was full, so Kenny and I went ashore to check out the only other lodging place on the island. We had to walk a couple of miles to reach it.

Sweating, we gratefully accepted two chilled Hinanos from the young woman at the desk in the small lobby. She plunked herself down uninvited and joined us in a beer, eager to get acquainted, her eye on Kenny. Then began a nearly incomprehensible conversation, punctuated by elaborate hand gestures, in which each participant grasped only an occasional word of the other's language.

Almost immediately she spotted my gold chain bracelet with its four pavé diamond hearts, the last gift Kelly'd given me for what he'd mistakenly thought was our tenth anniversary. By now I knew the Marquesans had a "thing" about gifts. One was expected to hand over anything asked for. Generous Kenny had given away everything he'd brought—his watch, his Nikes, his Swiss Army knife, even a folding mountain bike, and his cassette, headset, and tapes. Along with the gift tradition went a total naiveté as to intrinsic values. Instinctively I covered the bracelet with my hand and said a firm, "Non!" I wasn't even polite. She gave a little shrug, got up, and came back with a half green palm frond hat and a bottle of homemade suntan lotion in an old salad dressing jar, intended as a trade. She knew about these tan-obsessed tourists. She pointed again to my bracelet and with a casual wave of her hand said, "Quand vous allez," meaning, "When you go." She didn't have to get the bracelet that very minute.

Kenny brought the mad-hatter-like barter scene to an end by asking to see a room. There was only one available. We ascended a steep staircase and the girl threw open the door to a small, clean room with a stripped double bed. "Non, mademoiselle," I said in my pidgin French. "Il est nec-essaire pour deux chambres ou deux lits."

She leaned close, taking my arm. I understood her French this time. "Madame, with a man like this, why do you want two beds?"

"Because he is my son," I snapped. She had the decency to blush. This brash young woman was finally silenced.

Kenny's greatest embarrassment was being mistaken for my husband or lover. It seemed inconceivable, but it happened often. With their child-like perceptions, the islanders were sufficiently misled by my blond hair and slender figure to misjudge my age by several decades.

We put Willie and Doris up at the little inn for the next two nights.

"I need a last night aboard alone, Kenny," I said.

"No Mom. I'm staying here with you. In fact, I have a surprise. Theo gave me lobsters and his mom picked us fruit. I'm making a langoustine dinner with salade du mangoe et pomplemousse." He produced a long baguette, which he used like a baton to emphasize the French words he pronounced with an exaggerated accent. "Even champagne. A bon-voyage gift from Bernard." He looked at me with affection. I knew Kenny was trying to make our last night festive, not somber.

"Thank you," I said. "Kenny—you have brought me so much these nine weeks."

After he set the lobster pot boiling he joined me in the cockpit. He'd gotten out the crystal glasses etched with schooners he'd remembered from Christmas, as if to keep Kelly's traditions alive. He popped the champagne cork over the side, where it landed with a small splash then bobbed gaily to the surface.

So many corks over the side...

"This is more like a celebration than a farewell," I said to reward my son's efforts.

"Yup."

"Kelly would have wanted it like this." I looked out to sea toward the sunset.

"Well, there she goes." In a moment's lull, we both looked out to the horizon and saw it—a brilliant flash of emerald encircled the red ball of the sun just as it set—we were too awed to speak—then Kenny shouted,

"The green flash! I always thought it was a fake! We've seen it, Mom! We've seen the green flash!"

"At last," I breathed. "At last." We clinked glasses and Kenny said, "Here's to Kelly!"

"To Kelly. Now prepare to be impressed," I warned him as I began to recite from memory: "The green flash can occur when an atmospheric change in air density creates a blend of the light as it passes from cool to warm, as in a prism. Green and blue refract more light than yellow and red. If the green is properly positioned, the red ball of the sun may display a magnified rim of brilliant emerald as it sets in the sea. Extreme clarity of atmospheric conditions is necessary for the green flash to be seen."

"Wow, Mom! I am impressed!"

"Yes. I memorized that to have it ready for when Kelly and I saw the green flash together. Of course, now that will never be."

"Mom, you did see it together—from separate shores. That was the miracle we just toasted."

I walked the familiar dirt road that ran along the bay past the governor's house, picking flowers as I went. It was our last day. How could I possibly say goodbye? Kelly's grave was complete. It surpassed my expectations. Beneath the massive curved headstone made of rocks meticulously fitted by Kenny and Theo. Finally, it bore Kelly's name— SPEAR spelled out in Porcelaines and the nine cowrie shells set into the concrete slab arched above it. It was exactly right. In the strength and simplicity of its materials and design, it was a fitting monument to a man who epitomized those qualities. I scattered my flowers thinking sadly that I'd be gone before they wilted. I looked across the bay to where the *Vagabundita* lay anchored. How different was this day from that of our arrival—sailing in, exalting over our achievement. Now one of us would go, the other stay.

At the sound of a motor I looked down toward the entrance to the cemetery. Bernard on his scooter jounced up the hill. "Bonjour, Tomee. I thought you would be here to say au revoir. I know you are very sad."

"Yes, I didn't think it would be so hard to leave. Kenny said someday it would make me smile to remember our odyssey and this place where Kelly lies, but I'm afraid I have a long way to go. I loved him from the first moment—then my life was shattered in an instant."

"Ah, oui. Une coup de foudre, we say—a thunder clap. There is of course no consolation when you lose your love. Perhaps I presume, but I will offer one word of comfort. You will never see him grow old."

"Or ill or infirm, never see his face change. Yes, I have thought of that—but..."

"Cold comfort one could say." He made a sad little smile.

"Bernard, I see you brought leis. How thoughtful. In Hawaii the lei is the symbol of return."

"Yes, here too."

"And I will return in one year with a bronze dolphin plaque to tell our story."

"I will watch over Kelly's grave. On the date of November one, we celebrate what we call La Toussaint. All Saints' Day. A day to honor and remember the dead. Everyone comes here to tend the graves. We bring flowers and light candles here at night. It is very beautiful. Please know I will do this for you." Deeply touched, I draped the white lei over Kelly's headstone, inhaling the fragrance of frangipani for the last time.

"This other is for the baby's grave," Bernard said. "I am having a cross carved with his name, if he had one, and the dates 4 Mai a 5 Mai 1991. A life of one day. I can't get him out of my mind."

"Yes, I too think of him with his short little life, and Kelly with his sixty-five years so full of energy and achievement. I come here every day and sit and ponder what it all means—as if there is a connection between them."

"Both families coming by boat from far away, each leaving someone here. The man and the newborn dying the same night, as if they were meant to be together in the hereafter." Our eyes met and there was a silence—the sound of the sea swelling in my ears.

"The baby is the grandson Kelly never had in life. Such a disappointment to a man who reveled in raising his own children. Such a blow when
he lost the one that was on the way."

"Then let us think of it like this." Bernard bent down and placed the
yellow lei on the barren dirt of the baby's grave, the other on Kelly's. "It
is beautiful to think of them together in paradise." He took my hand and
we walked away from the graves. As I climbed on the scooter I thought, *I
will not look back*—but at the last minute my head turned, and I caught a
quick breath, felt an irregular beat in my heart. The verdancy of the grave-
yard pulsed with the intensity of the green flash—the essence that was
Kelly. I looked ahead, out to sea, watching the white hull of the
Vagabundita turning and turning of her anchor rode.

I felt no wind. I felt only Kelly's presence with me and I knew we
would walk together hand in hand forever.

PHOTO GALLERY

Kelly and Tommie

Kelly below in Vagabundita's *cabin*

Tommie's sons, Kenny and Billy

The yacht Vagabundita

The cruising cat Morris

Lost cat poster, Manzanillo, Mexico

Vagabundita *at sea*

Kelly cleaning a dorado, Sea of Cortez

Tommie and Morris as "shellbacks" crossing the equator

Kelly before his rope gave way and he was lost at sea for 14 hours

Kelly studying charts

Entering Taiohae Bay, Nuku Hiva

Making landfall in the Marquesas

The church where Kelly's service was held

Kenny, Bernard, Marceline, and Nadia Au Maitre

Flower lei on the baby's grave

Rock grave monument built by Kenny and Theo

Kelly's grave with his name spelled in shells from the local reef

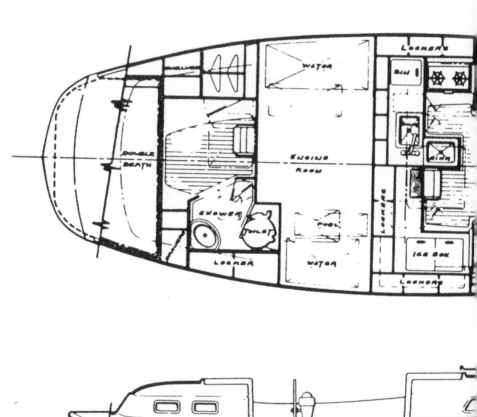

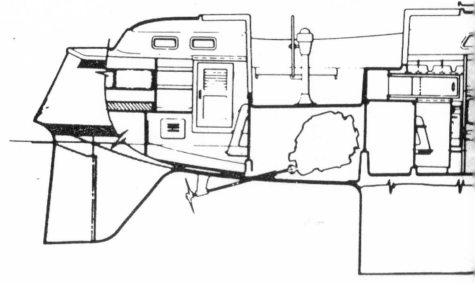

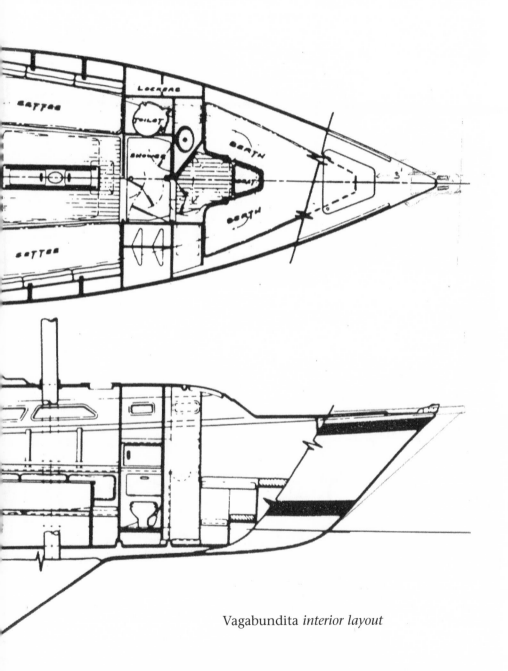

Vagabundita *interior layout*

GLOSSARY

BEAT—to sail into the wind (close-hauled) at about a 45° angle

BOOM—a piece of metal or wood running horizontally at right angles to the mast, along which the bottom of the sail runs

BOWSPRIT—a large, tapered spar extending out over the water from the bow of a boat

BROACH—to be swung (usually by a wave from astern, so that the beam of the boat faces the waves and wind) vulnerably in danger of capsizing

CLEW—the after lower corner (closest to the mast) of a fore and aft sail

CLOSE-HAULED—when a boat is beating or sailing close to the point from which the wind is coming

CROSS SEAS—resulting from storm condition or where currents cross, causing severe water disturbance

DOG—a device for holding or grappling

DOLDRUMS—ocean regions noted for dead calms and fluctuating breezes, located between the belts of the NE and SE trade winds

FIX—boat's position obtained from celestial observation (sun or star sight) by use of a sextant

GUY—a rope, chain, or rod attached to something to steady it

GENOA—a large jib, used in lieu of the standard jib, usually in light winds

GREENWICH MEAN TIME—mean solar time of the meridian—the sun's highest point at Greenwich, England—used as a basis for standard time throughout most of the world

GIMBALS—devices enabling equipment such as the compass, stove, and hurricane lanterns to swing freely, keeping level with the boat's gyrations

GYBE—the action of passing the sails from one side of the boat to the other, sailing downward; if accidental, it can prove disastrous

HALYARD—a rope or tackle used for raising or lowering a flag or sail

HANK-ON—to snap a sail to a stay using a spring-loaded sail-snap

HEAVE-TO—a heavy-weather maneuver to stop the vessel's forward movement

HORSE-LATITUDES—so named because sailing vessels transporting horses to the West Indies had to throw horses overboard due to water shortages while becalmed in the Doldrums

LEEWARD—the downwind side of a sail, vessel, or coast

LORAN—a device by which a navigator can locate his position by determining the time displacement between radio signals from two known stations

LUFF—a sailboat is said to luff when she comes up into the wind, causing the canvas to shudder as the wind spills out

MIZZEN—a fore and aft sail set on a mizzen mast, forward of the main mast

POOPING—a violent engulfment of water coming from the stern

REEF—to reduce the area of sail exposed to the wind by roller-reefing, an automatic process by which the sail is rolled up vertically or hand-reefed by tying small cords through reinforced eyelets, pulling down a section of canvass

SEXTANT—an astronomical instrument used in measuring angular distances of the sun and stars at sea in determining latitude and longitude

SHEET—a line (rope) by which a sail is controlled

SHROUDS—wire cables running from the deck to the mast, mounted port, and starboard to provide lateral support to the mast

SOLE—cabin and cockpit floor

SPREADER—a horizontal wooden strut attached to the mast to hold shrouds away for increased support (yardarm—term used for square riggers)

STANCHIONS—a series of upright steel posts supporting the liferails

STAYSAIL—a sail set between the main and jib, sometimes used as a storm jib

TACK—a boat is on the port tack when the wind is coming over her left
    side, on the starboard tack when it comes over her right side
VANE or WIND-VANE—a self-steering mechanism
WINCH—a crank or handle used for raising and lowering
YAW—when a vessel deviates from a strait course
ZEPHYR—a gentle, mild breeze; the west wind personified

WWW.LITTLEMOOSEPRESS.COM